A CUTTING DECEIT

By the Author

Beulah Lodge

A Cutting Deceit

A CUTTING DECEIT

by
Cathy Dunnell

2022

A CUTTING DECEIT

ISBN 13: 978-1-63679-208-8

THIS TRADE PAPERBACK ORIGINAL IS PUBLISHED BY
BOLD STROKES BOOKS, INC.
P.O. BOX 249
VALLEY FALLS, NY 12185

FIRST EDITION: OCTOBER 2022

CREDITS
EDITOR: BARBARA ANN WRIGHT
PRODUCTION DESIGN: STACIA SEAMAN
COVER DESIGN BY JEANINE HENNING

To Bex—for being my biggest fan.

Chapter One

Valeria stood for a moment and let her gaze linger on the salon's sign. It was her own name, rendered in curvy blue writing across the front of the building. There had been a time where the sight of it had thrilled her to her core. Her very own salon with her own name on it.

Yet she looked at it now and felt only a dull stab of pain that the sign proclaimed the salon to be hers, but in reality, it was Sirvan's. It had always been Sirvan's.

She could see Katya frowning at her through the window. It was time to get back to work. She steeled herself and opened the door. The familiar noises and chatter greeted her, and she went over to the front desk where Katya sat to check the appointments for the afternoon.

"What were you day-dreaming about?" Katya demanded.

"I was thinking how happy the sign used to make me."

"Used to?" The wrinkles on Katya's forehead deepened. "It still should. You got your name above your own business. You always dreamed of that."

Valeria looked up from the computer screen. She still felt a rush of affection for Katya whenever she looked at her. Katya's face was the first friendly face she had seen when she had first arrived in London. Katya had been the first to speak to her in Russian, making Valeria instantly homesick. She had relied on Katya from the first, and the remembrance of how Katya had looked out for her, advised her, and had generally always been there would never leave her.

But lately, all their interactions were beginning to grate on her. Katya knew perfectly well that Sirvan owned the salon, but whenever Valeria referenced it, she brushed it aside as if Valeria was quibbling over something minor.

"Yes," Valeria said. "I always dreamed of owning my *own* business." Katya opened her mouth, but Valeria cut her off. "Has anyone come in about Dalia's job?"

Dalia had been the salon junior. Her job was to assist the stylists, sweep up the cuttings, and generally keep the place tidy. She had been constantly late for work and had grumbled about being given all the menial tasks. Katya had muttered to Valeria that she wouldn't last long.

It was annoying when Katya was right. Valeria had a serious chat with Dalia in her office one afternoon, and Dalia had never showed up for work again. She had lasted less than six months, but Valeria was relieved to see her go.

"No one has come to apply," Katya said, "but her mother is waiting to see you."

"Dalia's mother?"

"Yep." Katya jerked her head to indicate one of the chairs in the corner. Valeria could see a visibly nervous woman glancing at them. "You better go talk to her," Katya continued. "The woman is having kittens."

Valeria sighed and walked over. Fear was etched into every line of the woman's face. Valeria drew up another chair and sat next to her. She assumed a kindly expression and asked how she could help.

The woman launched into an apology for her daughter's conduct. She assured Valeria that this behaviour was quite out of character and that Dalia really was a good girl. She said she knew how much trouble Dalia must have caused, and if Valeria had lost money because of her daughter, she only had to say, and she and her husband would cover the cost.

Valeria held up a hand to staunch the flow of words. "You do not need to worry," she said. "Girls come and go in that job. They try it for a bit, and lots of them realise they don't like this kind of work after all. And that is okay. They leave for something else, and it is no big deal."

"But she left with no notice," Dalia's mother said, her voice trembling. "I told her she should not have done that. I tell her I want her to come and apologise to you—"

Valeria held up her hand again. "That is not necessary. She is young, she makes a mistake. We have all done this, yes?" She smiled, encouragingly. "I am not angry. I hope she finds another job soon that she likes better."

After a few more minutes of reassurance, Dalia's mum finally stopped trembling. Valeria explained she had clients to take care of, and the woman retreated backward out of the salon, thanking Valeria profusely over and over.

"She thinks you're the bloody Queen," Katya remarked, watching her hurry away down the high street.

"I'm not queen of anything," Valeria said and went to speak to her next client. She washed and cut the woman's hair with practiced ease, keeping up with the client's chatter and responding in the right places. Years of experience had enabled her to keep half her mind on the job whilst the other half was occupied elsewhere.

She thought about Dalia's mother. The woman hadn't been afraid of Valeria. It was Sirvan she feared. She feared that Valeria's displeasure would somehow be reported back to Sirvan, with dire consequences for her family. Valeria often found that the fear Sirvan inspired was often transferred to her. She noticed shopkeepers looking anxiously at her as she browsed and rushing to serve her with unseemly haste. Young men made way for her in the street, their eyes lowered respectfully because she was Sirvan's wife. Valeria had begun to actively avoid going out to the shops because it made her so uncomfortable.

She finished her client's cut and sent her over to Katya at the front desk to pay. She was busy sweeping the hair from the chair when she heard a voice say, "Hey, Valeria? Anyone come about Dalia's job yet?"

Shanaz had emerged from the hair-washing room behind her,

shepherding her customer back to their chair. Shanaz was the other stylist, a vivacious, gossipy woman in her mid-thirties, and she had the knack of being able to talk to anyone about anything. All the customers, from the dour old widows to the fashionable young women, loved her.

"No, not yet."

"Let's hope we get someone good, eh? That Dalia." Shanaz shook her head. "She was a right 'mare. I never heard someone complain so much in all my life. You'd think this place was a chain gang, the way she went on about it. Kids today haven't got no work ethic, ain't that right, Mrs. Ali?"

Mrs. Ali nodded vigorously and proceeded to tell Shanaz about her daughter-in-law who cooked too many meals from the freezer.

As Valeria finished clearing up, she took a quick break to make herself a cup of herbal tea from the big shiny machine that sat on one side of the arch in the wall. On the other side of the archway was the area of the salon where Azad worked.

He had been shaving men's faces on the high street for forty years, and when Sirvan had given her the salon, he had made it clear that Azad came as part of the package. He had his corner where he took care of the male customers, enough removed from the rest of the salon that the men could talk in peace without being disturbed.

Valeria hadn't liked this, but she didn't question it. She never questioned Sirvan in anything. The salon was a useful place for Sirvan to come and discuss business without seeming to do so. He could sit in the chair, be shaved by Azad, and talk casually to the man next to him.

As Sirvan had insisted on Azad, so Valeria had insisted on Katya. Katya was fantastically grumpy and barely adequate as a receptionist-cum-tea maker, but Valeria had asked for Sirvan's special favour. It was not often that Valeria asked Sirvan for anything, and he had nodded his assent. Valeria had been almost overwhelmed with relief. In the earlier days of their marriage, she had never been entirely sure how he would react to anything.

The door rang and Valeria glanced up from her tea. A well-muscled young man with a partially shaved head entered and grinned at Katya. "All right, darling?" he said.

Katya scowled in response, and he laughed. He walked through the archway without acknowledging Valeria and went straight to Azad, clapping the older man heartily on the shoulder.

Katya came up to Valeria and spoke quietly in Russian. "What is Sirvan doing with a guy like Zoran?"

"Sirvan does whatever he likes," Valeria said. But it was true that Zoran was different from the other men Sirvan surrounded himself with. He was flashier and liked drawing attention to himself, all the qualities that Sirvan usually despised.

Valeria had been astonished when Sirvan had first brought Zoran to their house for dinner. Dinner at his house was a mark of favour, a sign that Sirvan was taking someone seriously. Within a few minutes of meeting Zoran, Valeria had found herself completely baffled as to what Sirvan could possibly want with him. He was loud and obnoxious. He made crude jokes and bragged constantly about his cars, his TV, and all the other things he owned.

It was when Valeria heard Zoran talking about "his girls" and how he kept them profitable for Sirvan that Valeria realised precisely which aspect of Sirvan's business he was involved with.

Shanaz walked past in time to see Zoran settling into a chair by Azad. She frowned. "Why is he always in here nowadays?"

Katya shrugged.

"His hair must grow very fast, no?" Shanaz grinned, but it faded quickly when she caught Valeria's eye. She busied herself sweeping up some hair from the floor.

A few minutes later, Sirvan himself came in. As always when he entered a room, people sat up straighter. They followed his movements from beneath their eyelashes, watching him to see what kind of a mood he was in. He was not physically imposing, but he cut a noticeable figure, nonetheless. There was something about the exquisite tailoring of his suits and his subdued, severe manner that drew all eyes to him.

Valeria felt his presence as forcefully now as she had when

she had first met him. She had been living a precarious existence since first arriving in London, moving through a succession of jobs in seedy bars with occasional escort work. She had arrived with dreams of building a better life, but these had been slowly worn away until her sole focus had become survival.

Sirvan had first come in with one of the regulars at the bar where she'd worked on weekends. It had sticky floors and regular brawls on Saturday nights. Sirvan had looked out of place from the moment he walked in. His tailored suit was a stark contrast to the leather and denim jackets worn by the other men. His dark hair was receding and already peppered with grey. His eyes were slow-moving and steady, and his air of calm self-assurance was a pleasing contrast to the frenetic, edgy energy of the younger men.

Even in that dark, dingy bar, Sirvan had commanded attention, just as he did now. Valeria remembered how impressed she had been by him. To her, it was as if he had stepped into her life from an entirely different world, one that was calm, well-ordered, and above all, safe.

His dark eyes scanned the salon and rested briefly on Valeria. She smiled reflexively, as if she was pleased to see him, though in reality, she hated it when he came into the salon. His presence acted as a reminder that he was the true owner.

He nodded to Valeria and went through the arch to join the men. Valeria watched him greet Zoran and settle into the chair beside him. She could hear the low murmur of their talk whilst Azad drew his razor carefully along Zoran's chin.

Valeria's jaw tightened. Where once Sirvan's presence had made her feel safe, now his appearance inspired only anxiety. She finished her tea just as her next client arrived, and she forced her thoughts back to hair.

❖

The girl came in later that day, clutching her CV. The advert in the window had only been up for a day, and Valeria was pleased that there was interest already. She came over to the reception desk when Katya called her.

"This girl wants Dalia's job," said Katya, jerking her thumb at the leather sofa that sat beside the desk. Valeria glanced briefly at the dark-haired girl.

"Okay. Will you go and wash my lady's hair whilst I speak to this girl about the job?"

Katya grudgingly agreed. "Hey darlin'," she called to the customer. "I'm gonna wash your hair for you. I don't got much feeling in my hands these days, so you gotta tell me if the water is burning your scalp, right?"

Valeria winced. She turned her attention to the sofa and saw that the girl had seemingly caught her expression. She smiled sympathetically. Valeria summoned up her professional persona and sat on the sofa. She extended her hand and smiled brightly.

"Hello, there. I am Valeria, and I run the salon."

"Hi, I'm Athena." She took Valeria's hand and shook it. She was exceptionally pretty. An oval face was framed by thick dark hair that was pulled into a plait. Her large eyes were almost black and rested on Valeria's face with a hopeful expression.

Valeria realised she'd held on to Athena's hand for slightly too long. She let go and took the CV. She scanned it with a practised eye, taking the opportunity to settle herself. She couldn't fathom why she was so flustered after exchanging only a few introductory words. Athena's work history consisted of the usual assortment of retail and waitressing jobs. She had spent some time working in a salon, but there was no evidence of any formal training.

"You haven't done any hairdressing course?" she asked, looking up.

"No, but I plan to. I really liked working in the salon, and I'd like to pursue hairdressing as a career." She spoke with a London accent, and although her voice was girlish, Valeria judged her to be at least twenty-five, slightly older than the girls who usually worked this position.

"What do you like about hairdressing?"

"I like meeting new people and making them feel good about themselves. Like, you can't feel good if you have crap hair, right?" She smiled, and Valeria felt herself almost lean back under its force.

"Yes. Hair is very important." Valeria looked back at the CV, feeling flustered.

"I can start straight away," Athena continued. "And I can work whatever hours you need."

"You know that this is a junior position, right? We try to give some basic training, but you'll be mainly sweeping up, washing hair, and making the coffee."

"I am totally fine with that. I love making coffee, anyhow." Valeria raised her eyebrows, and Athena laughed self-consciously. "No, I'm serious. You know how gutting it is when you're looking forward to a really good cup, and then it's no good, right?"

"Yes. I look forward to my morning coffee a lot."

"Exactly. You gotta get the coffee right. And if you have clients with great hair *and* great coffee, well, then you're unstoppable."

Valeria found herself smiling, her first genuine smile of the day. "Okay. You've convinced me that you take coffee making seriously. But what would you do if you get a customer who says they don't like their cut?"

Athena seamlessly switched into a more serious manner and talked Valeria through the steps she would take to address the customer's concerns. Valeria asked her more questions: what would she do if she double-booked an appointment for two people, and how would she cope with a customer being rude to her? Athena answered the questions with an easy self-assurance that impressed Valeria. She showed none of the nervousness or timidity that usually characterised the applicants for this job.

"So," Valeria said as she finished her questions, "do you live locally?"

"Kind of. I'm up in Enfield." That might explain the lack of nerves, Valeria thought. If she didn't live locally, she maybe had no idea who Valeria's husband was.

"How did you hear about this job?"

"I've got mates who live down this way, and one of them sent me a pic of the ad. She knows I've been looking for a job in a salon."

"Okay. Well, we will give you a trial," Valeria said. Athena beamed with delight and Valeria felt a surge of pride at being the cause of it. "One week, starting tomorrow. We pay you in cash for the week, and if you do all right, then we will see."

"Thank you," Athena said breathlessly. "I really appreciate it. I won't let you down, I promise."

"Be here at half-eight tomorrow morning. Don't be late."

"I'll be here bang on time."

"Good. I will see you tomorrow." Valeria stood and offered Athena her hand. Her grasp was firm.

"Thank you so much, Valeria." Her dark eyes were shining as they met Valeria's, who was careful this time not to hold on too long to Athena's hand. She didn't want to appear to be giving her any special mark of favour before she had even started.

Valeria watched her walking away down the high street and jumped as Katya appeared at her elbow. "Why do you give the job to a Greek? Turks and Greeks hate each other."

"I've only given her a trial. And if she is a good worker, then I don't care about anything else."

Katya jerked her thumb in the direction of Azad's corner, where Zoran and Sirvan were still talking. "You could have asked Sirvan what he thought of her."

Valeria's temper flared. "I don't need to ask him," she said, keeping her voice low. "I decide who gets to work here."

Katya raised her eyebrows and slid back behind the reception desk. Valeria went to prepare for her next client, trying to push down her annoyance. As she cleaned and tidied her station, she looked up at where Sirvan and Zoran remained deep in conversation. They had been talking for a long time, and she felt a stirring of unease in the pit of her stomach.

CHAPTER TWO

Athena arrived early the next day, and for the whole week, she scrupulously swept hair, made coffee, and answered the phone. She was unfailingly polite, even when Katya was at her grumpiest. She was never late and never gave any attitude.

Valeria spent a good deal of her time watching her and noting how she interacted with customers. Athena seemed to have a knack for putting people at ease. She encouraged customers to talk if they felt like it or was quiet if it was clear that they didn't. Valeria liked the way Athena found out if she or Shanaz needed help with anything rather than waiting to be asked. She could see Athena even trying to coax smiles from Katya.

Valeria found that she enjoyed watching Athena work. She brought a fresh energy to the salon that made the days seem brighter. At the end of the week, Valeria handed over her week's pay and told her she had the job. The delight that shone from her face was almost blinding.

That same Friday evening, Valeria stood in the kitchen at home, chopping onions for chicken stew. Sirvan was sitting at the kitchen table, working on his laptop. He looked up abruptly and said, "You give Dalia's job to the Greek girl?"

"Yes. She did good this week."

"Does she speak Turkish? Or Kurmanji?"

"I don't know."

"But she is Greek, yes?"

"I have no idea. Everyone tells me she is."

"She got a Greek name. And she looks Greek. With that hair. And that face."

Valeria nodded absently. She could picture Athena's face easily after a week of working with her. She could call to mind the curve of her brows, the small mole on her left cheek, and the perfect bow of her lips. Valeria smiled to herself as she scraped the chopped onions into the frying pan.

"You hear what I said?" Sirvan asked.

"What?"

"I said you must make sure she is definitely okay."

Valeria turned to look at him. His face was impassive, but Valeria could tell from a slight tightness around his jaw that he was tense for some reason.

"Sure. If she does anything wrong, she's gone." And then, because she could not help herself, she added, "I don't have bad workers in *my* salon."

"I know, darlin'. You run the place well." He turned his attention back to his laptop, signalling that the conversation was over.

Valeria stirred the onions and felt the unease return. Sirvan had never before shown any interest in who took the most junior role in the salon. He came into the salon for his occasional business chats, but that was as much interest as he ever took in the place. Valeria did not know why he should suddenly be concerned about who her staff were, but she did not like it.

❖

Valeria set out early for work the next morning, as she always did. She liked to be the first to arrive so she could spend a while in the silence of the salon, relishing the opportunity to be alone somewhere that felt at least nominally like her own space.

The house she shared with Sirvan was comfortable, but Valeria was always acutely aware that it belonged to him. When they were married, he had told her to do whatever she wished with the place, but Valeria had never been able to summon up much enthusiasm for decorating a place that wasn't hers. And she knew that despite his words, Sirvan disliked anything ostentatious. As a result, the house was sombre, plain, and soulless.

The salon had been the first place that had felt like her own space. She had a free hand and had furnished and decorated in her own style, a style she knew Sirvan did not favour. Azad's corner looked different from the rest. The gilt-framed mirror had quietly disappeared, and the plush chairs had been replaced by more utilitarian black and chrome pieces.

Valeria bit her lip as she rounded the corner onto the high street. Sirvan had bought the salon outright for her and had assured her that it was hers. At the time, she had accepted his word and had been genuinely grateful that she had been given her own business. The stipulation that Azad be allowed a corner had seemed a small enough thing. But it had not taken long for her to understand that the salon was hers only in the sense that her name was above the door. As the years passed, this knowledge ate away at her, and she had become aware of a gnawing resentment at the way Sirvan waltzed in and held his meetings in Azad's space. It was a constant reminder that the salon was still his in all the ways that really mattered.

She frowned, and with the practice of many years, pushed the unwelcome thoughts away. As she approached the salon, she was surprised to see Athena waiting by the front door, scrolling on her phone. Valeria was always the first person to arrive, without fail.

"What are you doing here?" Valeria asked, feeling put out that her usual routine had been disrupted.

"Shanaz has two appointments for hair extensions this morning, so I wanted to check that everything is ready for her. And I need to call some clients about coming back in, and it's easier to do that first thing before it gets busy."

"About coming back in?" Valeria repeated, unlocking the door.

"Yeah. You can see on the system when their last appointment was, so if it was three months ago or longer, and they haven't got one booked, I can give them a call and see if they want to come back."

Valeria opened the door and walked through the darkened salon to her tiny office at the back. It was a grand name for a windowless space the size of a cupboard, with room only for a filing cabinet, a cheap desk, and tatty swivel chair. Athena went to the tea and coffee station, and Valeria heard the whirring noise of the coffee machine being switched on. She came back out and said, "Did Katya or Shanaz tell you to make calls?"

Athena shook her head. "No. I just thought it was a good idea." She said it with the easy confidence that seemed to characterise her whole existence.

"It is a good idea. We probably should have been doing it before now."

"That's the benefit of new eyes, eh?" Athena turned to the machine and said over her shoulder, "You take your coffee black, don't you?"

"That's right." Valeria was pleased that Athena had noticed and remembered; she was clearly trying her hardest to make a good impression. "So," she said as Athena fiddled with the machine, "everyone says to me that you look like a Greek."

"I know. Katya said that to me at least ten times this week." Athena shrugged as she pressed the buttons for a black espresso. "I don't mind. I mean, it's true, after all."

"Do you speak Greek?"

"Not much. Just enough to understand my nan. And you're Russian, right?"

"How can you tell?"

Athena turned and handed Valeria her coffee. "'Cos you look Russian."

"I do?"

"Yeah. The fur hat, the long bushy beard…it's a dead give-away."

Valeria laughed. "Come on, be serious."

"All right. I guessed from the accent."

"Ah, yes. It does not fade, even after all this time."

"How long you been in this country?"

"I came when I was nineteen. My mother had died, and there was nothing left for me at home. And I decided to come to London. I spoke no English and knew no one here." She laughed, remembering her younger self. "But I was so confident. I thought I would easily make my fortune."

"Looks like you've done all right for yourself," said Athena, nodding at the salon.

"Yes. I have done okay." She was not in the habit of talking about her past. Even with Katya, she preferred not to think about her younger self, so full of hope and optimism. It was painful to be reminded of all the dreams she had cherished in those early years, dreams of independence and of making a life for herself.

She looked around the salon and felt a stab of bitterness; despite all the apparent security which she had prized so highly when she had said yes to Sirvan, her younger self would have been disappointed that Valeria had nothing that was truly hers.

Athena seemed to notice the change in her mood and looked at her uncertainly.

Valeria forced a smile, not wanting to make Athena feel uncomfortable. "Well," she said, "I should let you get ready for Shanaz's clients. Thank you for the coffee." She moved back into the office and left Athena checking the supplies for later.

Athena seemed to have a talent for making people talk. Valeria watched her chatting to the clients as she washed their hair. Even the more taciturn regulars opened up with Athena and talked animatedly as the shampoo was rinsed from their hair.

And it wasn't just the customers. Shanaz and Valeria were cutting hair when they were both startled by an unexpected sound. Shanaz turned to where Katya and Athena were talking at the front desk.

"Did you just *laugh*?" Shanaz asked in disbelief.

Katya shrugged defensively. "What? This girl does good impressions." Athena smiled sheepishly and made a show of rearranging the magazines by the sofa.

"I ain't heard you laugh in all the time I been here," Shanaz said. "I thought you lot got sent to gulags for laughing."

"You cannot be Russian without a sense of humour. Look at Putin. He is the biggest joke of all." They were all still chuckling when Sirvan came in. Then the laughter ceased abruptly.

"What are you all laughing at?" he asked Valeria, looking around at them in surprise.

"Katya made a joke," Valeria explained. Sirvan raised his eyebrows and then motioned Valeria over to Azad's side of the salon. She followed him through the archway. She knew she should be focusing on what he wanted, but she couldn't help being very aware of Athena watching nearby.

"Listen," Sirvan said, lowering his voice. "I got some people coming I need to talk with later."

"They are coming here?"

"Yes, it will be nice for them. They have a shave, a coffee, we talk."

Valeria nodded, her mind still occupied with the thought that Athena had seen Sirvan come in and effectively act as if he was in charge. What would Athena make of that? Would she pity Valeria for being ordered around in her own salon? The thought of Athena pitying her made her so uncomfortable that she struggled to pay attention to what Sirvan was saying.

"Okay," she said distractedly. "That's fine."

"Good, good. Maybe the new Greek girl can bring us some coffees, eh?" He patted her arm and went off to speak to Azad. Valeria suppressed a sigh as she returned to her client.

An hour later, Sirvan's guests arrived. Zoran was with them, talking animatedly to the two men and gesturing expansively at the salon as if he owned it. The men were both in their fifties. They were grizzled, solid, and unsmiling. Valeria had never seen them before, and she was familiar with all of Sirvan's regular contacts. They nodded gravely at Valeria as they walked past. After they had settled themselves with Sirvan on Azad's side, Valeria called Athena over.

"Go see if they want any drinks," she said, nodding at the men. One of them was already being prepared for a shave whilst the other lounged on the sofa. Sirvan sat beside him, talking to them both.

"Who are they?"

"They are customers. Now, go get them some coffee." Athena stiffened at the sharpness of her tone, and Valeria was on the point of apologising when Athena walked over to the men. They looked up as she approached, and Valeria saw their eyes linger appreciatively over Athena's body, particularly Zoran, who might as well have had his tongue hanging out. Valeria clenched her jaw angrily. Now she knew why Sirvan had wanted her to serve the coffee.

She glanced at herself in one of the salon mirrors. Although her hair had retained much of its natural ash blond colour, her face was all angles compared to the soft round beauty of Athena's. And although Valeria could be charming when required, it did not come as easily to her as it once did. Too many years of reserve and caution had crystallised around her.

She shook herself and looked away. She of all people knew the effect that pretty young women had on men, and Sirvan was canny enough to use that to his advantage. One of the men said something to Athena. Zoran laughed a little too loudly, and Athena laughed along obligingly, flashing her brilliant smile. When she returned to the coffee machine, Valeria came and stood beside her.

"Are they being okay with you?" she asked quietly.

"Yeah, they're fine. Just the usual. You know what men are like."

"I do. And you must know too, yes?" Valeria imagined that Athena was constantly fending off attention from men, but she shrugged.

"I don't pay any attention to men."

"Ah, I see. You have a boyfriend?"

"No." Athena removed one full coffee cup from the machine and replaced it with another.

Valeria was genuinely surprised. A girl as good-looking as Athena would surely have plenty of male admirers. "But you must have lots of boys asking you out."

"Yeah, but I don't like boys."

"What do you mean you don't…" Valeria stopped herself as she realised what Athena meant. Athena looked up and smiled, the kind of amused smile that Valeria had seen youngsters give their grandparents who couldn't work a smartphone. "Oh," she said and then tried to appear nonchalant, as if she had known all along, and the knowledge hadn't caused a surge of excitement within her. "But you must have a girlfriend? Pretty girl like you?" Athena looked curiously at her, and Valeria felt her face grow hot.

"No, not at the moment. I'm enjoying being single."

"Of course. Of course, you are," Valeria muttered, trying to cover her confusion.

Athena carried the coffees to the men. She stayed there for a few minutes, chatting and laughing. Azad, who could be grumpier even than Katya, was warming under Athena's charm, breaking into the conversation with his own anecdotes.

Valeria looked on with a mixture of admiration and incredulity. She was amazed that Athena could be so confident about her sexuality, amazed and not a little envious. Valeria had always been aware of her own attraction to women but had simply pushed the feelings aside. She had grown up in an environment where such things were not spoken of, and she had simply put that part of herself into a box and had sat firmly on the lid.

Athena turned and walked back. Valeria watched the bounce of her hair as she went and knew that the lid of the box was being rattled. She moved away and busied herself checking the appointments for the afternoon.

The men stayed for an hour, then left. Their jovial laughter and banter as they departed implied that all had gone well. Sirvan stayed, talking with Azad and Zoran for a few minutes, and then he too left. Valeria glanced at his face, but as usual, it gave nothing away.

Zoran strolled casually over to the coffee machine. His very presence set Valeria's teeth on edge. His hands were in his pockets, and his eyes roved around the salon as if wanting to ensure that he was seen and noticed.

Athena came out from the hair-washing area with a client and guided her back to the seat.

"Hey, Greek girl! How about another coffee?" Zoran called.

"You're standing right next to the machine," Athena pointed out amicably.

"Yeah, but I don't know how to work it. And it will taste better if you make it."

Valeria tensed. She did not like Zoran ordering her staff around, but she was also acutely aware that he was one of Sirvan's men. And from the way he was constantly around these days, it was clear that Sirvan had plans for him.

"Can you believe this guy?" Athena said to her customer. "I got to show him how to press a button?"

"I've never met a man who knew how to press a button properly," replied the woman, winking in the mirror at Zoran. Shanaz hooted delightedly.

"That's one-nil to you, darlin'." The woman laughed, and Athena walked over to the coffee machine, stuck a mug in, and pressed the button for a black coffee. She smiled at the irritated-looking Zoran and went back to combing her client's hair.

Zoran sipped his coffee as the loud exchanges and laughter between the women continued. Valeria came to stand beside Athena and spoke in a low voice as she talked her through the cut the woman had asked for. She was dimly aware of Zoran from the corner of her eye. He finished his coffee and walked past them, slapping Athena on the behind as he did so.

Athena yelped, and all eyes turned toward her. Zoran grinned rakishly and made to carry on his way. Without thinking, Valeria grabbed his wrist. She yanked hard, pulling him toward her. Her other hand held the scissors, and she brandished them in his face. Her anger was so intense that it took all her reserves of self-control to keep from stabbing him.

"No," she said, clearly and loudly so that everyone heard. "You don't do that here."

His face darkened, and he pulled free. He pointed in Valeria's face. "You—"

"Think very carefully about what you say next. I don't want trouble here," Valeria interrupted calmly. She could see Zoran choking back his words, could see him weighing up the consequences behind his eyes.

"Come on, now." Katya walked over from behind the front desk and took Zoran's arm. "People are here to have their hair cut. They want to relax, chat about their holidays, right?" She gently but firmly steered him toward the door. He looked as if he wanted to argue, but he caught Azad's eye and seemingly thought better of it. The older man was looking at him with barely concealed contempt.

Zoran shook off Katya with an annoyed sound and left the salon. There was a collective exhalation of breath.

"Are you all right?" Valeria asked Athena.

"Yeah, I'm okay. Thank you."

Shanaz nodded her head approvingly. "That's why she the boss, eh?" she said, addressing her client. There was a low murmur of approval, and gradually, the conversation rose back up to normal levels.

Valeria continued her tutorial with Athena and then left her to get on with it. She walked to the desk and checked through the remaining appointments for that afternoon.

"It's not good to make trouble with him," Katya murmured beside her in Russian.

"You want that I let him treat my staff like that?" Valeria snapped.

Katya scowled. "No. He should not have done that. But you should have just told Sirvan and let him deal with it."

"Yeah? And how are Athena and Shanaz gonna respect me after that? After they see that I let a dog like Zoran feel them up whenever he wants?"

"I'm just saying that I think—"

"I don't care what you think." She could tell that her words hurt. Katya had long played the role of mentor and almost surrogate mother to her, but Valeria was too angry to apologise.

She walked to the coffee station and made herself an herbal tea in an attempt to calm down. She watched Athena as she sipped it. Her face was constantly moving as she talked to her customer, a smile flashing out, eyes widening in surprise, or forehead creased with concern as she sympathised. Valeria felt herself soothed by the very sight of her.

When she got home later that day, she could hear Sirvan upstairs on the phone. She began making dinner as she did every evening, and when Sirvan emerged later, she watched him closely for signs of displeasure, for any indication that he had heard about the incident with Zoran. But there was nothing. Sirvan read the paper with his meal as he always did.

As she was clearing the plates, Valeria said, "We had an issue with Zoran today in the salon."

Sirvan's head snapped up. "What issue?" he demanded. Valeria told him briefly what had happened, and his face darkened. "What did you do?"

"I told him he could not do that kind of thing to my staff."

Sirvan nodded approvingly.

"But I was holding my scissors at the time. I think he did not like that."

Sirvan raised his eyebrows. "Did you stab him with your scissors?"

"No. But I wanted to."

Sirvan grunted. "You did right. He does not treat girls well."

Valeria's hands tightened on the plates as she stacked them on the side of the sink. "Is that right?" she asked casually.

"Yes," said Sirvan with a heavy sigh. "I already have to tell him not to knock them about so much. If he keeps showing up with them at the hospital, the doctors are gonna ask questions."

Valeria remained turned toward the sink so he would not see her fighting to keep her face under control. She had always known that Sirvan made his money in illegal ways, but she had been so grateful for the security he offered that she had not dwelt too long on the nature of his business. Illegal money was, after all, better than no money. Valeria had known poverty, and Sirvan had rescued her from it exactly as if he had plucked her from quicksand.

But as the years went by, she found his so-called business intruding into her consciousness more and more, like a nagging pain that only intensified the longer she ignored it. What made it worse was that Sirvan's trust in her increased as time went on, and he began to talk more openly about what he did on a day-to-day basis.

He talked about the problems he faced with shopkeepers who wouldn't pay the money they owed him. And then he began to complain of the problems that the girls in his business caused him, and Valeria knew exactly what he was referring to. And once she knew, there was no way she could go back to being oblivious. The knowledge of what Sirvan did ate away at her, and she found herself willing the girls to cause him more problems so he would be forced to give it up. But Sirvan had decided instead that he needed someone to take charge of that area of the business, and that was when Zoran had started cropping up everywhere.

Valeria had disliked Zoran from the moment she'd met him, and the knowledge that he was running a prostitution racket for Sirvan deepened her dislike into hatred.

"I hate that you do business with him," she said. She felt Sirvan's gaze on her back and turned to face him.

He regarded her steadily. "I know, darlin'," he said. "But these girls, they would have it much worse if I didn't keep Zoran in check."

Valeria bit her lip. Sirvan had just given her an opportunity to agree with him, to smooth over the fact that she had dared to voice criticism of how he conducted his business. But she could not let it go. She could only think of all the desperate, despairing girls she had known when she had first arrived in London.

"I wish you weren't involved in that kind of business at all," she said.

Sirvan's eyes darkened. "I can't stay doing one type of business all the time. If I run a video store, and then everyone stops buying videos, what am I gonna do? I got to do a different type of business."

"But *that* business?"

"I know you don't like it, but trust me, these girls don't have it so bad compared to what they come from. They work for Zoran for a little while, they pay off their debts, and then they're free. It's a good deal for them."

Valeria turned back to the sink and turned on the taps. Anger coursed through her, and she knew how dangerous it would be to let Sirvan see even a glimpse of it. Alongside the anger, she was aware of a creeping sense of shame. The food she ate, the clothes she wore were all funded by the fear that Sirvan inspired. She had always known it, but up until recently, she had been able to ignore it, to push it into the box where she stored all the feelings that she was unable to face.

"But you did right with Zoran in the salon," Sirvan said. "He can't treat your girls like that."

Valeria knew this was his way of offering an olive branch, and she could not afford to brush it aside. She turned back to him and forced a smile. "Thank you. I never want to make any trouble for you, but I have to look after my staff."

Sirvan rose from the table and put his arm around her waist. He kissed her lightly on the lips. "I know, darlin'. You did good." And then, satisfied that all was well between them, he returned to his chair and the paper.

Valeria dropped her smile and turned back to the sink. Anger simmered within her, and she focused all her energy on pushing it down where Sirvan wouldn't see it.

Chapter Three

Athena was waiting by the front door again the next day, this time saying that she wanted to clean the coffee machine before the first appointment. As Valeria unlocked the door, she said, "You sure you're okay about what happened with Zoran yesterday?"

"Oh yeah," said Athena as they entered the salon together. "Guys like him are two a penny." She stuck her hands in her pockets and leaned nonchalantly against the reception desk in a perfect imitation of Zoran's affected manner. "But the coffee will taste better if you make it, darlin'," she mimicked.

It was so spot-on that Valeria laughed out loud. Athena grinned and shrugged self-consciously. "What an idiot, eh? But did you see his face when you pointed those scissors at him?" She pulled a face that exactly replicated Zoran's shocked expression: eyes wide and mouth hanging slightly open.

Valeria laughed again. "Yes, he is an idiot," she agreed when she had regained her breath.

"Is he a friend of your husband?"

"No, more of a business contact."

"Oh, okay. And what line of business is Sirvan in?"

Valeria looked at her sharply. She was never asked directly about Sirvan's business. Everyone around here just knew. But if Athena wasn't local, then she wouldn't necessarily know. Her face was open and guileless, and she looked expectant.

"Sirvan has interests in all kinds of local businesses."

"What, like waste disposal?"

"No, that is not one of them," said Valeria, confused. "I just mean he has lots of business interests."

"Sure. Don't worry, I was just being stupid." Athena walked to the coffee machine and opened the back panel. "God, look at the state of this. I'd better get started before the customers arrive."

❖

Athena's Zoran impression was in demand for the rest of the week at the salon, and it gradually evolved to more ridiculous heights until Athena's Zoran was calling Katya "sweet cheeks" and asking her to clip his toenails. Laughter rang out, and Valeria reflected that it was an unusual but not unwelcome sound. She would occasionally catch Shanaz glancing at her as if to check that it was all right to laugh and then relaxing when she saw Valeria herself laughing uncontrollably.

The Zoran impression had taken on such a life of its own that it was quite a shock when the man himself reappeared in the salon later that week. He was again accompanied by Sirvan and the two unsmiling men. He kept his eyes down and muttered a greeting as he headed to Azad's corner. Azad grinned at him; he too had been enjoying the impersonations.

Sirvan came up to Valeria and asked for Athena to get them drinks.

"I don't know if she wants to," Valeria said, "considering what Zoran did."

"No, it's okay, Valeria. I'm happy to do it."

Valeria jumped, not realising that Athena had been standing quite so close.

"Good girl." Sirvan smiled at Athena and went to join his guests. She followed and spent a few moments with the men, taking their orders.

She smiled at Zoran. "You gonna give me a hand now you know how the machine works?" she said. He looked nonplussed and began to stammer an answer before Athena laughed and said, "Don't worry, I'm only messing."

Valeria looked at her with new admiration as she returned and began to make the drinks. "You were very nice to him, considering," she said, fetching some mugs.

"It's all part of my commitment to excellent customer service," Athena said, flicking her plait over her shoulder.

"I do not think I could talk so nicely to him. I am still angry with him for the way he treated you."

"I loved the way you stuck up for me. Seriously, you were amazing." Her eyes rested on Valeria's face, and Valeria fumbled with the mugs, almost dropping one.

"That's okay," she mumbled, feeling her face grow hot.

Athena took the drinks to the men and stayed chatting with them for a while. Valeria watched, fascinated. Athena's smile took in each of the men in turn, and she joked easily with Zoran as if nothing untoward had ever happened.

Katya ambled over to where Valeria was standing. "She got a winning way with her, eh?"

"Yes," Valeria said, feeling flustered. "She has a nice manner."

"She's a good actress too. To act like that with Zoran."

"I know. I couldn't be so nice to him."

"He's a goat." Katya's nose wrinkled as if she had just smelt something appalling. "I don't know what he does for Sirvan, but it must be important." There was a hint of a question in the final word, and she looked expectantly at Valeria.

"Why are you always fishing for information about what Sirvan does? You know I can't be gossiping about his work."

"I just worry for you, sweetheart. Time was, Sirvan would not have touched men like Zoran with a barge pole. Now, he's all pally with them. I don't like it."

Valeria wanted to tell Katya that she didn't like it either. There was a time when she would have told Katya everything that she was thinking and feeling, but in recent years, she had got out of the habit of confiding in her friend. It was because she always knew Katya would tell her that Sirvan was safety, security, and all the things that had been missing from their lives before. Katya was steadfast in her advice, and that advice had never changed. What was best for Sirvan was best for them.

"Sirvan makes his money, and that keeps all of us in a job," Valeria said, shutting down the conversation. Katya opened her mouth to reply when Athena returned from Azad's corner.

"They all good with you?" Valeria asked.

"Yep, all perfect gentlemen," Athena said. Katya snorted and moved back to the front desk.

"Good. Now you can help me with Mrs. Dogan. She wants a fringe."

"A fringe? Yeesh, that won't look good on her."

"I know, it would be a terrible mistake. But I think you will have a better chance of convincing her."

"Let me at her," Athena said, rubbing her hands.

It was a busy day, and Valeria only vaguely noticed Sirvan and his group departing. Azad left shortly afterward. His exact working hours were somewhat mysterious, but he never stayed much past midday.

Shanaz left at three as she always did to collect her children from school. Valeria took the late afternoon appointments, with Athena taking charge of the washing and blow-drying. The last appointment of the day was overrunning, and Valeria could see Katya fidgeting at the desk from the corner of her eye.

"You can go, Katya," Valeria called. "I will close up. Almost finished, darling," she said to her client as she finished the blow-dry.

Katya didn't need telling twice, and the door swung to after her a few moments later. Valeria finished up with her customer, took the payment, and put up the "closed" sign as the woman left. As she was cashing up the till, Athena emerged from the sink room. She took the brush and began sweeping up the cuttings from Valeria's client.

"You can go if you want, Athena. I'll finish here."

"It's okay. There's only a few things left to do." She was wearing a sleeveless vest, and Valeria found herself admiring the smooth curves of her arms. She shook herself and focused on the cashing up. "Those guys were here a while, huh?" Athena said.

"Men are just the same as women. They get their shave, then they like to sit around and gossip."

Athena bent to push the broom right underneath the sofa. "Yeah. I bet their talk is different, though. More football and less holiday chat, I reckon."

"Azad says he hears a lot about cars."

"Urgh. I'd take a loft conversion over cars." Athena straightened and swept the dust and hair into a tidy pile. She bent over with the dustpan, and Valeria's gaze lingered on the stretch of her jeans across her thighs.

She blinked rapidly and tried to focus on counting the cash. But her brain refused to cooperate, and eventually, she gave in. "Did you ever have boyfriends?"

Athena looked round in surprise. "Me?"

"Yes, you," Valeria said, smiling. "Who else would I be talking to?"

Athena leaned on the broom. "One or two. Why do you ask?"

"I just wonder if you have always known that you preferred women."

"Yeah, pretty much," Athena said breezily. "But I went out with a few boys just to make sure, you know?" She grinned, and Valeria gave a nervous laugh.

"I don't really know. I mean, where I come from—"

"Oh yeah, sure," Athena said quickly, "I mean, you're married and everything, right? You're all set."

"Yes. I'm all set." Valeria felt the words falling heavily. She was set, like being set in stone or in an unbreakable mould. "Well," she said, trying to lighten the mood, "for someone who doesn't like boys, you can sure act like you do." She winced; that had not come out as she had intended.

But Athena didn't seem to take any offence. "You mean with Zoran? Sure, but it's all acting in this job, right? You have to act like you're interested in what the customers are telling you, even if it's super dull. In the last salon, I had a lady tell me all about her urinary tract infection. In great detail." She dumped the contents of the dustpan into the nearest bin. "And it's the same with guys. I don't date them, but I know what they're like. You have to act interested to keep them sweet. Pretend to care about how fast they can run a 5K or whatever." She pulled the bag out of the bin. "It's an interesting setup you've got here, having a bit of the salon just for the men. I haven't seen that before."

"It was Sirvan's idea," Valeria said shortly.

"Oh, okay." Athena seemed to be waiting for more. "Seems to work well, anyhow." She bent to tie a knot in the top of the bin bag.

Valeria finished cashing up and placed the takings into her handbag just as Athena looked up.

"That's a lot of money to be walking about with," she said.

Valeria shrugged. "The cash gets taken home every night. We have a safe."

"But why don't you just take it to the bank?"

"Sirvan does that."

"Okay. Just seems like it would be safer for you to take it during the day. That's what they did where I used to work."

"Sirvan says it is better this way. He knows about these things." Valeria fiddled with her handbag. She looked up and met Athena's black eyes.

Athena held her gaze for a moment and then flashed her smile. "Sure. He knows what he's doing, doesn't he? I'll stick this out the back, and then you can lock up."

"No, leave it. I will do it."

"You sure?"

"It's good for the boss to take the bins out sometimes."

"You're keeping it real." Athena placed the dustpan and broom in the corner and took her jacket down from the coat stand behind the door. "You're definitely going to be okay?" she asked, nodding at Valeria's bag.

"Yes, I'm always okay. I will see you tomorrow."

"All right. See you tomorrow." Valeria watched her disappear into the busy high street and looked around at the empty salon. She thought about what Athena had said: "You're all set."

There had been a time when nothing in her life had been set, when everything had seemed fluid and brimming with possibility. When she had first arrived in London, it had seemed a golden opportunity to remake herself in a place where no one knew her.

It was during those first heady months in a new country that she'd had her first experiences with other women. Away from the oppressive, small-town surroundings of her childhood, Valeria had felt almost drunk with the possibilities before her. She had revelled in the freedom she had to date and sleep with whoever she wished. The gay bars and clubs of London had been a revelation to her, places that she could hardly believe actually existed.

But the needs of survival had pressed in. Money had poured like water through her fingers. There was always something to pay for: rent, food, bus fare. She'd worked multiple different jobs to cover her bills, and the grind of always thinking about and counting money had begun to wear her down. She'd taken on precarious jobs that had involved pleasing men in order to get paid.

She had always lived in a world where the value of a woman was determined by how attractive men found her, and she'd become adept at the art of putting forward a false version of herself.

Becoming Sirvan's girlfriend and then wife had freed her from needing to think about money constantly. It had also meant that any feelings she had for other women over the years were pushed away because they'd served no useful purpose. She knew how fortunate she was to have escaped and could reel off a list of girls who had not been so lucky. When she met women she was attracted to, she simply pushed the feelings into the box inside her and did her best to forget about them.

She shook herself and slung her handbag over her shoulder. Then she hauled the bin bag out to the alleyway behind the salon and locked the back door.

She checked that everything was in order and then switched the lights off and closed and locked the front door behind her. She heard

Katya's voice echoing in her head, telling her how lucky she was, what a good life she had. Alongside the tug of shame at how this life was paid for was an ache of sadness at the thought of her younger self, with all that possibility laid out before her.

Chapter Four

Sirvan and his new business associates made another visit to the salon the following week. Athena again served them drinks and lingered longer this time, chatting and laughing. Valeria cut her clients' hair as usual but looked into the mirror continually to see what was going on.

Athena was being her usual charming self, and the men were noticeably more relaxed around her. Even so, Valeria was astonished when she saw Athena take her phone out and snap selfies of herself with the group. Her eyes flicked at once to Sirvan, thinking that he would rebuke them. But he wore an indulgent expression, like an uncle at his favourite niece's eighteenth birthday. Valeria was so taken aback that she lost her concentration and sliced her finger open. She swore in Russian, making her client jump.

"Sorry, darlin'," Valeria said. "Just give me a moment, yeah?" She went into the back and ran her hand under the tap in one of the sinks.

After a few moments, Katya sought her out. "What's the matter with you?"

"I cut my finger, that's all. It's not deep."

Katya looked at her suspiciously. "You're all jumpy. You don't like Sirvan talking to those thugs either, right?"

"He can talk to whoever he likes." She pressed the cut hard with her thumb, knowing perfectly well that this was not what was distracting her.

"Yes, but these are new men, right?"

"How do you know they are new? Maybe Sirvan knows them all really well."

"Nah. You can tell he's trying to sweeten them up. That's why he got Athena hanging round them."

Valeria's jaw clenched. It irked her that even Katya could see it. She turned off the tap and sucked hard on her finger. "It's none of your business," she said curtly.

Katya folded her arms. "I think that we are all here because of his business. This salon is *his* business."

It was the first time that Valeria had heard Katya acknowledge this fact. Even though she had been annoyed before that Katya had skirted the issue, Valeria now felt pained to hear Katya say it as though it was self-evident. She knew it was illogical, but she couldn't help feeling irritated. "And you are here because he is *my* husband," she said. "You think he would have given you a job if I hadn't asked him?" She was struggling to keep her voice down.

At that moment, Athena appeared in the doorway. "Mrs. Karim needs her treatment washing out. Can I do that now?"

"Yes darlin'," Katya said, her eyes flashing at Valeria. She walked past Athena and back out to the main salon. "And make sure you don't go bleeding into it, eh?"

Valeria pressed a piece of tissue paper against her cut, furious with herself and Katya.

"Are you okay?" Athena asked.

"Fine. I just cut my finger, that is all. No big deal."

"You're dripping blood on the floor," Athena said gently. Valeria looked down and swore again.

"Here, let me see." She took Valeria's hand and turned it over, her fingers gently cradling Valeria's. "I did a first aid course once, so you're in safe hands." Valeria didn't reply. Athena was so close that she could smell the scent of her hair. It was something vaguely floral, like lavender. "It doesn't look too deep. We just need to stop the bleeding. Is there a first aid kit somewhere?"

Valeria blinked at her stupidly before registering the question. "A first aid kit?" she repeated.

"Yeah. You know, the thing you should have shown me during my health and safety induction."

"Yes, there is one. It's in my office." Valeria clamped her fingers around the cut and led the way. The first aid kit was on top of the filing cabinet, and Athena made Valeria sit on the chair whilst she rifled through the kit.

Athena drew out a dressing and took her hand again. She held very still, doubting that she would be able to control her own body. Athena wound the bandage carefully around her finger, head bent to concentrate on the task. Her eyebrows were a shade lighter than her hair and her eyeliner was a bit wonky on her right eye. The skin of her face was perfectly smooth, and Valeria imagined what it would be like to touch it. She was so close that she could simply reach out and brush Athena's cheek. Her hand had begun to rise as if of its own accord when Athena stepped back with a satisfied sound.

"There," she said. "I reckon an actual doctor couldn't have done it much better."

Valeria blinked and looked. Her finger was bandaged so thoroughly that she could barely move it. "That's a good job," she said, trying to collect her thoughts from where they had been straying. She could feel the heat in her face, and her office felt unbearably small.

She stood abruptly, and then they were once again very close. Athena seemed to register this and took a step back. Valeria swallowed. "I must get back to my client. And you should wash Mrs. Karim's hair."

"Sure." She looked at Valeria with a vaguely quizzical expression, as if she was trying to work out what had just happened. Valeria coughed and motioned at the door where she was standing. "Right. Sorry." Athena turned and went back out through the sink room and into the main salon, Valeria following close behind.

"Sorry about that, Mrs. Karim," Athena said to the stern old lady in one of the chairs. "Had a minor medical emergency to see to."

Valeria returned to her own client, murmuring apologies and

trying to her best to grip the scissors round her bandaged finger. She could see Sirvan still deep in conversation with his new friends, but she kept her eyes resolutely on her client's head. She could sense Athena standing a little way off and could hear her easy patter. Amazingly, it seemed she could make even dour Mrs. Karim laugh. She really did have the power to charm anyone.

Valeria bit her lip and focused intently on the task before her. She didn't know what had come over her just now, but she was certain that whatever it was needed to be suppressed, to be fought against. Sirvan and his associates stayed a long time and left just after lunch, looking very pleased with themselves. Once they had gone, the rest of the day passed as normal, except for Katya being even more sour than usual. She left without saying good-bye, slamming the door so hard that the hinges rattled.

At closing time, it was again just Valeria and Athena. Athena watched her put the cash into her handbag and said, "I don't like to think of you walking home with all that money on you. It's not safe."

"I've been doing it for years. Everyone knows I am Sirvan's wife."

"So?"

"So Sirvan is well-known and respected. Nothing will happen to me."

Athena chewed her lip. "I think it would be better if I walked you home."

"Walked me home?" Valeria repeated, amused. "You gonna escort me through the mean streets, is that it?"

Athena laughed, a slight blush coming to her cheeks. "Yeah, I'm well hard, me. But seriously, we took a lot today. I'll sleep better if I know you're okay."

Valeria didn't reply, pretending to focus on closing her handbag. Her instinct, reinforced by the habit of years, was to brush Athena off. She did not cultivate friendships or any kind of personal relationships. Katya was her only real friend, but Valeria rarely saw her outside the confines of the salon. Sirvan preferred people to be kept at arm's length.

The tendency to keep people at bay had become so ingrained that no one even attempted to make friends with her. Concealing herself, her thoughts, and her feelings, had become second nature so that now, she found it almost impossible to be relaxed in someone else's presence. Admittedly, Athena didn't exactly make her feel relaxed, but her offer to walk Valeria home had been the first time that anyone had suggested doing anything with her outside of work. What harm could there be in walking home with a colleague?

"Yes, all right," Valeria said quickly before she could change her mind.

Athena blinked as if she hadn't been expecting Valeria to agree. "Cool. I'll get my stuff."

They locked up the salon and walked down the high street together. The restaurants were already filling up with people getting early dinners, and drinkers stood outside the pubs, clutching pints and bottles.

"It's always buzzing round here," Athena remarked.

"But not where you live?"

"No one ever called Enfield buzzing."

"You live with your parents?" Valeria wanted to be able to picture the sort of home that she went to each evening.

"Nah, I've got a house share with some mates. How long have you lived here?"

"Almost fifteen years. When I first came from Russia, I lived in Stockwell. Then I met my husband and came to live here." She thought ruefully of how much life could be glossed over in a single sentence. They turned off the high street into the quieter residential roads.

"Do you ever want to go back?"

"Go back to Stockwell?"

"No," said Athena, laughing. "To Russia, I mean."

"I don't know. I never think about it. I don't think it could happen."

"Why? You could go if you wanted to, right?"

"Sirvan," Valeria began and then stopped. She was acutely aware of how this must sound, that Sirvan controlled everything in her life, that she couldn't do anything without his consent. But wasn't that true? She pushed the thought away.

"Oh, I see." Athena filled in for her: "Sirvan wouldn't like it."

"No, it's not that," she said, feeling like she had to explain, to get Athena to understand. "He has been a good husband. Everything I have, he gave me. Without him, I would still be in Stockwell. And that was not a good life."

"Is that where you met? In Stockwell?"

"Yes. I was working in a bar at the time, and one night, he came in."

"And that was it? Love at first sight?" Athena's tone was teasing, and she tried to force a smile.

"No. But he was a striking man." She could remember the impression he had made from the moment he had first entered the dive bar where she'd worked. He wore the air of a successful man. She could see the esteem in which he was held by those around him and noted how other men made room for him, inconspicuously removing themselves from his path.

"Was it a whirlwind romance?" Athena persisted.

"No. There were no whirlwinds. He was just different from the other men."

He had noticed her at once and had gone out of his way to talk to her, asking her about where she had come from and what her aspirations were for life. She had found his gravity and serious manner reassuring. She'd felt safe in his company, and it had been so long since she had felt safe that she had reciprocated his initial advances out of gratitude. And once she was his acknowledged girlfriend, he had looked after her every need. She no longer needed to work in seedy bars, and the men she was around now were Sirvan's men, who treated her with scrupulous courtesy.

Athena blew out her cheeks. "Wow. You're making it sound very Mills and Boon."

"It wasn't a great romance. But we suited each other very well."

Sirvan had told her he had been married before and had grown children living in Turkey. Valeria knew that an older man often wanted a younger woman on his arm but was still unsure why he had picked her from all the more beautiful woman he could have had. When he had made a proposal of marriage, she had asked him this directly.

He had looked at her gravely and said, "You're a smart woman. You're not a bimbo. I have seen that you don't go shooting your mouth off. You keep things to yourself."

She had understood. He'd liked her because of the qualities she had developed throughout her tough beginning in life: caution, watchfulness, reserve. These qualities ensured that she would never embarrass him, would never be indiscreet, and most importantly, would never betray him.

"Well," Athena said, "I guess there's more to love than all that *Romeo and Juliet* bollocks."

"Exactly. Katya told me that Sirvan would look after me and keep me safe. And she said that was worth more than hearts and flowers."

At the time, the safety that he had represented seemed to be the most precious thing in the world. And so, she had accepted his proposal.

They were silent for a moment as they walked past the rows of almost identical terrace houses. Accepting Sirvan's proposal had seemed inevitable, as though there was no other choice that she could possibly have made. But sometimes, just sometimes, she wondered if there had been a choice and if she could have chosen differently.

"Still," Athena said, "It seems like you should be able to go back and visit your own country if you wanted to."

"I could go if I wanted to," Valeria said. "It's just, there is nothing there for me." She knew she sounded defensive, and she was aware of Athena glancing at her. She ached to know what she thought of her, if she regarded her with pity or just plain confusion.

She slowed as they reached the house. It was at the end of the street, with the neighbouring house and the house that backed on to it both also owned by Sirvan.

"Here we are," she said awkwardly.

Athena looked the house up and down as if she had been expecting something different. In keeping with Sirvan's dislike of overt displays of wealth, the house was entirely nondescript. "It's nice."

"Yes." She felt like she was trying to end a rather awkward date. "Well, thank you for the escort."

Athena executed a mock bow. "My pleasure. Pretty sure the sight of me scared off a tonne of potential robbers." She shuffled one foot over the other and said haltingly, "Look, sorry if I was a bit out of order with the whole Russia thing. I know it's none of my business but it's just…well. You're an intelligent, beautiful woman. Seems like you should be able to do anything you want. I mean, you should be able to do anything you want anyway, even if you were ugly and stupid. Which you're not, obviously."

Valeria barely heard her. Had Athena just called her beautiful? Her mind couldn't progress past this, and she realised she was staring at Athena, open-mouthed.

Athena looked mortified. "Look, just forget I said anything, okay? Let's just pretend I walked you home in complete silence. God, you must think I'm an idiot."

"No, no. I don't think that." She was aware that they had been lingering outside the house for a while, and she began to worry that Sirvan or someone else would see them and ask questions.

Athena seemed to pick up on this and said, "Okay, good. 'Cos I wouldn't want to be sacked for being a dork."

Despite her anxiety about being spotted, Valeria couldn't help smiling. "A dork? Do the kids still say that?"

"Only the deeply uncool ones. But look, I won't keep you any longer. You've got a home to go to."

"I'll see you tomorrow, okay?"

"Sure. Have a nice evening." Athena gave a cheery wave, having recovered her usual self-assurance, and walked back the way she had come. Valeria watched her go with the painful realisation that tomorrow was still a long way away.

❖

Sirvan was back late that night, and Valeria had already finished her coffee the next morning when he emerged. He greeted her and took his usual place at the table as she prepared the eggs and the cured sausage he liked for his breakfast.

"How'd it go in the salon yesterday?" he asked.

"Good. Mrs. Karim came in for her cut and colour. She says her boy Yusuf will be getting out next month."

"Yusuf," he said thoughtfully. "He the one who went down for armed robbery?"

"Yes. Mrs. Karim wants to know if he can get work when he is out."

He stroked his chin thoughtfully. "That's difficult. He went down because he was bad at his job."

"But he kept quiet, no?"

"Yes, he did one thing right." He leaned back in his chair and sighed. "Maybe I can find him work that he cannot fuck up. Driving or something." He made an impatient noise and flicked the pages of his paper. "Boys these days are no good. They want everything on a plate. They're not prepared to work like I did. What did you say to her?"

"I said I would let you know."

He nodded his approval and turned to his paper.

She finished frying the eggs and placed them on a plate with the sausage. It was not uncommon for her clients to speak to her about their husbands, sons, and nephews, hoping that Valeria would be able to convey their concerns back to Sirvan. Clients would say things to her in the salon chair that they would never dare to communicate to Sirvan directly. She had early on understood that the esteem in which he was apparently held was based on fear. She could read it on the faces of her clients, in the way their eyes anxiously scanned her face as they told her about their sons and husbands who were caught up in Sirvan's world. She sympathised with their sense of powerlessness and tried to use what little influence she had with Sirvan to help them.

She placed the plate before him and self-consciously cleared her throat. He put down his paper and raised his eyes to her.

"So," she began, "I was thinking last night that maybe I want to go back to Russia sometime."

"Go back to Russia? What for?"

"For a visit. I haven't been back there since I arrived in this country."

"Why would you want to go back? There is nothing there for you."

"But it's where I'm from."

He shrugged dismissively. "I'm from Diyarbakir. But I don't want to go back there."

"You wouldn't have to come with me. I could go alone."

"What about the salon?"

"Shanaz and Katya can look after it."

"I wouldn't trust those two to run a piss up in a brewery."

"I trust them," she retorted, trying her best not to sound petulant.

He folded his paper and leaned on his forearms. "What's this all about? You want that we take a holiday?"

She shook her head. They had never been on holiday. The most they had done was go to Southend for the day once. "No, I don't want a holiday. I just want to go back and see home once more before I die."

"You're afraid of dying now? Why? Who has said that?" There was an edge in his voice, and he was half-risen from his seat.

"No one has said anything. I mean just what I say. I want to go visit Russia sometime."

In the silence that followed, he sat back down, his eyes never leaving her face. "Okay," he said quietly. "You want to go to Russia. I tell you, it's not a good idea. Our home is here. And we need to work. We need to work all the time to keep what we have."

She picked up her coffee from the side and sipped it, steeling herself for the question she was about ask. "But you wouldn't stop me going?"

He looked at her from under his thick, grey brows. "I told you. It's not a good idea." He picked up his paper with deliberation, indicating that the conversation was over.

She took her coffee and went and sat outside in their small

patch of garden. She held herself very still, but inside, she felt feelings bubbling up that she had not felt in a long time. She could not remember the last time she had pushed Sirvan like that. Her usual default was to acquiesce to whatever he desired and not only that, but to never express any desires of her own. Asking for Katya to have a job in the salon was the last request she had made. Her hands tightened around her mug as resentment churned inside her. She wasn't sure that she even wanted to go to Russia, but Sirvan had shut down the mere mention of the idea.

She thought of what Athena would have made of the exchange in the kitchen. Athena, with her easy confidence and self-assurance. "You could go if you wanted to, right?" She felt her face burn with shame. She was a grown woman who could not go anywhere without Sirvan's express permission. If she had ever doubted the fact, the brief exchange with him had confirmed it.

She thought again of the woman she had been when she had first arrived in London, all those years ago. Perhaps she had been like Athena, full of easy optimism and confidence. And somewhere along the way she had become this person. She took another sip of her coffee, but it tasted bitter in her mouth.

Chapter Five

The next day, Valeria's eyes followed Athena around the salon as she swept hair, made tea, and did the countless other small tasks required to keep the place running smoothly. Valeria was in no doubt that it had been their conversation that had led to her questioning Sirvan about an entirely theoretical trip to Russia. It bothered her that Athena might think that she was completely under his control.

She lingered on the outline of Athena's body, and her blood warmed with pleasure at the sight. It had been a long time since she had felt such an attraction to anyone. Her world was a narrow one, and new people were automatically regarded with suspicion. But Athena's smile and easy charm had broken down her usual aloofness. And then Athena had called her beautiful. She kept recalling that moment and feeling herself redden with the memory. She had never considered herself beautiful, merely adequate for the needs of survival.

When the time came to close up for the day, she cashed up and prepared to slip the takings into her bag as usual. She paused and considered all of the money she had taken home over the years. She handed the cash to Sirvan, who placed it in the safe in the cupboard under the stairs. He told her he paid the money into the salon's account, the same place where all the credit card payments went.

Valeria did not know the combination of the safe, and she had no access to the salon's account. She stood for a moment, her hand halfway into her bag. She had always known this, and yet now, she was looking at it in a new light. It was as if she had spent her life skirting a corpse in the middle of the room and someone had finally pointed it out to her and made her look at it.

Even if she wanted to go back to Russia, she had no access to the money to do so. Sirvan paid for everything. On the rare occasions that she wanted new clothes, she simply asked him for cash, which he always gave to her.

Up until now, she had never considered herself hard done by this arrangement. It had made sense that Sirvan should have charge of the finances as everything was his. She'd understood that he did not want the kind of wife who spent ostentatiously, showing off her husband's wealth as a sign of status. So she rarely asked him for money, and this pleased him.

She took the money out of her handbag and recounted it. There was around three hundred and fifty pounds, which was about average for a weekday. Without even thinking about it, she took out fifty pounds and stuffed it into the pocket of her jeans. She zipped up her handbag, walked through the hair-washing room and into her office by the back door.

The filing cabinet was lockable, and she occasionally used it to store odd bits of paperwork. She held the key and reflected that this battered cabinet represented the only secure space she had. She unlocked it and shoved the fifty pounds into the back of the top drawer before relocking it. She walked back out into the salon before she could change her mind.

Over the next week, she began setting aside small sums from the daily takings. Sirvan never questioned the amount she came home with. This slow secreting of money gave her a thrill and a precious feeling that there was something in her life that was entirely hers, something that Sirvan did not know about.

❖

Valeria hoped that she had seen the last of Zoran for a while, but he showed up at the salon at lunchtime on a Tuesday.

It was a particularly busy day, and she was so intent upon her clients that she didn't register his presence until Shanaz muttered, "Oh God. He's back again."

Valeria looked up and saw Zoran standing by the front desk. He had a girl with him, and something about the way she stood with her eyes downcast made Valeria's stomach lurch with misgiving.

Zoran waved at her, indicating that he wanted to talk to her. Valeria resolutely ignored him for a few minutes, determined to make him wait. She finished the foils on her client and excused herself for a moment.

She walked over to where Zoran was standing. Katya was sitting behind the desk, looking at him coldly.

"Azad has left for the day," Valeria said.

"Yeah, I know. But I ain't come for me. It's her." He gestured at the girl, who kept her eyes lowered. "She needs a haircut."

Valeria looked at the girl. Her reddish-brown hair was long and tied up in a low, messy ponytail. With her practiced eye, Valeria could see that her hair was in a bad state, with split ends everywhere.

"What do you want done, darlin'?" she asked.

Zoran answered for her. "Just give it a trim and tidy up, yeah? Make it look less messy."

Valeria fixed him with a steely gaze. "Did you make an appointment?"

He rolled his eyes. "Come on, Valeria. It won't take you two minutes. Sirvan wants it done."

She clenched her jaw angrily. She knew that he had invoked Sirvan's name to get her to do what he wanted. And she couldn't simply tell him to get lost, however much she wanted to. For reasons that only he knew, Sirvan seemed to want him around.

"All right," she said. "I'll try to fit her in. We need to wash the hair first, though. You can come with me, sweetheart." The girl finally raised her eyes to look fearfully at Zoran. He nodded, and Valeria led the girl out to the sinks. As she went, she could hear Zoran asking Katya to get him a coffee.

She settled the girl into a chair and called Athena over. "Can you wash this girl's hair for me? I need to check my lady's foils."

"Sure." Athena eased the girl's head back and turned on the showerhead. Valeria looked at the girl's tense, miserable posture and went out to check on her client. A few minutes later, she went back to the sink room. The girl was sitting up whilst Athena gently patted her wet hair with a towel.

"That feel better?" Valeria asked. The girl looked up. She looked very young, younger than Athena. Her eyes were full of fear, and Valeria had a misgiving that perhaps this girl was afraid because she was Sirvan's wife. The thought sickened her. "Are you all right?" she asked, lowering her voice.

Athena looked at her sharply, no doubt picking up on her tone.

"Yes," the girl said.

"You know what you want done with your hair?"

"I don't care. Just whatever Zoran says." Her voice was heavily accented and sounded faintly familiar.

"Do you speak Russian?" Valeria asked in that language.

The girl's eyes widened with surprise. "A little," she replied.

"Okay. Listen. I'm going to take you out there and sort out your hair for you. I'll speak to you in Russian, and you can tell me about yourself, okay?" The girl nodded slowly, some of the fear calming in her eyes.

Valeria turned to Athena, who had watched the exchange with a puzzled expression.

"She came in with Zoran," she said. "I want to talk to her whilst I do her hair. Perhaps you can chat to Zoran for a bit?"

Athena nodded. "Sure. Whatever you want."

Valeria was grateful that she asked no further questions. She led the girl to one of the stylist chairs whilst Athena sauntered over to where Zoran was lounging on the sofa in the window. Despite everything that was going on, Valeria couldn't stop her eyes lingering on the sway of Athena's hips as she walked.

Athena greeted Zoran as if she was delighted to see him, and Valeria could see him respond instantly, his face breaking into a broad grin. Valeria pushed down the spark of jealousy that flared within her, telling herself she was being ridiculous.

She turned her attention to the girl in her chair. She unwrapped the towel and began to gently comb the hair out. "What's your name, sweetheart?" she asked, still speaking in Russian.

"Inna."

"And where you from, Inna?"

"Ukraine."

"How long have you been in this country?"

"A couple of years." Inna watched Valeria cautiously in the mirror.

Valeria glanced to the front and could see Athena chatting away with Zoran, who seemed to be completely absorbed by whatever she was saying. "How did you end up working for Zoran?"

"I had a job picking fruit for a while. But then there was no more work. Then my boyfriend told me he had found me a job. He took me to Zoran's house." Inna's voice trembled.

"Where's your boyfriend now?"

"I don't know. He disappeared, and I haven't seen him since."

Valeria's jaw tightened, but she made sure she kept her combing gentle. "How is it in Zoran's house?" she asked. Inna stiffened at once, her eyes dropping. "It's okay. You can tell me." Inna didn't reply. Valeria took out her scissors and began tackling the mass of split ends. "You know, when I arrived in this country, I didn't know anyone. But I knew everything would work out okay because I was prepared to work hard." Inna looked up and met her eyes in the mirror. "And I did work hard. But it wasn't enough. There was never enough money, and there were always bad men around me."

She kept cutting Inna's hair and waited. Finally, Inna said in almost a whisper, "Zoran is a bad man."

"I know."

"He says we owe him money, and we have to work to pay back the debt. But no matter how much we work, the debt is never paid."

"That is how he keeps you there."

"You are married to Zoran's boss?" Inna asked as if she couldn't quite believe it.

"Yes," Valeria said, her face flushing with shame. "But I don't like what he does." That was the first time she had ever said that out loud to anyone. Inna's pale blue eyes regarded her intently in the mirror. Valeria was about to say more when she heard a shout from Zoran.

"Hey! How long is this gonna take?"

"Almost done," Valeria snapped.

Athena broke in. "You can't rush a good haircut. It's not like with you guys, like shearing a sheep. A lady's hair has to be done just right."

Valeria finished up the cut and blow-dried Inna's hair and then held up a mirror so Inna could see the back. She met her eyes again in the mirror.

"Thank you," Inna said.

"Please don't thank me," Valeria said gruffly. "I've done nothing for you except cut your hair."

Inna opened her mouth to reply, but at that moment, Zoran strolled over. He ran his eyes up and down Inna as if he was appraising a piece of furniture he wanted to buy. "That's better," he said. "Now, come on. We have to get going."

Inna slid from the chair, and Zoran marshalled her from the salon without another word. Valeria walked to the window to watch them leave. Inna looked over her shoulder as Zoran marched her down the high street.

"He didn't pay for the cut," Athena said.

"Don't worry about it," said Katya quickly. Valeria could feel Athena's eyes on her, could feel the questions from them pattering against her back like raindrops. She turned and walked back to her original client and began unwrapping the foils from her hair.

Everyone seemed to sense that it was best to give Valeria a wide berth for the rest of the day. Even her clients seemed to pick up on it and were quieter than usual. She did her work mechanically, dwelling on Inna and the misery that had seeped from her.

She said the briefest of good-byes to Shanaz and Katya when they left. Athena was washing up the coffee mugs in the small bathroom sink whilst Valeria cashed up at the till. She counted the cash out into the takings bag and set aside a small amount, as had now become her habit. She went through to her office and was just placing her small cut into the filing cabinet when she heard Athena's voice at the door.

"I'm just heading off, okay?"

Valeria turned with her hand still grasping the notes. She pushed them hurriedly into the drawer and slammed it shut, but she could tell that Athena had seen.

They looked at each other for a moment in silence, Athena's large dark eyes resting on Valeria's. Finally, Valeria cleared her throat. "I like to keep some money in the salon in case we need it," she said. "For a float and stuff."

"Sure." Athena's eyes didn't move from her face. "Are you all right?"

"Yes, I'm fine."

"I thought perhaps that girl who came in with Zoran had upset you?"

"I'm not a fan of his. I would rather he didn't come into the salon."

"Was she his girlfriend?"

"I don't know." Valeria turned aside to lock the cabinet, avoiding Athena's gaze.

"I thought she was at first. But then...I dunno. There was a weird vibe between them."

There was a hint of a question in her tone. Valeria wondered how she would react if Valeria told her everything. The thought of being able to talk to someone was a tempting prospect.

"You wanted me to keep Zoran busy whilst you spoke to her," Athena pointed out.

"Yes," Valeria admitted. "I wanted to see if she was okay."

"And was she?"

Valeria looked at her for a long moment. Her face wore its usual, open expression. "Zoran...does not treat girls very well."

Something shifted in Athena's eyes, a brief flash, and then it was gone. "That doesn't surprise me."

"No." Valeria sighed and ran a hand through her hair. "I gave her a haircut, but I should be able to do more. I should be able to help her. You know she told me thank you for the cut? She thanked me." She shook her head.

"Hey." Athena stepped forward and laid a hand on her arm. "You were kind to her. That counts for a lot. And it's not like you can control what Zoran does, right?"

Valeria was painfully aware of how small and cramped her office was. She could smell Athena's perfume in the confined space, and the closeness raised the hairs on the back of her neck. "No," she said. "I can't control Zoran's behaviour."

"Right. You shouldn't feel bad."

How easy she made it sound. She couldn't know that Valeria felt bad all the time, every time she looked at Sirvan, every time she came into the salon that wasn't hers, and every time she encountered someone who had been touched by Sirvan's so-called business.

Athena's hand was still resting on her arm, the warmth of it seeping into her skin. Athena's face was turned up, and Valeria's eyes moved inexorably to her lips. She was standing so close, and Valeria was desperate to not feel bad, just for a short while.

She dipped her head and pressed her lips against Athena's. Athena stiffened and pulled her head back. Valeria's stomach clenched as she saw the shock written across her face.

"Valeria, I—" Athena began, but Valeria held up her hand to forestall her.

"Sorry," she said. "Sorry. I didn't mean...I only wanted..."

"No, it's okay." Athena recovered quickly. "I mean, I like kissing beautiful women as much as anyone. You just took me by surprise."

Valeria felt a flush of pleasure at Athena calling her beautiful again but composed her face into a serious expression. "Of course. You weren't expecting your boss to kiss you."

"Well, yeah." Athena laughed nervously, and Valeria took up her bag.

"I'm sorry. Please, forget it ever happened. I don't know what came over me."

"It's okay, really. But I should probably get going now if that's okay?"

"Yes, yes, you should go. I'll lock up."

"And you'll be careful on your walk home, yeah?"

Valeria smiled, touched that Athena was still concerned for her, despite the awkwardness she had introduced. "Yes, I promise. I will be on high alert."

"All right. I'll see you tomorrow."

"See you tomorrow."

Valeria followed her out and closed and locked the door behind them. She watched Athena walk down the street and then turned back to the darkened salon. She was amazed at herself. She could not remember the last time she had acted so impulsively. It made her stomach flutter with nerves but also with exhilaration. She had done something purely because she had wanted to, without reference to anyone else. For the first time in as long as she could remember, she had acted without weighing the consequences, without sifting through all the possibilities of how people would see and react.

She picked up the cash bag and stuffed it into her handbag. She couldn't be sure what Athena really thought about what had happened. It was perfectly possible that she would resign. Valeria was, after all, her boss, and kissing her had been unprofessional. Valeria wondered briefly whether Athena would be likely to spread the story around, but she found she was not unduly concerned. She had an innate sense that it wasn't the kind of thing Athena would do.

Valeria replayed the kiss in her mind, feeling again the soft lips that had brushed so briefly against hers. She could feel herself growing aroused, and she pulled her thoughts in sharply. She had to get home. Sirvan would be waiting.

Chapter Six

Valeria told herself that Athena wouldn't just quit, but she couldn't quite banish the tension in her stomach. She was distracted in the morning, but fortunately, Sirvan seemed too preoccupied to notice.

Katya was first to arrive, and Valeria tried her hardest to focus on what she was saying. She wanted to make amends, to regain some of the old intimacies of their friendship. Despite her best efforts, she couldn't prevent her eyes from straying over Katya's head to watch the door. Katya grumbled about her being away with the fairies.

Valeria almost cheered when the door opened, and Athena arrived, but she managed to keep her face under control.

"Morning, darlin'," Katya said, bestowing one of her rare smiles on Athena.

"Morning, all," said Athena cheerfully. She smiled at them both, and Valeria was sure she detected something knowing in the way Athena met her eye. But then Athena moved off to start the coffee machine, and Valeria wondered if perhaps she had imagined it after all.

The day progressed along the usual rhythms. Over the years, Valeria had found that she could tell what time of day it was without looking at her watch. All she had to do was listen to the sounds of the salon. The morning buzzed slowly and built to a crescendo by lunchtime, with people popping in during their lunch hours for a quick trim or blow-dry. The afternoon had more of a sleepy feeling until around five o'clock, when there was a mini rush as people came by after work.

Today's mini rush had been longer than usual, and by the time Valeria was finishing off the final client, it was almost a quarter past six. Katya was still answering phones and emails on the reception desk whilst Athena began to clean down for the evening.

Valeria brushed the hair from her client's shoulders. "You all done, darlin'," she said. "Remember to use the conditioner on the ends, yes?" She sent the woman over to Katya to pay and rested her hands on her hips for a moment, rolling her tired shoulders.

Athena was cleaning out the grounds from the coffee machine. She stretched up to take the filter out, and Valeria found herself admiring the flexing of the muscles down the back of her legs.

"You worried she ain't cleaning that machine right?" Katya asked in Russian.

Valeria started and felt her face flame at having been caught ogling Athena. "No," she said. "I mean, maybe. I like to keep an eye on things." Katya looked at her curiously, and Valeria felt even more flustered. She cleared her throat and began to put her scissors and other things away. "If you're all done, you can go," she said.

"You are letting me go earlier and earlier these days," Katya said.

"Why not? You work very hard. And I have Athena now to help with the closing up."

"That's true. She is a better worker than Dalia, no?"

"Much better," Valeria agreed as casually as she could.

"All right. I'll go home then and soak my feet." Katya shrugged her coat on and said her good-byes.

Athena finished cleaning the coffee machine and then emptied the bins whilst Valeria deposited her customary cut of the cash into the filing cabinet. She came out of the office just as Athena was closing the back door. They both stopped as if to let the other pass; both laughed nervously, then stood there.

Valeria cleared her throat. "I thought perhaps you wouldn't come back."

"What?"

"I thought you might quit. Because of...what I did."

"No way." Athena shook her head vigorously. "I love this job." A faint colour rose to her cheeks, and her eyes slid away from Valeria's face, as if it was too difficult to look directly at her. "And as for the kiss, well, I didn't hate it."

The air seemed to grow thicker. Valeria swallowed. "You didn't?" she said faintly.

"No. I kind of liked it, actually." She put her head on one side and smiled. It was as much of an invitation as Valeria had ever received, but she felt paralysed by what it meant. And as the moment stretched out, she could see doubt enter Athena's eyes, and her smile began to falter. Any moment now, Athena would turn away, thinking that she had misread the situation. And it would become another missed opportunity, just another occasion where Valeria had stood by and done nothing.

She stepped forward, and Athena seemed to understand. She tilted her face up, and Valeria kissed her. This time, Athena relaxed against her. Valeria put her hands on the sides of Athena's face, losing herself in the feel of Athena's mouth beneath her own. She felt Athena's hands resting on her waist, and the feel of being touched by her was almost too much to bear.

Valeria felt as if years of suppressed feelings were at risk of being unleashed. She told herself to go slowly, but her hands were already sliding beneath the hem of Athena's shirt and running across the soft skin of her hips.

Athena broke the kiss, and Valeria withdrew her hands at once. She had gone too far, too fast. She was opening her mouth to apologise when Athena cut her off. "Do you hear that?"

"What?" It took a moment for Valeria to drag her focus back to the dark, cramped corridor. But then she heard it. Someone banging on the front door of the salon. It wasn't unheard of for people to knock after closing time, but this was different. This was someone thumping on the door for all they were worth.

Valeria tutted in annoyance and walked back through the sink room and into the main salon. She could see a huddled figure by the door, its arm raised to knock again.

"We're closed," Valeria called as she approached. And then she stopped.

Inna's pale, frightened face peered through the glass at her. Without hesitation, Valeria unlocked the door, and Inna bolted through. Valeria closed and relocked it. "Please," Inna said in Russian. "Please, help me." She was wearing a scruffy-looking parka and folded her arms protectively.

"What's happened?" Valeria asked.

"I have run away from Zoran's house. And he will be looking for me. I didn't know where else to go."

Athena came through from the back, and Inna whirled at the sound.

"It's okay," Valeria said, quickly. "It's only Athena."

"What's going on?" Athena asked, her eyes flitting between Valeria and Inna.

"Inna has left Zoran."

"He will kill me," Inna whispered, still speaking in Russian. Valeria's blood ran cold because she knew it was true.

Athena must have seen something change in Valeria's face, for she said, "What do we need to do?"

Valeria's mind raced. She knew exactly what she was expected to do as Sirvan's wife. She was expected to call him or Zoran and tell them that Inna was here. But Valeria knew with perfect clarity that she could not do that. She could not look at Inna's terrified face and send her back to Zoran. "You need to get away from here," she said to Inna, switching to English. "Get out of London. Do you know anyone else in this country?"

Inna's eyes were wide as she considered. "On one of the farms I worked, there was an English woman who was kind to us. She would bring us cake sometimes while we were working."

"Do you remember where the farm was?"

Inna nodded slowly. "Yes. It was near Grimsby."

"Okay. You should try to get there. You can take a train."

"But I have no money."

"I'll give you money. Come." She led Inna into her small office. She unlocked the filing cabinet and gave her the wadge of cash.

Inna looked at it with wide eyes. "That is too much," she said.

"No. Take it all. You never know what you might need." Valeria shut the cabinet drawer with a bang. Her mind was whirling. A part of her knew that what she was doing was extremely dangerous. If Sirvan were to find out, there would be no excuse that she could offer. And yet, she had no other choice; there was no way she could hand Inna back to Zoran. She took out her phone and looked up the route Inna would need to take.

"Okay. You need to take the Tube to King's Cross and get the train to Doncaster. Then another train to Grimsby. Can you do that?"

Inna's hands were shaking, but she nodded.

"You know this woman's name?"

"No, but I think I can remember where the farm was."

Valeria bit her lip. It wasn't much to go on, not much to pin hope on. But it would have to do.

There was another knocking sound at the door. Valeria froze. She heard Athena calling, "Okay, Zoran! I'm coming!" She knew at once that Athena was letting them know, warning them. She bundled Inna behind the door of the tiny office.

"Stay here," she said. "Don't move or make a sound. I will come back and tell you when it's safe." Inna nodded, her eyes wide and frightened. Valeria walked back out in time to see Athena opening the door to let Zoran in. He looked pissed off, as if his night had been ruined by an unavoidable inconvenience.

"Hey, Zoran," Athena said, as if he was the one person in the world she had hoped to see. "You're a bit late for a shave."

"I don't want a shave," he snapped. "Has my girl Inna been here?" He addressed Valeria, who shook her head.

"She was the one you brought in for the haircut, right? No, she has not been here since then. Does she need something else doing?"

"She needs a fucking good kicking," he said. Valeria felt fury course through her. She glanced at Athena, and he seemed to read the gesture. "Sorry, darlin'," he said to Athena. "I'm a bit old-fashioned like that."

Even Athena, who could act so well around him, seemed to struggle to keep the disgust from her face. That seemed to annoy

Zoran, and he kicked at one of the salon chairs. "She's caused me a shit tonne of trouble tonight. And now she's done a runner." He glanced again at Athena and made a visible effort to calm himself. "I need to find her and make sure she's okay, don't I? That she don't do something stupid. Or something that she'll regret." He looked hard at Valeria.

She nodded gravely. "Sure. I understand."

"She needs to realise that she's better off with me." He spread his arms wide. "I know I ain't a saint, but it's much better with me than it is out there." He gestured to the high street beyond the window. "There's nothing out there for her."

"If we see her, we'll let you know," Valeria said.

He didn't reply. His eyes moved around the salon. "You're here late," he said. It was exactly how Sirvan would have said it. A small, innocuous sentence but with danger weighing down every word.

"Yes. We had a run of late appointments, and so we're later finishing up."

"And you ain't seen her? She ain't come in here?"

Valeria feigned surprise. "No, I haven't seen her. Athena, did anyone come in while I was out the back?"

"No. We locked the door after Katya, left so no one could have come in without us knowing."

Zoran looked from Valeria to Athena and back again. His eyes drifted to the back of the salon. "What's out the back?" he asked.

Valeria widened her eyes. "The sink room, the toilet, and the bins. Do you need the toilet?"

"Nah."

"Okay. But you want to see the bins, perhaps?" Valeria made a show of taking her phone from her pocket. "Let me call Sirvan. I'll check with him whether it is okay."

Zoran's eyes narrowed. "There's no need to bother him."

"Yes. I'm sure he has much more important things to be dealing with." Valeria locked eyes with him, and the two of them stared at each other for a long moment. She hated that she needed to invoke Sirvan's name, but she knew it would work.

He finally gave a shrug, as if the whole thing didn't matter much anyway. "If you see her, you let me know. She's much safer with me than out there on her own."

"Sure. If I see her, I'll tell you."

He turned to Athena and winked. "I'll see you later, gorgeous." He glanced at Valeria as if daring her to object. She pressed her lips tightly together to control her anger.

Athena locked the door after he left. "What do we do now?" she asked.

"You don't need to do anything. You should go home."

"What? I can't just go home."

"Yes, you can. Thank you for all you've done, but this is nothing to do with you. You don't need to be involved. And you shouldn't mention this to anyone, you understand?"

"But what are you going to do?"

"I'll help Inna get to the station and get away from here."

"I want to help."

"And you have. But the rest is for me to take care of." Valeria set her face into determined lines. She did not want to drag Athena into the sordid reality of her life. Athena looked at her for a long moment, and Valeria could almost see the different arguments crossing her mind. But the set of Valeria's face must have convinced her.

"Okay," she said. "But will you at least text me to let me know that everything is all right?"

"I don't have your number."

Athena grabbed a pen and Post-it from the reception desk and jotted it down. She handed it over, her fingers brushing against Valeria's. "If you need me, you call me. Promise?"

"I promise."

Athena lingered for a moment, her eyes searching Valeria's face before she unlocked the door and let herself out.

Valeria went back to the office and found Inna trembling behind the door. "Has he gone?" she asked.

"Yes. But we need to get you out of here."

"I could hear his voice, and I thought he might come back here and—"

"He's gone," Valeria said, ducking her head so she could look into Inna's eyes. "It's okay. I'm going to help you."

"Why?"

"What?" Valeria was startled by the question.

"Why are you doing this for me? You would be in trouble if Sirvan found out."

"Yes, but that doesn't matter. Not when I think that my only other option is letting you go back to Zoran."

"He has other girls," Inna pointed out sadly.

Valeria closed her eyes. "I know. It's in my power to help you now, so that's what I'm going to do. Maybe I'll get the chance to do the same for the others one day. Now, you got the cash I gave you?"

Inna nodded.

"Okay. Now listen to what I'm going to tell you. I have to go home. Otherwise, Sirvan will wonder where I am. When I leave, I'll lock the front door. But I'll leave the alarm off. That means you can go out the back through the fire exit. Wait for a few hours before you leave, though, 'cos Zoran will still have people looking for you. Take the bus to the Tube and then to King's Cross. Find this farm and this woman and see if she will help you. But don't come back to London if you can help it. Do you have a phone?"

Inna shook her head. "Zoran keeps our phones. And he has all my documents as well." Valeria felt a twist of pain as she looked at the frightened girl before her. Inna had so little to go on. As if reading her thoughts, Inna raised her chin defiantly. "I know," she said. "But I will be free."

"You are very brave." And definitely braver than me, Valeria thought to herself.

❖

Valeria returned home to an empty house. She walked about the rooms restlessly, with a tense, nervous energy. She thought about trying to eat something, but her stomach was too tight. Eventually, she sat in the front of the TV, staring at it without seeing anything.

It was gone midnight by the time Sirvan came home. He was

accompanied by Mesut, his most trusted associate. Mesut was taller and broader than Sirvan but had the manner of a kindly uncle. He smiled frequently, the corners of his eyes creasing when he did so.

Neither of the men was smiling now, though, and Valeria could tell by the set of Sirvan's jaw that he was very angry indeed. She rose to offer them drinks and food. They refused food, but Sirvan asked for coffee to be brought to them. When Valeria returned, the two men were sitting on the sofa, talking in low voices.

As Sirvan took his coffee cup from her, he said, "I hear that Zoran came to see you earlier."

"Yes." She guessed from his face that he must have heard about Inna's escape. "He said he was looking for his girl. Athena was there, so he didn't say anything more."

Sirvan grunted. "Good. He is not a complete idiot, then." Mesut shook his head sorrowfully. Sirvan took a sip of coffee and looked hard at Valeria. "I don't like that he came to see you when the salon was closed." He paused and took another sip. "But Zoran thinks the girl must be getting some help from someone."

His tone was casual, conversational, even, but she knew that he did not throw words around with abandon. She gave a wry smile. "Yes, he seemed to think that we might have hidden her in the toilets."

Mesut snorted with laughter, and some of the tightness in Sirvan's face eased. "He was just being thorough and checking all the places where she had been recently."

"Sure. Has he found her?" She mirrored the casualness of his tone.

"No," said Sirvan. "But he will." There was a cold certainty in his voice that chilled her.

"He knows he has messed up," Mesut explained.

"He told you that he'd lost her?" Valeria asked.

Sirvan nodded grimly. "That is the only reason he is not—" He stopped himself and took a deep breath. "He did good to own it. There have been others who have tried to cover things up and told me lies. That only makes things worse." Mesut echoed the sentiment by nodding solemnly.

Valeria put her hands behind her back to hide their shaking. "Well, now that you are home safe, I'll go to bed." She went upstairs and sat on the edge of the bed, breathing deeply and praying that Inna was on her way out of London. She looked at her phone and saw a message from Athena, sent several hours ago.

Is everything okay?

Valeria replied, *All okay.* She knew better than to write anything more explicit than that.

Athena messaged again almost immediately. *Good. Talk to u tmrw. x*

Valeria spent a long time staring at the final x. She thought about how good it would feel if she could call Athena and hear her voice, could hear Athena breezily assure her that everything would be fine.

CHAPTER SEVEN

Valeria struggled to sleep and rose early to go for a jog. Her early morning runs were one of the few occasions where she had time to herself, where she felt free from Sirvan's oppressive presence. Even when he was out, the house, his house, seemed to retain his essence, and she always felt as if he was somehow still watching from the very walls.

When she got back, he had already gone out. She had a brief text from him saying he would not be back until late. It was unusual for him to be out for the whole day, but she was more relieved that she could go straight to the salon without having to make his breakfast.

She went to the back when she arrived and found it empty, with no sign that Inna had ever been there. She stood in the darkness and quiet and prayed that Inna had made it. And then, her thoughts drifted inexorably to the kiss that she and Athena had shared. What would have happened if Inna had not banged on the door? She felt the heat rise up her throat as she set about the tasks to get ready for the day ahead.

Katya was the first to arrive. She took one look at Valeria and said, "What's the matter with you?"

"What do you mean?"

"You look awful."

"I didn't sleep very well."

"You worried about these new men, eh?"

"What?"

"They are always coming in here. People start to notice. They start to talk. They say, 'Why are these guys coming down here? This is not their area. Why are they talking to Sirvan?'"

Valeria looked toward the door, hoping that Athena might come in at any moment.

Katya droned on. "He needs to be careful. These men are not good. You touch pitch, you gonna get defiled."

"What are you on about? Sirvan is just doing his business as usual."

"No, not as usual." Katya wagged a finger in her face. "You're away with the fairies at the moment. You haven't even noticed. This is not business as usual. These are new men, so that means it's new business for Sirvan. Why is he doing new business now?"

"If a man runs a video store, and everyone stops buying videos, he has to change his business."

Katya stared at her. "You're speaking Greek to me, sweetheart."

"He has his business to do, and we have ours." As if on cue, the phone began to ring. Valeria looked pointedly at it.

Katya made an impatient noise and picked it up. "Yes, darling, how can we help? You want to sort out your do, hey? Getting to be a bit of bird's nest, is it? When you wanna come in?"

Valeria escaped and busied herself making coffee. She was distracted by wondering if Inna had made it on to the train and by thoughts of Athena and the brief kiss they had shared. It all felt like too much for her brain to process. She had no spare headspace to worry about what Sirvan's meetings with what Katya called the "new men" meant.

She heard the door open and looked up to see Athena enter. She felt her body jolt as if she had touched a live wire. Athena looked no different. She wore her usual skinny jeans and vest top, but Valeria felt her presence in a completely new way.

Athena smiled and said good morning. Katya, still on the phone, gave her a brief nod. Athena came over to the coffee machine where Valeria was standing. "All right?" she asked, quietly.

"Yes," Valeria said, and it really did feel like everything was okay now that Athena was here.

"Is she okay?"

"I hope so. I gave her the money, told her to wait a while before going. I pray she makes it."

"Me too." Athena's face was serious as she made coffee for herself and Katya. It made her look older, as if she had seen more of the world.

Katya finished on the phone, and Athena went over with her coffee. Her face instantly returned to its usual sunny expression. "You been hard at work already, eh?" she teased Katya.

"Someone has to concentrate on the job," Katya said.

Valeria clenched her jaw and took her coffee to her office.

The day wore on, but she felt tense and edgy. She kept expecting to be discovered, that Zoran would come storming in, having somehow found out about her helping Inna. Every time the door opened, her head shot up.

She conducted small talk with her customers on autopilot and was vaguely aware that she had missed something important when Mrs. Kochar began talking about her husband planning to sell his shop. The thought crossed her mind that Sirvan would want to know about this. In the past, Valeria would have passed on this information without question, but now she felt this was no longer an option. Inna's frightened face was before her, and any thought of helping Sirvan in his business seemed like a betrayal of Inna and girls like her.

Her gaze strayed around the salon as she nodded along sympathetically with Mrs. Kochar, and she briefly locked eyes with Athena. Athena smiled, and Valeria was sure she could detect something special in the smile, a subtle difference from the smiles that Athena normally bestowed on everyone, and it made her glow with pleasure.

Katya reprimanded her several times throughout the day for not paying attention, but Valeria was too caught up in thinking of Athena to care. She replayed their kiss in her mind over and over again, and the memory of it made the blood sing in her veins.

As the hours passed, Valeria found herself rushing to finish her appointments. Shanaz glanced across at her and said, "You're cutting like a demon today, Valeria."

Valeria smiled as she brushed the hair from her client's shoulders. "Yep. Less chatting, more cutting."

Once Azad and Shanaz had left, Valeria took her final appointment of the day, which was a blessedly quick trim for the Sahin's youngest daughter. Katya sat moodily at the front desk, resisting all attempts by Athena to chat with her. Valeria could feel her dissatisfaction emanating from across the salon.

The Sahin girl was done in under half an hour, and as Katya bade her farewell, Valeria said, as casually as she could, "You wanna go now as well, Katya?" Katya looked pointedly at the clock. "What? That was the last appointment. Athena and me can clear and close. You could go and soak your feet."

"My feet are fine," Katya snapped.

"Okay, so go and relax some other way. You look like you need to relax." Valeria tried a smile, but Katya was having none of it.

"I never relax. You start relaxing, you start losing your grip on things."

Valeria rolled her eyes. "Jesus. Give it a rest, would you?"

"I'm looking out for you, like I always do."

"I know," Valeria said, feeling a momentary pang at how horrified Katya would be if she knew all that had happened last night. "But you don't need to worry. Everything is fine."

"I don't know what's got into you. You've gone daft."

Valeria didn't reply. She was busy cashing up the till so she would be able to close up a few minutes early. Katya sighed and stumped out of the salon, the door closing behind her.

Once she had finished cashing up, Valeria locked the front door and flipped the sign to "closed." Then she gathered the cash into her bag and walked through to her office at the back. She deposited her usual cut into the filing cabinet and then went back into the sink room. Athena was in there, half-heartedly rinsing a sink. She stopped when she saw Valeria, and they looked at each other for a long moment.

Valeria felt her throat tighten. She had been waiting for this precise moment all day, had been hurrying through the minutes and hours as quickly as possible to get to this point, but now she was here, she wasn't sure what to do.

Athena took a slow step toward her. Valeria could not stop her gaze from lingering over the outline of Athena's breasts and hips. Athena stood before her and looked up into her face. "Inna wasn't Zoran's girlfriend, was she?"

Valeria blinked. She did not know what to say. The secrecy around Sirvan's business had become so ingrained that she had no idea how to talk about it.

"Look," Athena continued, "I'm thinking that Sirvan's work... may not be strictly legal. Am I right?"

Valeria kept her face very still. "What makes you think that?"

"Little things I've overheard from the clients. The way everyone acts around him. The way he doesn't go anywhere alone. And everyone knows about this area. And about how things work here."

Her eyes rested on Valeria's face. And they were very beautiful eyes, Valeria thought. The temptation to let go of her reserve was strong, but she held herself in check. She couldn't talk to Athena about this. Athena was an outsider in every sense.

"I take it Zoran works for Sirvan?" When Valeria didn't reply, Athena simply carried on. "Okay, I'll assume he does. And he brings in a girl who is clearly terrified. Later, that girl turns up, desperate to get away from him. But she doesn't have any money and is pinning her hopes on some farmer up north somewhere. That sounds to me like she wasn't with Zoran out of choice." Athena waited, but Valeria still said nothing. "It seems to me that Zoran and Sirvan are involved in exploiting women like Inna. Am I right?"

Valeria closed her eyes briefly, finding it hard to look into Athena's at this precise moment. "Yes," she said quickly, before she could change her mind. "You are right."

"About all of it?"

Valeria nodded. She sat on the edge of one of the chairs and leaned her face into her hands. Now that Athena had spoken the words out loud, shame curdled in her stomach. She was dimly aware of Athena kneeling before her and placing a hand on her knee.

"I guess Sirvan doesn't know that you helped Inna leave?"

Valeria shook her head. When she looked up, Athena was sitting back on her heels and looking intently at her.

"What would happen if he found out?"

"He would be angry," Valeria said.

Athena's dark eyes rested on her face. "You did a brave thing."

Valeria shook her head. "No, it was not brave. It has been years, and I have not done anything. I have helped. I have told Sirvan things—" She broke off and put her face back in her hands. She thought of all the times over the years that she had passed on snippets to Sirvan, feeling relieved as he gave his slow nod of approval. She thought of all the money the salon made, money that went straight to him. She felt like curling into a ball on the floor.

Athena gently took hold of her wrists and moved her hands from her face. "Hey," she said. "But you helped Inna. And you faced down Zoran. You did that. No matter what has happened before, you made a choice yesterday. A good choice."

It had not seemed like a choice. It had seemed like something inevitable, that it would have been impossible to do anything else. She looked into Athena's eyes and felt that something else inevitable was tugging at her.

She laid a hand against Athena's cheek. Athena's eyes seemed to shift and grow darker as Valeria leaned forward. She paused, her face inches from Athena's. Although her mind was in turmoil, her body was very clear about what it wanted, cutting through her churning thoughts with ice-sharp clarity.

She waited, but she did not have to wait long. Athena leaned forward and pressed her mouth against Valeria's. She could hear the blood pounding in her ears as she cupped Athena's face. Her skin was impossibly smooth, and as their kiss deepened, Valeria told herself to be gentle, to be slow.

As she felt Athena's tongue brush against her own, her resolve began to crumble. She grasped the waistband of Athena's jeans and pulled her up, drawing Athena into her lap. Desire flared with a white-hot intensity as Athena's weight settled against her. Athena shifted so she was straddling Valeria, her head bent to explore deeper in Valeria's mouth. Valeria ground her hips against Athena's, growing more and more aroused.

Valeria slid her hands up Athena's top. She fanned her fingers over Athena's breasts, trying to remind herself to go slow, but she couldn't. The feel of the soft, firm flesh only inflamed the ache at her core, and she squeezed Athena's breasts.

Athena whimpered, and the sound drove Valeria to new heights of arousal. She pulled at the button on Athena's jeans, but Athena reached down and placed a hand between Valeria's legs.

Even through the fabric of her jeans, Athena's touch felt as if it was against her bare sex. She gasped as Athena pushed the heel of her hand upward to brush against her clitoris. She squeezed her eyes shut as tremors of pleasure radiated from Athena alternately pressing and releasing. Valeria pushed her hips up and ground against Athena's hand. Athena moved slowly back and forth, catching on Valeria's clit each time. Valeria gripped Athena's hips, and her head fell back as she rode the rhythm, every part of her being reduced to this insistent, urgent need.

It had been so long since she'd experienced desire like this that her body was soon overwhelmed. She thrust her hips as her orgasm broke over her, and then she was still, shuddering convulsively against Athena's hand, her mouth open as the release swept through her.

Athena kissed her neck as the last pulsations ebbed away. She inhaled the scent of Athena's perfume, now with an undertone of something sweaty and earthy. Her mouth found Athena's, and they kissed again.

Finally, Athena slowly unfolded herself from Valeria's lap. Valeria stood and found her legs were shaky, and her clitoris still throbbed deliciously. There was a moment of awkwardness as they stood looking at each other.

"Sorry," Valeria said, "I meant to be slow but…it has been so long."

"You don't have to be sorry. I'm sorry that it's been so long since someone made you feel like that." The veiled reference to Sirvan made her blush even deeper. "I guess this is another thing that you probably don't want Sirvan to know about."

"Yes," Valeria said, running her hands through her hair. She wasn't quite sure how she had gotten to this point. A few weeks ago, her life had been trundling along, just as it always had. An anxious look crossed Athena's face, and Valeria hastened to reassure her. "But don't worry about that. It's not your problem. Besides, he is so focused on his new business now that he doesn't notice anything I'm doing."

"Okay," Athena said, sounding unconvinced. "Because I wouldn't want to get you into trouble."

Valeria was touched and stroked Athena's hair from her face. "Don't you worry about me, darling. I know what I am doing." She kissed Athena again. The kiss lingered, and she was just beginning to feel her ardour rising again when Athena gently broke off.

"I have to go," she said. "I'm having dinner with my parents tonight." Valeria released her reluctantly. She went with Athena to the main salon and unlocked the front door. "Good night," Athena said with a smile.

"Good night," Valeria said, fighting off the impulse to embrace her again. She watched Athena move off amongst the busy crowds of the high street and closed her eyes, savouring the lingering feel of Athena's touch. As Athena's figure became ever more distant, she felt the confines of her life begin to tighten, and she thought again of Inna, out there alone with nothing but the slenderest hope to rely on.

Chapter Eight

Sirvan was out when Valeria got home, and she was relieved that she didn't have to face him with the feel of Athena still fresh on her skin. She showered and made herself some dinner, but Sirvan was still not back by the time she was ready for bed.

She had a restless, charged night. Her mind whirred incessantly with everything that had happened in the last forty-eight hours. At some point, she was dimly aware of Sirvan coming to bed, and she instinctively moved away, bunching into the smallest space on the edge of the bed. She awoke feeling bleary-eyed and sluggish.

She was sipping her morning coffee when he came downstairs, dressed in his usual well-tailored suit. "I haven't started breakfast yet," she said. "I had a bad night."

"Don't worry. I will eat breakfast out today." Despite his own late night, he looked his usual dapper self. He grabbed some grapes from the fruit bowl and popped them into his mouth. "Tomorrow," he said, between mouthfuls, "there will be some guests for dinner."

That was enough to wake her up. "Who's coming?"

"There will be four guests."

"It's the guys who have been coming to the salon, right?"

He looked at her for a moment and then nodded. "And Mesut and Zoran."

"Zoran is coming?" She couldn't keep the surprise from her voice. She had assumed Zoran would still be in the doghouse from having "lost" Inna.

"Yes. He has a chance to make up for his mistakes."

A cold fist of fear clenched around Valeria's heart. "Did he find his girl again?" she asked as casually as she could.

He grimaced. "No. But the girl had no money, so she won't last long on the streets." He said this as if it was a relief. "Zoran knows he fucked up. And he knows that he can't afford to do that again. He will be on his best behaviour at dinner."

Despite trying her hardest, Valeria must have made a face.

"I know you don't like him, darlin'. Especially after he groped your girl."

She felt the blood rush to her face and turned aside to fiddle with the kettle so he would not see.

"But you know what you are good at?" When she didn't reply, he nudged her playfully with his elbow. "Hey. What are you good at?"

"Cutting hair," she said, turning back to him.

"True. But also, you're good at being nice to everyone, making everyone feel happy and okay. Even if you don't like them. You're good at hiding your feelings."

"Yes. I'm very good at that."

He nodded approvingly. "And when Zoran comes, you'll be nice to him and make him forget the time you almost cut his balls off."

"The scissors were nowhere near his balls," she protested.

"Wherever they were, you can make him forget about it. And we can all have a nice dinner and can do some good business, yes?"

"Of course. Is there anything these guys like to eat?"

"You'll make your roast lamb and some *kunefe*. They will like that."

"Okay."

He dug into his pocket and drew out a wadge of cash. He handed it to her. "And maybe you can get yourself a new dress or something. Doll yourself up for a special occasion."

She was wide-awake now. It was clear that this dinner with his new business associates was a big deal to him and that everything would need to be spot-on, including her own appearance. "Absolutely. I will make sure I am in good nick for them."

He smiled genially and gave her a peck on the cheek. "I know you will, darlin'." He glanced at his watch. "I've got to go. I'll see you tonight."

Valeria said good-bye and drank deeply from her coffee as the front door slammed. For the first time in what felt like ages, something else had driven thoughts of Athena from her mind.

She was preoccupied with the upcoming dinner as she walked to the salon. She ran through the to-do list in her head and realised with a pang that she would need to take the next day off work in order to get everything ready. She grimaced as she rounded the corner onto the high street. She rarely spent a day away from the salon. Despite what she had said to Sirvan about trusting Katya and Shanaz, in reality, she felt jittery at the thought of not being there to oversee things.

She reached the salon and unlocked the door. Inside, she savoured the silence and emptiness for a little while. She turned as she heard the door open, and her stomach flipped at the sight of Athena entering.

"Morning," said Athena, grinning at her.

"Good morning." Instinctively, Valeria stepped closer and then pulled herself up.

Athena seemed to catch the movement. "Guess we gotta keep it professional. Till later," she said and winked.

Valeria felt the urge to giggle like a teenager, but she repressed it and took a deep breath. "Yes. We must be professional today."

Athena mock saluted and shrugged off her jacket.

Azad and Katya arrived in quick succession, and the usual daily bustle of the salon began. Valeria cut hair and chatted with customers, her thoughts alternating between planning Sirvan's dinner and noting every single movement Athena made. Valeria was hyper-aware of her and could have pinpointed her exact location at any given point during the day.

Her attention was so focused on Athena's whereabouts that it took her a while to register that Katya was calling her from the front desk. "Hey," Katya called in obvious irritation. "There is a phone call for you."

"Who is it?" Valeria called back, still working on her client's cut.

"I dunno. Some girl who wants to talk to you."

Valeria was about to bark an annoyed reply when she felt Athena's eyes on her. She turned and saw Athena looking at her intently from where she was making coffee. Then Valeria understood.

She went over to the front desk and took the phone. "Hello?"

"Valeria?"

"Yes. Who's this?"

"It's Inna."

Valeria gripped the phone tightly but kept her face under control. She was very aware that everyone in the salon could hear what she was saying. "Ah, hello. Are you okay?"

"Yes, I'm fine. I found the farm again, and the woman I remembered is still there. She recognised me and has been very kind to me."

"That's good to know."

"She wants me to go to the police."

Valeria turned her face away from the salon so she was looking out at the traffic crawling up and down the high street. In normal circumstances, any mention of the police in connection to Sirvan's activities was strictly taboo. Valeria took a deep breath. She was already way beyond the normal parameters of her life. "What do you want to do?" she asked.

There was a brief silence. "I think that I have to. For the other girls."

Valeria thought of all the other girls she had known when she had first arrived in London. Where were they now? Had they disappeared into lives such as the one Inna had led? "Yes," she said. "I think that would be the right thing to do."

"But I know that it may cause problems for you."

"Don't worry about that. I can take care of everything."

"Okay."

There was a pause, and Valeria could hear movement in the background of wherever Inna was. A chink of crockery, like someone was making tea. It was a homely, domestic sound, and she felt a wave of relief that Inna was somewhere safe.

"Well, that is what I'll do. Thank you again."

"No problem," Valeria said, keeping her tone light. "We'll see you soon." She hung up the phone.

"Who was that?" Katya demanded.

"Just a girl. She wanted some extensions done."

"Why couldn't she tell me that?"

"She wanted to speak to me, to check that we could do it."

"Of course, we can do it. We're a bloody hair salon," Katya grumbled. "It's like ringing up the butcher and asking if he sells sausages."

Valeria walked back to her client and resumed her cutting and small talk. What would happen if Inna went to the police? Would Zoran be arrested? Valeria watched the snippets of hair fall to the floor. The thought of him being arrested was immensely satisfying. It would be a major upset to Sirvan. But things like that had happened before. Occasionally, someone was arrested and might even go to prison. But no one ever talked, and so Sirvan was always protected. And he simply replaced whoever it was and carried on the business. There seemed to be an endless supply of men desperate to work for him.

During her next appointment, Athena came and stood by her as she demonstrated how to cut layers. The client was a young woman who spent the whole appointment looking at her phone. Valeria glanced at the Instagram photos scrolling past and said quietly to Athena, "You'll never guess who called earlier."

Athena drew a lock of hair between her fingers and cut it carefully. "Our friend from a few days ago?"

"Yes. She called to say everything had worked out well."

"That's good to know." Athena's face was a picture of concentration.

Valeria lingered on the soft outlines of Athena's cheeks and on the adorably rounded end of her nose. Pulling her mind back to the haircut was like trying to pull her feet out of quicksand.

For her part, Athena gave no hint of anything untoward. She behaved exactly as she always did: friendly, open, and unfailingly professional. Valeria wondered if she had once possessed such unflappable self-assurance and if so, where it had gone.

Lunchtime came and went, and by the time Shanaz was getting ready to leave, Valeria was beginning to think maybe she had imagined everything that had happened the previous evening. Either that, or Athena was even better at concealing her feelings than Valeria was.

"I'll see you tomorrow, yeah?" Shanaz said, pulling on her coat.

Valeria started as she remembered her necessary day off. "No, you won't," she said. "I have to take tomorrow off to help Sirvan with something."

Katya's head snapped up from the front desk, and Athena paused in her sweeping.

"Oh, okay," said Shanaz. "That means I'm in charge, then?"

Valeria saw Katya open her mouth and said quickly, "You and Katya can look after things. It's only one day."

"We could make some changes round here, couldn't we, Katya?" Shanaz joked. "Introduce a hundred-quid minimum spend, maybe?"

"We could make it women only for the day," Katya said.

"Yeah. When was the last time old Azad had a day off?"

"I see that it's in safe hands with you two," Valeria said, smiling.

Shanaz said her good-byes, and Valeria went back to her client. She felt Katya looking at her, but she said nothing, and Valeria was relieved. It seemed like she could not have a conversation with Katya these days without it turning into an argument.

Katya left a short while later, saying to Athena with mock sternness, "No showing up late tomorrow just because the boss is away, eh?"

"No sir," Athena replied, snapping smartly to attention.

Katya smiled indulgently. "You're a good girl. Better than the last girl we had. She would have been late to her own funeral." Katya left, and Valeria finished her last appointment, and then it was just Valeria and Athena in the empty salon.

Athena swept and tidied whilst Valeria cashed up. She took a slice of the takings to the filing cabinet in her office and paused for a moment. She had been reminded this morning of what Sirvan expected of her as his wife. It was nothing she hadn't done before, but it seemed more of an imposition this time. She looked at her watch and wondered what time he would be home. Would he notice if she was a bit later than usual? She heard a sound behind her and turned to see Athena standing in the doorway.

"You stashing the cash?" Athena asked.

Valeria closed the filing cabinet and turned the key. "Yes. Katya and Shanaz will need a float for tomorrow."

Athena put her head on one side. Her face wore its usual affable expression, but Valeria could tell there was something more behind it. "Is it really for a float?"

"What?"

"The money you stash in here. We've never taken any of it out."

"Well, some of it is for a rainy day."

"A rainy day?"

"Yes. You never know when it might rain."

Athena's expression grew serious. "Is that the only money you have?"

"What do you mean?"

"I mean, what about the money from this place? We cut hair from morning till night. The salon must be making a nice profit, right?"

"I suppose so," said Valeria with an over-casual shrug. She didn't like this line of questions. It brought her too close to having to admit the level of control that Sirvan had over her life.

"But you must know if it makes a profit," Athena pushed. "'Cos it's your salon, right? And the money it makes is yours too. Right?"

"Why do you even want to know?" Valeria said defensively. "What does it have to do with you?"

Athena folded her arms. "Nothing, I suppose," she said. "But why would you need to stash money in here? The only reason I can think of is 'cos you don't have any of your own."

She said the words gently, but Valeria winced as if she had been stung. She leaned back against the desk, feeling the energy drain from her. Athena had already guessed at the truth about Sirvan. What was the point in trying to pretend?

"Fine," she said, blankly. "You're right. The salon isn't really mine. The money all goes to Sirvan. I take the cash takings to him every night. But recently, I started to think that maybe it would be good for me to have a little something tucked away, just in case. There. You happy now?"

"'Course I'm not happy," Athena said. "'Cos that isn't right, Valeria."

"Maybe not," said Valeria with a shrug. "But it's the way it is." Athena tried to hug her, but Valeria pushed her gently away. "No. I don't want you to pity me."

"I don't pity you."

Valeria looked at her sceptically.

"I don't," Athena insisted. "You helped Inna get away from Zoran, even though that might be dangerous for you."

Valeria closed her eyes briefly. She could feel the sincerity, but the words were no comfort. She had done little enough to help Inna and nothing for all the other girls who worked for Zoran and ultimately, for Sirvan. He owned them just as he owned everything else.

When she opened her eyes, Athena was standing close, her scent sudden and sweet. Athena kissed her, hesitantly at first, as if unsure how she would respond. She wondered briefly if Athena was doing this out of pity to try to make her feel better. And then she decided that she didn't care.

She returned the kiss and put her arms around Athena's waist, pulling her close. As Athena bent her head, Valeria pulled her top free from her jeans and ran her hands over the pleasing flatness of Athena's stomach.

Athena broke the kiss briefly and pulled the top over her head before returning to Valeria's mouth. Valeria ran her hands over Athena's breasts, smoothing over the fabric of her bra. Athena responded to her touch. She cupped Valeria's face and kissed her more deeply than ever.

Valeria reached around and fiddled with the clasp on Athena's bra for what felt like an age before it finally released. Athena shrugged it free, and Valeria took Athena's breasts in her hands, revelling in the feel of them. She kneaded and fondled, and Athena's breath quickened in her mouth.

Valeria pulled her head from the kiss and transferred her mouth to Athena's breast. She kissed around the nipple before taking it gently into her mouth. Her tongue teased and flicked as Athena gasped. And then she began to suck, and Athena gave a small cry. Valeria raised her eyes. Athena's were closed, and she was biting her lip.

Keeping her mouth firmly on Athena's breast, she undid Athena's jeans and eased them down until she could slip her hand easily into Athena's knickers. She felt the warm wetness of her and trailed her fingers gently across her sex. Athena gasped again and clutched the back of Valeria's head.

Valeria slipped a finger inside and worked it steadily back and forth as she continued her remorseless sucking on Athena's nipple. Athena's hands clenched into fists amongst Valeria's hair as her hips rocked back on forth in time with Valeria's rhythm.

"Valeria," she choked. "I—" But it was too late because she was coming, crying out as her legs shook, and she pressed Valeria to her. Valeria held her steady with one arm whilst the waves passed, and Athena was eventually still.

Valeria withdrew her hand gently. Athena's hands were still about Valeria's neck, and Valeria looked into her face. Her eyes were closed as she regained her breath. She opened her eyes and looked into Valeria's. And then she took a step back, covering her breasts and looking for her bra. She retrieved it from the floor and turned away as she put it back on.

Valeria felt a surge of dismay. "Is something wrong? Was that not okay?"

Athena was doing up her bra but turned back. "No, it was fine. I just didn't expect…I mean, I didn't think—"

"What? You did not think I could make you come?" Valeria asked, smiling.

Athena blushed to the roots of her hair. "I just wasn't expecting it," she mumbled.

Valeria looked at her in amusement. This was the first time she had ever seen Athena lose her easy self-assurance. If she was honest, she was somewhat relieved. It drew some of the sting from having had to admit that Sirvan owned everything in her life. Well, almost everything.

She straightened and went over to Athena, who was struggling with her top, becoming flustered as she tried to get it over her head. Valeria gently pulled it down and smoothed the hair from Athena's face. "I've been with women before," Valeria said, trying to be reassuring. "A long time ago but I still remember what to do."

"Like riding a bike, yeah?" said Athena with a nervous laugh.

Valeria kissed her, but she could feel how tense Athena was. She drew back and released her. "You want tea?" she asked.

Athena looked at her as if she had just suggested slaughtering a goat. "Tea? Now?"

"Sure, why not? We have some herbal teas, right? Something that can help you feel calm."

"What about Sirvan? Won't he be expecting you back?"

He probably would be, but Valeria's overriding priority at this moment was to make sure Athena felt at ease. "I'll text him and say I've been delayed," she said soothingly. "Come on, I'll make you some tea."

She headed back through the sink room and into the main section of the salon. The evening traffic on the high street continued past the large glass windows at the front, but the light was already beginning to fade, giving the empty space an eerie aura.

Valeria pressed the button for hot water and made two cups of mint tea. Athena emerged from the sink room looking more like her usual self. She took the proffered mug and blew on it. "Are you feeling okay now?" Valeria asked, leaning back against the counter.

"Yes. Sorry, I don't know what happened there."

"It is not your first time, is it?" Valeria asked, panicked because that had never occurred to her.

"No, no. It was just...unexpected. This whole thing wasn't what I was expecting."

"I understand. It's the same for me."

Athena sipped her tea and said, "Why are you doing this, Valeria?"

"Are you fishing for a compliment now?" Valeria teased.

"No," said Athena, her face deadly serious. "It's a genuine question. It seems like you have a lot to lose."

Valeria looked away. It was a good question, one that had been lurking at the back of her mind but that she had avoided facing. "Do I? You already figured out I don't have my own money. This salon has got my name, but that's it. Everything belongs to Sirvan, right down to the teaspoons." She picked one off the counter and waved it to emphasise her point.

"So, what? This is a 'fuck you' to Sirvan?"

"Maybe. But it's also the first time in years that I've felt alive."

Athena looked at her over the rim of her mug. "Really?"

"Yes, really. I wasn't expecting it, but I meet you and suddenly start feeling things that I have not felt for years. It's like there is a whole part of me that has been sleeping until now." She looked seriously at Athena and steeled herself for what she had to say next. "But if you don't want us to carry on, if you want to stop—"

"I didn't say that," said Athena. "I just want to be sure that you know what you're doing. I mean, there are risks, right?" Her usual lightness of manner was entirely gone, and Valeria had the disorientating impression that she was speaking to an entirely different person, someone older and wiser.

"Yes," she admitted. "But they're for me to worry about. Not you." Athena chewed her lip and didn't look convinced. "Look,"

Valeria said, anxious to reassure her any way she could, "I won't be here tomorrow, so you can have the day to think. Whilst I'm not inflaming you with my animal magnetism."

That finally coaxed a smile. "Okay. It will be nice to have a day without you distracting me. What are you doing tomorrow? Anything fun?"

"I have to make dinner for some of Sirvan's business colleagues. I need the day to go shopping, make all the food, and get everything ready."

"What are you going to cook for them?"

"Roast lamb and then some kunefe. You know kunefe?"

"Hell, yeah. Love that stuff."

"Let's hope they do too."

"Is it those guys who have been coming to the salon?"

Valeria took a sip of tea before replying. Her habitual caution in talking about Sirvan's business was hard to shake off. But she reminded herself that Athena already knew the worst of it. Plus, she had just regained some ease between them, and she didn't want to endanger that. "Yes," she said. "And Zoran."

"Oh." Athena wrinkled her nose in disgust, and Valeria nodded. "My feelings too."

"Don't suppose you could slip some laxative into his kunefe?"

"Don't tempt me."

"I hope it goes well for you. Do you have to sit there and make polite small talk with them all evening?"

"Yes," said Valeria with a sigh. "I must be nice and chatty with them, put everyone at their ease. I used to be good at that sort of thing but not so much now. And especially now that I have to do this with men like Zoran. I just hope these new men are not like him."

She drained her mug and glanced at the clock on the salon wall. She felt a twinge of alarm as she realised how late it was.

Athena seemed to read her expression and put her own cup on the counter. "Let's call it a night. Good luck for tomorrow."

"Thank you. I hope it's all okay here. Don't let Katya bully you."

"Don't worry. She'll be too busy vying with Shanaz for control." Athena grinned and was once again her usual, confident self.

Valeria unlocked the door and saw Athena out onto the street. Then she checked the salon over once more before heading home, formulating explanations for Sirvan as she went.

In the end, she needn't have worried. He came in some time later. He looked tired and was even quieter than usual, refusing all offers of food and drink and retiring to his office upstairs. Valeria cleaned the kitchen, relieved that she did not have to use any of her invented explanations.

As she scrubbed the hob, her mind replayed the day's events. It had been an extraordinary day. Inna was safe and would be telling the police all about Zoran's work. Valeria felt a thrum of excitement at the thought of Zoran being removed from her life.

And then there was whatever was happening with Athena. She smiled to herself, replaying the moments of their encounter. It was reckless and dangerous, but Valeria found that she was delighting in the thrill, in the rush of feelings breaking in upon her carefully guarded and sealed-up self.

She could conjure up Katya's voice in her head, telling her how stupid she was being, how she was endangering all the safety and security she had worked so hard for. She pushed the voice firmly away.

Chapter Nine

Valeria looked at herself in the fitting room mirror and smoothed the dress over her hips. It was beautifully tailored, as it should have been for the price. She turned around and viewed herself from all angles.

The dress highlighted her narrow waist and skimmed close to her thighs. It was a tad shorter than she normally went for, but she felt the high neckline balanced that out. Plunging, scooping dresses had never suited her. She did not have the cleavage for them. Not like Athena, she thought, thinking of the low vest tops Athena favoured.

Valeria's thoughts drifted inexorably to the outline of Athena's body and the feel of Athena's breasts beneath her hands. She shook her head, trying to chase the thoughts away. She turned once more and looked at the dress from the side, noting the skim of it over her buttocks. She thought of Athena looking at her in this dress and could almost feel the imagined gaze as a touch grazing over her skin.

She roused herself from her reverie. She had too much left to do to allow herself to be distracted. She took the dress off and went to pay. As she stood in the queue, she couldn't resist sending a text to Katya to check that all was well.

Katya's texts were like telegrams. She replied in capitals: *ALL FINE*. Valeria doubted whether Katya would tell her if the salon was on fire, but she pushed those concerns to one side. She had to stay focused on the task ahead.

It was only much later that day, when the lamb was roasting and everything was prepared, that Valeria felt it was safe to change into the new dress. She spent some time styling her hair and applying makeup and was just taking a final look in the bedroom mirror when Sirvan walked in. He stopped as soon as he saw her and gave a low whistle.

"You look stunning, darlin'," he said. He came and stood behind her and kissed the back of her neck.

She stiffened. It was not often that he touched her in this way. When they were first together, sex had been more frequent and always prompted by him. She'd always had the sense that he'd initiated sex because that was what was expected of him rather than because he especially desired it. It was power that gave him the thrill other men derived from sex. She had even heard Mesut once half-jokingly tell Sirvan that he should have been a priest.

In recent years, his desire seemed to have lessened even further, much to Valeria's relief. She understood that part of her role was to look good as his wife, and so she continued to be meticulous about her appearance. She endured his caress now, exerting all her willpower to prevent herself from flinching away.

"Are they here yet?" she asked to distract him.

He released her and went over to the wardrobe. "No. Mesut is bringing them and Zoran over in fifteen minutes. I got time to get changed and get some drinks ready."

"You seem relaxed."

He flicked through the shirts in the wardrobe. "The deal is as good as done. Tonight is about the final details and making everyone feel good." He looked at her over his shoulder, and she knew that there was an unspoken question being asked.

"Everyone is going to feel good," she assured him. "Even Zoran."

He gave his slow nod of approval and went back to perusing his shirts.

When the doorbell rang, Valeria had painted on a smile that clung to her face as tightly as the new dress clung to her hips. She opened the door to find Mesut and Zoran waiting with the two men who had come to the salon.

She invited them in, and as they stood in the hall taking off their coats, Mesut introduced the two men to her as Omer and Galip. She shook their hands and apologised for not having introduced herself in the salon.

Omer waved his hand gallantly. "No, no. We know you are working, and we would not want to distract you."

Valeria was about to reply when the doorbell rang again. She looked questioningly at Mesut and Zoran.

"Dunno who that is, sweetheart," Zoran said.

Her smile became even more forced at "sweetheart," but she went to open the door, already feeling annoyed that Sirvan might have added another guest to the dinner without telling her.

Athena was standing there. Valeria was so surprised that she couldn't say anything. For her part, Athena also seemed flummoxed. Her mouth dropped open as her eyes travelled down Valeria. "Wow," she stammered. "You look—"

"What are you doing here?" Valeria asked as she felt her skin prickle.

Athena blinked and made a visible effort to pull herself together. "Yes, right. Sorry. I brought the takings." She held up a canvas cash bag. "I didn't want to leave them in the till, and I know you always take them home, so I thought I'd bring them round."

She stepped into the doorway, making Valeria take a step back. Athena looked over Valeria's shoulder and called, "Hi, Zoran!"

Valeria was surprised to hear her greet him so enthusiastically.

He turned from where he was speaking to the others. "All right?" he said, with studied nonchalance. "You coming for dinner too?"

"I'd love to. I hear Valeria's kunefe is to die for. Are Omer and Galip here too?"

"How do you…" Valeria began and then stopped herself. She did not want to draw attention to the fact that Athena knew their names when she did not. Omer and Galip came forward and greeted Athena cordially.

"I just came to drop off the takings from today," Athena explained. "But I'm not stopping. I'll leave you to have your dinner.

I'm gonna get an Uber home." She drew her phone out and tapped at the screen as Mesut started saying something about coffee.

Athena's scent seemed to fill the hallway, and Valeria felt dazed by her closeness. At the same time, she felt irrationally anxious that somehow, Mesut or Zoran would guess what she and Athena had done together. Her thoughts were still on this when Sirvan descended the stairs at the far end of the hallway. Her stomach lurched.

He took in the crowd in the hall and at once greeted his guests and ushered them into the living room. He looked questioningly at Athena and then at Valeria.

"I brought the takings round."

"She brought the takings." They both spoke at once, broke off, and then looked at each other. Valeria spoke again hurriedly. "Athena has brought the cash from today. She's just leaving."

"Yes. Sorry for interrupting your evening, but I wanted to make sure the takings were safe."

Sirvan nodded gravely. "You did good," he said. He turned to Valeria. "I will get some drinks and then you can join us."

"I'll be right there."

He disappeared into the living room, leaving Athena and Valeria alone in the hallway. "Why didn't you message me?" Valeria demanded.

"I knew you had a busy day. I thought it would save you trouble if I just came over with them." She looked at Valeria uncertainly. "Sorry, was that the wrong thing to do?"

"No," said Valeria, taking a deep breath to calm her jangled nerves. "I just wasn't expecting it."

"You look gorgeous, you know that?" Athena murmured.

Valeria felt the heat rising up her neck. "I have to go and look after our guests. I'll see you tomorrow."

"All right. Have a good evening." Athena walked down the path to the front gate. She looked back and waved.

Valeria raised her hand in reply and closed the door. She stood for a moment in the empty hall, Athena's scent still lingering in the air. She placed the bag with the takings in the cupboard under the stairs. And then she forced the smile back on to her face and went into the living room.

She topped up the men's drinks and sat with them for a while. She asked Omer and Galip questions about their families and showed a keen interest in their replies. Galip mentioned his garden, and Valeria chatted amicably with him about his vines and fig trees. After about ten minutes, she excused herself to check on the food.

The food was all prepared and being kept warm, but she waited in the kitchen until Sirvan indicated that they were ready to eat. He paused for a moment as Valeria busied herself taking the enormous joint of lamb from the oven.

"Did you tell Athena to come here with the takings?"

"No," she replied, hefting the lamb onto the counter. "I didn't tell anyone what to do with the takings. I should have done. But Athena knows I take them home. And she walked me home once so…" She prodded the lamb, checking that it was cooked. She knew perfectly well that it was, but it gave her a reason not to have to look at Sirvan. She didn't trust her face to remain neutral when talking about Athena.

"She walked you home?" He sounded amused.

"Yeah. She said she didn't like me walking around with all that money."

He grunted, and she risked a glance over her shoulder. "She's a good girl. You did well hiring her."

She made a noncommittal noise that she hoped masked her relief.

He helped her carry in the dishes, and they sat down to dinner. The conversation over the meal continued in a similar vein as before. Valeria carried on with polite enquiries of Omer and Galip, knowing there would come a point when Sirvan would turn the talk to business.

There was a lull in the conversation once Omer had finished describing the patio he was laying, and Sirvan said, "We have a good deal here, no?"

Galip sat back and patted his stomach. "We do. I think it's

going to work out well for both our businesses. We get the girls from our end, and you give them the new life they are always so desperate for." He smirked, and Valeria's stomach turned over.

Sirvan raised his glass of wine and proposed a toast. "To good health and prosperity." Everyone chimed in with their own glasses raised.

Sirvan sipped his wine thoughtfully and then said, "You know that Zoran runs this side of the business for us." Zoran preened as Omer and Galip nodded their understanding. "This is a big move for us. We have never done business across borders like this. Sure, we have sent money abroad, but this is different. Getting the girls direct from you guys will be a big benefit to us."

Omer dipped his head in acknowledgement. "It works well for us too. We know we will always have a buyer for our goods."

Valeria looked at her plate as she thought about Inna's frightened face. Inna had been merely "goods" in their eyes, a thing to be bought and sold. She tightened her grip on her knife and fork as she thought of Inna fleeing in the night with nothing but the faintest of hopes to go on. But even that was better than what these men had planned for her. Her jaw tightened with anger, and she forced herself to relax her face.

Sirvan sat back in his chair and twisted his wineglass. Everyone waited in respectful silence until he would be ready to speak again. "I know I said originally that I would send Mesut out to work with you at your end. He has been with me for a long time. He is one of my best men." Mesut dipped his head in respectful acknowledgement of the praise. "But now, I think that it would be better if Zoran comes to work with you guys for this first shipment."

Zoran looked mightily pleased with himself, and judging from Mesut's expression, that was something Sirvan had already discussed with him. Valeria was astonished that Sirvan had seemingly forgiven Zoran so readily for the crime of losing Inna. Not for the first time, she wondered what Sirvan saw in him.

Galip and Omer both looked at Zoran, and their hesitancy was clear. Just as the silence was becoming awkward, Galip cleared his throat. "Okay. If you think that is best for you."

Sirvan inclined his head, and Zoran mimicked the motion. "I'm looking forward to working with you and learning from you," he said. Sirvan had clearly been coaching him, but Omer and Galip nodded politely.

Valeria noted that everyone had finished and decided this would be a good moment to clear the plates. She took them out to the kitchen and heard Sirvan proposing another toast. By the time she brought the kunefe a few minutes later, the talk had moved on.

"You get a flight next Thursday," Galip was saying, looking at his phone, "and we will have one of our guys meet you at the airport. He can look after you and take you across the border."

"Cool," said Zoran, grinning broadly. "I ain't never been to Istanbul."

"You will do exactly what you are told and keep your mouth shut," said Sirvan sternly.

"Sure, sure. You won't even know I'm there," Zoran said.

Valeria served the kunefe and was gracious with the praise that was heaped upon it.

"My mother could not make it better," Omer said.

"You better hope she never hears you said that," Valeria replied, smiling. "My own mother was a terrible cook, but she got so mad if you didn't eat all your food and say you loved it."

"It is good that not all things are inherited, eh? You get your beauty from your mother?"

"Obviously, I'm going to say that my mother was beautiful."

"All mothers are beautiful to their children," Omer agreed.

Valeria picked at her dessert, and her thoughts turned to her mother for the first time in a long while. Her mum had had very high hopes for her, had encouraged her to leave their little town and go and seek a better life. What would she think of the life Valeria had?

She looked around the table at the men, their faces flushed with wine and satisfaction. Everything between them was all friendliness and banter, but these were men who discussed trading in women just as if they were talking about cattle.

She felt her stomach lurch and set down her fork. She had been so focused on making things easy and comfortable for them that she had almost forgotten what it was they were discussing.

The food felt hard and leaden in her stomach. She dearly wished she could be gone from the room, from the presence of these men. With agonising slowness, they finished their dessert, and Valeria was able to escape to the kitchen with the dishes.

The men repaired to the living room, and Valeria cleared the table, relishing the chance to be alone. She thought of the photo she had of her mother in the drawer by her bed. It had been taken when her mum was about twenty and showed her posing on the shore of a lake, hands on hips and laughing. Valeria had discovered the photo amongst her mum's things when she had died. She knew nothing about where the photo had been taken nor who had taken it. Her mum looked happy, full of life, and doubtless with the same breezy optimism that Valeria had possessed at the same age. It was how she preferred to think of her mother rather than the careworn, ground-down woman she had known.

She washed the dishes, her thoughts far away. She started when Sirvan came to say their guests were leaving. She went out and said good-bye, receiving hugs and compliments on her food from Galip and Omer. Mesut thanked her with his usual gravity and then escorted Omer and Galip out to a waiting car. Sirvan placed a hand on Zoran's arm as he was about to follow.

"You understand that this is a big deal, right? I'm sticking my neck out for you, giving you a big chance."

Zoran composed his face into a serious expression. "I understand," he said gravely. "I won't let you down."

"No. You won't." Sirvan closed the front door after them and stood for a moment in the hallway, his hands on his hips.

Valeria went and retrieved the takings bag from the cupboard. She handed it to Sirvan. "I guess you better put this in the safe."

He roused himself. "Yes, I'll do that now." He took it from her and went into the cupboard under the stairs, hunching as he punched in the combination for the safe.

Valeria hovered in the hallway behind him. She craned her neck but could not see what the combination was. As he backed out of the cupboard and closed the door, she cleared her throat. "Perhaps it would be good for me to know the number for the safe. In case I ever need it?"

He smiled and patted her cheek. "Don't worry about it, darlin'. You leave all that to me. I'll always take care of you."

She forced a smile, pushing down the anger she felt at his patronising tone. He went back into the living room and collapsed with a loud sigh onto the sofa. A moment later, Valeria heard the sound of the TV.

She went back into the kitchen and continued the washing up, crashing the plates with more vigour than was strictly necessary. She thought again about her mother, about that smiling, optimistic girl and the hopes she had entertained for her daughter.

CHAPTER TEN

Sirvan must have been pleased with how the evening went, for the next morning, he was whistling as he came downstairs. Valeria served him his breakfast and suppressed a yawn. She had not slept well. Images and half-remembered impressions of her mother had plagued her dreams and left her feeling melancholy.

He devoured his breakfast with gusto and rose to leave. He kissed Valeria lightly on the lips and then downed the remains of his coffee. "You did good last night, darlin'. We got a good deal for our new business."

"*Your* new business," she corrected. "It has nothing to do with me."

He took her face in his hands. "It couldn't have happened without you." He gave her another kiss and was gone, still whistling as he closed the front door behind him.

She stood in the empty kitchen. She knew that his words had been intended as a sop, as a way of smoothing over her apparent pique. But she felt a cold weight in her stomach. "It couldn't have happened without you." Was that true? Had her kunefe and small talk contributed to sealing the fate of truckloads of desperate girls?

She went through the motions of clearing up and getting herself ready for a day at the salon. But the cold, hard weight remained.

She arrived early at work, as usual. Being back in the salon usually made her feel better, whatever the circumstances, but today, she looked at the familiar surroundings and felt a creeping horror at the thought that all her work went to fund Sirvan's activities. At some level, she had always known this, but now the naked truth of it seemed to be plastered onto the walls. She heard the door open, and her heart surged as she turned.

"Ah, you finally glad to see me?" said Katya as she came in.

"I'm always glad to see you," Valeria said.

Katya snorted as she hung up her heavy, faux-fur coat. "I get on your nerves. You think maybe you would be better off without me."

"That's not true. But I'm sorry if I have been off with you lately."

Katya looked somewhat mollified as she installed herself behind the reception desk. "What has been the matter?" Her keen grey eyes looked into Valeria's face.

Valeria sighed. How could she even begin to explain it? "I'm just feeling discontented lately."

"Discontented with Sirvan?" There was alarm in her voice.

"With everything. This just isn't what I thought my life would be."

"What? What did you think it would be?"

"I always dreamed of having my own salon."

Katya made a disbelieving noise and gestured around her. "What is this, then?"

"This is Sirvan's salon. He owns everything. Even the bloody teaspoons."

"You are discontented because you don't own the spoons?" Katya shook her head. "You've got a good life here. Much better than where you came from. And you remember what it was like in Stockwell?"

"Of course I remember."

"Then you remember all those other girls who weren't as lucky as you."

"Yes, I do," Valeria retorted, feeling her temper beginning to rise, "and I think of all the unlucky girls who have to work for Zoran and Sirvan."

Katya made a shushing noise as she glanced around the empty salon. "Don't go talking about that stuff here."

"I have to talk about it somewhere."

"No, there is no need to talk about it. Sirvan does what he does, and that keeps a roof over your head and food on the table. There is nothing more to it."

"Katya, there are terrified girls in Zoran's place. Doesn't that bother you?"

Katya looked toward the door. "Don't be naive, Valeria. The world is a cruel place. Terrible things happen to people all the time."

"You're saying I should just ignore it?"

"Be glad that you are in here instead of in there with Zoran's girls."

"I can't. I can't ignore what Sirvan does."

"You never cared before about what he does."

"That's not true," Valeria said hotly. "I just valued me being safe above everything else." As she spoke the words out loud, she felt the truth of them hit home like a punch to her stomach.

"Oh, so now you are not bothered about being safe?"

"Things are different now."

"How? How are they different?" Katya demanded.

At that moment, the door opened. Athena came in, and her easy smile faltered as she seemed to pick up on the tension. "Morning," she said uncertainly.

"Good morning," Valeria said, praying that Katya would not notice the heat that rose to her cheeks.

Athena glanced at Katya, who remained stone-faced and silent. "Did the dinner go okay last night?" Athena asked Valeria, taking off her jacket.

"Yes, I think so."

"Everyone wowed by your kunefe?"

"They seemed to like it."

"It was me who said Valeria should learn to make it," Katya interjected.

"Good advice," Athena said.

"Yes, Katya is always generous with her advice," said Valeria. There was a tense silence. Katya fiddled with the computer.

"I'll make some tea, shall I?" Athena said.

"Tea," Katya grumbled. "That is the British answer to everything."

"I thought I was meant to be the Greek one," said Athena. "But I forget that you guys prefer coffee anyway. You take yours black too, Katya?"

Katya nodded. Athena moved toward the coffee machine, and Valeria went out through the sink room and into her office. She sat in her rickety office chair and slowly turned round, watching the drab walls flow past. She heard someone approaching, and Athena appeared, holding a cup of coffee.

"I brought you this," she said, placing the mug on Valeria's desk. Her scent wafted into Valeria's face, and she resisted the urge to reach out for her. "And also," Athena continued with a quick look behind her, "I brought you this."

She reached into the back pocket of her jeans and withdrew a small wad of notes. "This is from yesterday's takings. I know you like to put some of it in here, so I kept a bit back for you. Didn't seem the right moment to try to give it to you last night."

She held the cash out, and Valeria's stomach lurched. "You shouldn't have done that," she said. "What if one of the others had seen? There would be no way to explain it." Panic surged painfully through her chest at the thought of the risk Athena had taken.

Athena's face fell. "Yeah, I guess that would've looked dodgy. Sorry, I didn't think. I just knew it was what you would've done."

Valeria took the bundle of notes, her fingers trailing across Athena's palm. Despite her alarm at what could have happened, she couldn't help being touched that Athena had done this purely for her sake because it was what she would have wanted. She couldn't recall the last time anyone had taken her thoughts or wishes so seriously. "You took a big risk," she said.

"I know. But it's your money. Or it should be."

Valeria couldn't help herself. She reached out and touched Athena's cheek, stroking the smooth skin. "Thank you," she said.

Athena leaned her cheek into the touch and then took a step back. "You've got a half head of highlights due in at nine," she said. "I'll get the colour sorted for you."

Valeria turned to the filing cabinet and stashed the wad that Athena had given her. She felt some of the melancholy that had dogged her all morning begin to lift.

Although some of her gloom eased, she was no nearer reaching a truce with Katya, who pointedly ignored her all day. So pointedly that Shanaz sidled up whilst Valeria was mixing up a colour for her client and said in a low voice, "Everything all right with you and Katya?"

"We've had a disagreement."

Shanaz nodded sympathetically, her large earrings swinging back and forth. "She ain't exactly a ray of sunshine, is she? But you guys go way back. You'll make it up."

"Sure," Valeria said breezily. "We'll be okay."

As Shanaz moved away, Valeria wondered if that was true. Katya had been almost like a substitute mother to her. When Valeria had first met her, she had simply accepted that Katya knew best. Their relationship had changed once Valeria had married Sirvan and had secured a place for Katya in the salon. That had placed Katya forever in her debt. Or rather, forever in Sirvan's debt. She frowned as she mixed the colour. Sirvan's ownership of everything extended even to her closest friend.

That afternoon, Katya left almost immediately after Shanaz without asking Valeria's permission. Valeria was sorely tempted to pull her up on it as she made for the door. She was still the boss in this place, after all. But she could not face another argument and so said nothing.

As the door rattled, Athena emerged from the sink room with Valeria's client. She settled the woman into her chair and remarked, "Katya gone already?"

"Yes," Valeria said, unwrapping the towel from her client's head. "Right, darlin'. Remind me what we're doing with this?"

The woman wanted a straightforward trim, and so Valeria called Athena over and talked her carefully through it. Athena cut the hair gingerly, taking the smallest amount off each time.

"Does she know how to cut hair?" asked the woman anxiously.

"Don't worry, darlin'. I'm watching her like a hawk. And it's a cheaper cut for you." The woman was mollified, and Valeria went back to coaching. She found it soothing to be standing next to Athena, breathing in her scent and watching her fingers move through the hair. She could forget the myriad of anxieties and frustrations and just focus on the simple task before her.

The client left pleased with her discounted cut, and Valeria locked the door after her. She cashed up whilst Athena swept up the hair from the cut.

"Did you manage to make nice with Zoran last night?" Athena asked.

"He was on his best behaviour." Valeria skimmed through the notes, mouthing the amount to herself as she went.

"His best must still be pretty gross."

"Yes," Valeria agreed. "But he's going away for a while, so we get a break from him."

"Is he off on holiday?"

"He's going to help out Galip and Omer." Valeria counted through the coins, piling them up in neat piles on the reception desk.

"Oh right. When's he off?"

"Next Thursday, I think. He was excited about seeing Istanbul." She swept the coins into the cash bag.

"I'll bet. You ever been?"

"No. I've not left the UK since I arrived here." She watched Athena sweeping out the final corners. "In fact, I have barely left London. Except to go to Southend."

"Istanbul won't be a patch on Southend. No two-penny machines there."

Valeria laughed. "If I ever make it to Istanbul, I will remind myself that it was better in Southend."

Athena grinned and swept the hair into the dustpan. As she emptied the bins, Valeria walked to her office with her cut of the cash. She placed it in the filing cabinet as Athena placed the bin bags into the back alley and closed the door.

Athena came and stood in the doorway of the office, watching as Valeria closed and locked the filing cabinet. "How much have you got squirreled away?" she asked.

"Not enough."

"Not enough for what?"

"For all the rainy days." Valeria ran a hand through her hair and sighed. The money seemed so small, so insignificant when set against the barriers that hemmed in her life.

Athena came over and tentatively put her arms about Valeria's waist. She raised her head and kissed Valeria lightly on the lips, then drew back and looked into her face. "Not feeling it?" she said.

Valeria shook her head. "Sorry."

"You don't have to be sorry. But is something wrong?"

"Just everything." Valeria leaned back against the filing cabinet and closed her eyes, feeling exhausted.

"You want to tell me about it?"

Valeria looked around the tiny office. She remembered how pleased she had been the first time she had set foot in it. A space that was properly hers, a space that defined her as a business owner. Except that even this crappy little cubbyhole wasn't hers. And the tiny stash of money she was hiding looked pathetic in the battered filing cabinet.

"I don't want to talk about it here." She wanted to get out of the salon. From being her most beloved place in the world, it now seemed like the symbol of how her dreams had curdled into something rotten.

"Okay. You wanna go get a drink?"

Valeria closed her eyes again. Athena made it sound so simple. But Valeria's presence in a pub or bar in the area would be noticed by someone who knew Sirvan. She never went out to eat or drink without him. He did not want a wife who went out drinking with her friends and ran the risk of forgetting who her husband was.

She could not face explaining all of this to Athena, so she simply shook her head. "No. I can't be seen with you in a pub."

"Okay," Athena said slowly. "But you must be allowed to leave your house sometimes, right?"

"Yes, of course," Valeria said defensively. "I go jogging some mornings before work."

Athena's face brightened. "Perfect. I love running, so I can join you. Where do you go?"

"Just through the park."

"Fine. I can go for a run with you tomorrow morning, then. That would be allowed, wouldn't it?"

Valeria felt objections spring to her lips like a reflexive action, but she bit them back. She would have control over this if nothing else. "Sure," she said. "Meet me at the park entrance at seven?"

"It's a date." And Athena smiled her winning smile, and Valeria felt herself melting under its warmth. She imagined what it would be like to feel that warmth every day and wondered if she could ever stop being dazzled by it.

Chapter Eleven

Valeria's regular jogs had been her salvation over the years. She made a point of emphasising to Sirvan their role in keeping her in shape, and he had never tried to prevent her from going. She did the same route each time, two laps of the park and back through the quiet streets. The steady rhythm of her feet on the ground soothed her mind and loosened her up for the long hours of being on her feet at the salon.

This morning, she rose earlier than usual to ensure that Sirvan's breakfast was ready for him. She did not want there to be any reason why she could not go. Fortunately, he was still asleep and had not stirred by the time she slipped out of the house. She jogged to the entrance of the park and saw Athena already there and waiting.

It had not occurred to her that Athena would be wearing running gear, and Valeria was momentarily nonplussed by how good she looked. The leggings outlined the shape of her thighs and tight top accentuated her breasts and waist.

Athena waved in greeting, and her eyes travelled appreciatively over Valeria. "You look good," said Athena in a low voice.

"You too," Valeria mumbled, looking about anxiously in case anyone might have heard.

Athena jerked her head toward the park. "Come on. Let's get going."

They set off side by side, gradually adjusting until they fell into an even pace together. Valeria relaxed into the rhythm as they ran around the edge of the park. It was quiet this early in the morning, with only a few dog walkers and fellow joggers about. A light fog hung in the air, and their breath came out in clouds as they went.

They completed one lap and started on the second. They were about halfway round when Athena put her hand on Valeria's arm and stopped.

Valeria came to a halt and looked questioningly at her. "Am I going too fast?" she asked.

"No. But we should stop for a moment so you can tell me what's going on with you." Valeria looked about her, and Athena rolled her eyes. "Come here," she said. She led Valeria off the path toward a band of trees and bushes that skirted the edge of the park. She pushed through them, and Valeria felt the ground begin to slope downward. Athena grasped her hand and guided her toward a fallen log that sprawled beneath a dense cluster of lime trees. They were completely hidden from the path, and it was dim under the thick canopy. It felt like a separate world, entirely cut off from the usual routines of her life.

Athena seated herself on the log and patted the space beside her.

"This is where you come for dates?" Valeria asked.

"No, I go on dates to pubs and restaurants, like normal people. This is where *you* come for dates."

Valeria sat down beside her. "Sorry," she said.

Athena tutted impatiently. "I wish you'd stop saying that."

"I would take you to a fancy restaurant if I could."

"But you can't?"

Valeria shook her head. She was aware of Athena looking at her, but she couldn't meet her eye. She felt ashamed that the best she could offer was sitting in cold, damp undergrowth that smelled of weed.

"And you can't because Sirvan wouldn't like it. He wouldn't allow it?"

She nodded.

Athena looked away, back up toward the line of bushes screening them from the path. "You're scared of him."

She didn't answer. She could hear the sympathy in Athena's

voice, or was it pity? She felt humiliated that Athena was naming the truths of her life so simply. Athena had seen it all so easily whilst Valeria felt she was only just waking up to the reality.

"Has he ever hurt you?" Athena asked.

"No. But I know he hurts other people." She had always been aware of things happening around Sirvan, things glimpsed in the periphery of her vision. People who seemed to disappear and were never mentioned again. Shops that opened and then suddenly closed again. Overheard snatches of whispered conversations in the salon or on the street as she passed. There was an aura of violence around Sirvan that went with him everywhere.

"What would he do if he found out about us?"

"I don't know." In truth, she did not want to think about it. "But he has so much on his mind with his new business that he doesn't notice what I do."

"Is that why Zoran is off to Istanbul? For this new business?"

"Yes."

Athena poked the toe of her trainer into the carpet of fallen leaves at her feet. "And what is this new business, anyway?"

"I can't tell you that," Valeria said as reflexively as drawing her hand away from fire.

Athena was silent for a moment, still rooting through the leaves with her foot. "If it involves Zoran, it probably involves girls like Inna. Right?" When Valeria still didn't reply, Athena placed a hand over hers. "It's okay," she said. "I understand. I know you probably feel like you can't trust me, or that I'm not smart enough to get it—"

"No, that's not it at all," Valeria said, taking Athena's hands. "It is simply that I don't speak about Sirvan's business. To anyone."

"Not even to Katya?"

"No. Katya doesn't understand. She told me to marry Sirvan because he would give me a good life. A life that was safe. Marrying him saved me from slipping into the kind of life these girls have. I would have ended up like Inna if not for him. And Katya thinks that is the end of it. I have a good life, so I should be happy. But I keep thinking about these girls and thinking that they were like me. And then I think, it's not just the girls in Zoran's place but all the other people too. All the shopkeepers that have to pay Sirvan money and their kids that are scared of him…" Her thoughts were running so fast that her words could not keep up. She looked at her hands, opening them so she could see the lines running across her palms. "I keep thinking of how I have nothing of my own, and then I think of all these people, and I'm ashamed."

All was quiet in the small belt of trees. The fog shifted and swirled, and Valeria felt the cold beginning to seep into her fingers and toes. But she didn't move, and it was only after a few moments that she felt able to raise her eyes and look at Athena.

Athena's face was solemn, once again making her appear older. "So Zoran going to Istanbul to help Omer and Galip. It *is* something to do with girls like Inna."

Valeria rested her head in her hands. She didn't want to say it out loud because if she did, it would mean it was real. She had a superstitious dread that by naming it, she would bring it to pass and doom countless women she had never met to misery. But Athena's gentle pushing was like speaking to a priest, being coaxed to confess her sins so that she could gain absolution. "They want to bring girls over from Turkey. Women who are desperate to come here for a new life. And when they get here, then they have to work for Zoran and Sirvan."

"Jesus," Athena murmured.

"I too wanted a new life here. I came so I could do something better. I wanted badly to have my own business, my own salon. Maybe these girls have similar dreams. And they have no idea what they are coming to."

Athena's face was set in grim lines, and Valeria almost wished she could take the words back so she could recapture the Athena who smiled at everything. Athena took a deep breath. "Now that stash you're saving up makes sense."

"What do you mean?"

"It's so you can get out of all this someday. Take a train and run away like Inna did."

She looked at Athena in stunned silence. She had never really considered what she would use the money for; she had only known that it felt good to have something that was hers. "I don't know. I couldn't...I mean, I've never even thought..." She stopped and blew her breath out in large white clouds. What had she been saving the money for? Some far-off, indistinct rainy day? Or so she could one day return to Russia? She thought of the small town of her childhood, of the apartment blocks and the patch of wasteland across the river where she and her schoolfriends had spent most of their time because there was nothing else to do. Was that what she had been saving her money for?

"Hey." Athena was leaning forward and looking up into her face. "Don't worry about that now. It doesn't have to be for any particular reason, does it? It can just be because it makes you feel good."

Valeria looked into Athena's face, her heart twisting at how beautiful she was. Athena leaned forward to kiss her. She returned the kiss, pulling Athena close and enjoying the warmth against her chilled body.

The kiss intensified, and all Valeria wanted to do was to lose herself in Athena, to obliterate herself and feel nothing but the pure ache of desire. She took hold of Athena's collar and pulled her off the log and onto the ground. The leaves were soft and slightly muddy, but Valeria was past caring. She sat astride Athena and kissed her again, her tongue moving deep within Athena's mouth. She pushed up Athena's top and ran her hands over the sports bra, feeling the nipples harden through the fabric.

Athena was squirming beneath her, and Valeria shifted so she was lying on top, her hips pressing Athena's into the ground. The smell of the damp decaying leaves pervaded everything, but Valeria barely registered it. She was entirely focused on the feel of Athena beneath her. She pulled impatiently at the waistband of Athena's leggings, tugging them down just enough to place her hand between Athena's legs.

Athena was wet, and Valeria wasted no time inserting a finger inside her. Athena arched, her neck bared to the grey half light filtering through the trees. Valeria moved inside her with single-minded intensity, leaves rustling with her movement.

Athena's teeth were bared as Valeria drove remorselessly on, and as she came, she clawed in the earth. Valeria buried her face in Athena's neck as she felt the pulsations from Athena's climax throbbing around her fingers.

Reality gradually seeped back into Valeria's consciousness. She became aware once again of the creeping cold, of the smell of rotting leaves and the faint hum of traffic as the city began to wake up. She thought of the day that awaited her in the salon, of Katya's sullen anger and having to watch herself to ensure that she did not allow her eyes to linger too long on Athena.

She groaned as she got to her feet.

"Bloody hell," Athena said as she sat up and brushed the leaves from her. "Was it that bad?"

"No, sorry. I was just thinking about having to go to work."

"You've got back-to-back appointments all day. You'll be too busy to think about anything but hair."

Valeria forced herself to return Athena's smile. They adjusted their clothing and emerged onto the path as casually as possible before resuming their lap. When they reached the park gates, they said a subdued farewell, Valeria scanning the faces of the people passing them. She jogged back along the still-quiet streets and let herself into the house.

She was unlacing her trainers when Sirvan appeared in the hallway, looking as if he was on his way out. "What happened to you?" he asked.

Valeria's head whipped up. "What do you mean?" she asked. There was a tremor in her voice, and she swallowed hard.

"You look like you fell over or something."

She looked down and saw the flakes of dried mud covering her leggings. She brushed them with her hand, but then saw Sirvan frowning as they fell onto the hall floor. She stopped. "Yeah, just a little tumble. Sorry, I'll clean it up before I go to work." She pulled off her trainers, fumbling over the laces as she felt his eyes on her.

"Hey." She straightened, and he came up to her, sliding an arm around her waist. "You look good," he murmured and kissed her.

She stiffened, unable to stop herself.

He drew back and looked at her. "What?" he said.

"Nothing," she said too quickly. He frowned. "I'm just all sweaty and dirty," she said, smiling in what she hoped was a coy way.

He leaned in again. "I know. And I like it." When he kissed her this time, Valeria was prepared. She couldn't relax entirely, but she was at least able to hold herself still and suppress the urge to recoil from him. After what seemed like an eternity, he finally disengaged and laid a hand on her cheek. "I'll see you tonight."

"See you later. Have a good day."

She almost collapsed with relief when the front door closed behind him. She stood for a few moments, taking deep breaths to still her trembling. She was getting to the point where she could hardly bear to be close to him anymore, and surely, there would come a time when he would notice this too.

Chapter Twelve

The day in the salon went much as she thought it would. Katya gave her a wide berth, but at least Valeria was so busy that she did not have time to worry about anyone noticing how much she looked at Athena. They locked eyes as they passed each other during the various tasks of the day, and Valeria was sure that Athena's smile contained something a bit extra for her.

As she cut hair and chatted to clients, her thoughts strayed to what Athena had said in the park. "It's so you can get out of this all someday." Perhaps that was what she was saving the money for, and she had simply not acknowledged it to herself. She turned her head and looked out of the front windows, at the buses crawling along the busy high street and the stream of people walking swiftly past. If she was to leave all this, where would she go?

Her imagination conjured up a small quiet house somewhere away from the city. Someplace where no one knew her, and no one would expect her to be anything at all. She smiled to herself, lost in the fantasy.

But then the client had to be finished to make way for the next one and so on until it was closing time, and she was again putting a laughably small amount of money into the filing cabinet. When she came back out into the main salon, Athena was putting her jacket on.

"I'm seeing my parents tonight," she said with a hint of apology in her voice.

"Sure, have a good evening." Valeria sensed that it would be no bad thing for her to get home on time tonight.

"You too. I'll see you tomorrow." Athena hovered in the doorway for a moment, as if unsure how she should take her leave. "If you want some company on a jog again…"

"I'll be sure to let you know," Valeria assured her.

Athena gave a final smile and left, the door clinking shut behind her. Valeria watched her walk away down the street as she did every evening. She allowed herself the luxury of imagining what it would be like if Athena did not have to walk away from her every day, if there could be some version of the future where the two of them walked away together.

❖

Over the next few days, Valeria spent a lot of time in her imaginary house. She furnished it in her mind's eye with lots of clean lines and accents of colour here and there. She pictured the large garden with fig trees and rosebushes. To begin with, she was alone in the house, moving through the rooms with the easy certainty that it was all hers. But there were times when she allowed herself the indulgence of putting someone else there too. Sometimes, it was her mother, and sometimes, it was Athena. Valeria did not dwell on the latter, feeling that there was something dangerous about letting her mind linger too long on possibilities that could never be.

Immersing herself in this imaginary other life had the effect of making her disassociate from her own. She felt the disconnect in the way she interacted with Sirvan and everyone at the salon. She could hear herself saying words as if they were a script, only a sliver of herself turned outward to face the world whilst the rest looked inward.

The salon that had once felt like the place where she could be herself now felt as if was another stage where she was required to perform. Perhaps it had always been that way, but it was only now that she was wearying of playing the part.

Sirvan gave no sign of noticing. He was home more often in the evenings, and she returned to the house promptly after closing every night, not wishing to risk any extra scrutiny. Yet, after only a few days, she found herself aching to see Athena properly. Working with her in the salon every day whilst playing her part was becoming intolerable.

She messaged Athena one evening as she sat on the sofa gazing vacantly at the TV whilst Sirvan made phone calls upstairs. She took an inordinate amount of time to craft her message, asking if Athena would join her for a jog the following morning.

Athena replied *Yes* almost immediately.

When Valeria saw her outside the park gates the next day, she felt a weight lifting off her. Finally, she could relax. She drew Athena into a hug, holding her close and breathing her in.

Athena made a surprised noise and gently disengaged herself. "I thought you were worried about people seeing us together?"

"I know. I just couldn't help myself." Valeria's cheeks ached from her smile.

Athena laughed. "Come on. Let's get going before you jump me right here."

They completed a lap of the park at a quick pace, and Valeria slowed as they approached the gates again. There was a small coffee kiosk that was just opening up, and she said, "Shall I get us a coffee?"

"Are we done running?" Athena panted, resting her hands on her hips.

Valeria permitted herself the luxury of looking her up and down and taking in every delicious part. "Yes. I don't want to run anymore." She bought two coffees and settled on a nearby bench.

Athena sat beside her, took the coffee, and they both watched the dog walkers and joggers coming past.

"I've been thinking about what you said," Valeria began.

"What did I say?"

"That I could get out of all this." The fog of the previous few days had cleared, and it was a crisp autumn morning. Valeria looked upward, enjoying the contrast of the yellow leaves burning against the dazzling blue of the sky. "Where would you go?"

"What?" Athena paused with her cup halfway to her lips.

"If you were to get out of all this. Where would you go?"

"I don't know. I don't want to get out of all this, anyway. I like working at the salon."

"But not forever, right? What do you want to do afterward?"

"Easy. Become a proper stylist. Like you."

Valeria shook her head. "No, not like me. You've got to make sure that everything you have is actually yours. You're saving your money, I hope?"

"Yeah, I put a bit aside each month."

"That's good." Valeria nodded as she sipped her coffee. "You've got to think about your future. You never know what might happen."

"True."

They were silent for a moment. A pair of middle-aged women walked past, talking animatedly to each other. There was a strong resemblance between them, and Valeria idly wondered if they were sisters.

"Do you have any brothers or sisters?" she asked.

"Just the one sister."

"And what's her name?"

"Briony."

"Briony? That doesn't sound very Greek."

Athena shrugged and looked out over the band of plane trees lining the path. "Yeah, I know. Dunno what my parents were thinking."

"Where does she live?"

"Newcastle. Look, why all the questions?" She was smiling, but there was a hard edge to her voice.

"I just want to know more about you, that's all. You know everything about me."

"I can tell you something about me, if you like."

"What?"

She leaned over and whispered in Valeria's ear. "I keep thinking about that clearing in the bushes and what you did to me there."

Valeria felt hot all over. She knew it was reckless, absurd even, but she didn't care. She threw the remainder of her coffee into the bin and stood. "Let's go," she said thickly. They jogged swiftly back to the belt of trees and pushed their way through, back to the same spot with the fallen log. The ground was drier this time, and Valeria lay down and pulled Athena on top of her.

They rolled in the leaves, kissing and caressing each other until Valeria guided Athena's hand between her legs. With Athena inside her, Valeria felt as if she lost and found herself at the same moment. She looked at the patches of blue that showed through the trees as Athena explored and unfurled inside her, and when Valeria came a few minutes later, she buried her face in the fragrant thatch of Athena's hair.

Athena lay on top of her, breathing hard and resting her head on Valeria's chest. Valeria revelled in the feeling and allowed her thoughts to stray again into her small, quiet house and to imagine Athena there, moving through the rooms with her easy grace.

She now knew Athena had a sister, which seemed to make Athena a more solid presence in the imaginary house. After a moment or two, Valeria said, "You've been with other women before, haven't you?"

Athena raised herself on her arms and looked at her. "What?"

"I'm asking about your ex-girlfriends," Valeria said, smiling.

Athena sat back on her haunches and pushed the hair from her face. "What's all this about, Valeria?"

"I'm just curious, that is all." She ran her hands up and down Athena's thighs.

"Well, yeah, I've had girlfriends before."

"When was the last one?"

Athena got to her feet and dusted herself off. "A year or so ago."

"And what was her name?"

"Sarah."

Valeria got slowly to her feet, savouring the smarting sensation from where Athena had been. "Were you in love with her?"

Athena started as if she had been slapped, and Valeria laughed.

"Why so coy? It's normal to be in love with your girlfriend, isn't it?"

Athena's usual assurance seemed to have completely deserted

her, and she shifted her feet. "No, I just wasn't expecting…I mean, I liked her a lot. But I don't think it was love."

"Have you ever been in love?" Valeria pulled her top back down. She raised her eyes and was caught off guard by what she saw in Athena's face. She looked stricken, as if Valeria had poured salt into an open wound. Valeria was confused and felt a twinge of misgiving. "Sorry," she said. "I didn't mean to make you feel uncomfortable."

"You didn't. I just don't know how to answer that question." Sadness welled up in her eyes, and Valeria stood there, unsure of what had happened exactly. Athena shook herself. "We should get going, yeah? We don't want to be late opening up."

She walked back up the slope to the path, pushing through the tangle of bushes. Valeria followed slowly, feeling as if a distance had opened up between them, and she could not understand why.

Chapter Thirteen

Everything followed its usual pattern over the next few days, but Valeria sensed that something had changed between Athena and her. Nothing changed in the salon. Athena was her usual, professional self and gave no sign that anything was amiss. Valeria sometimes wondered if she was imagining things, but then she would catch Athena's eyes darting away from hers. Athena had also ceased to linger over their tasks as they closed for the day. She swept up the hair and left with near-unseemly haste.

Valeria continued to go through the motions of life. She fought hard to keep her eyes off Athena, trying not to spend too long watching the sweep of her hips or the curve of her breasts. But still, she caught herself sometimes, lost in reverie. She tried her best to find out what exactly had happened, but there was no opportunity for them to be alone.

On Thursday evening, Valeria went home after closing. Athena had left as soon as she possibly could, giving Valeria the briefest of good-byes. Valeria felt heartsick but did not know what to do. She badly wanted to talk to Athena alone again but was racked by fears of inadvertently pushing her even further away.

She made Sirvan dinner mechanically, her own appetite having long since vanished. He spent the evening sat on the sofa with his phone, alternately texting or taking calls. He waved her away when she entered with a plate of food for him, and so she returned to the kitchen. She took out her phone and thought about messaging

Athena. But she could not think what to say. Should she say sorry? But she did not know what she was apologising for. Should she suggest another jog?

She put her phone down and tried to focus on a magazine, but she caught herself daydreaming about Athena, about the fall of her hair around her cheeks.

She threw the magazine away in frustration. Then she got up and changed into her running gear. She let herself out and ran her usual route around the park. She pushed herself hard, harder than she normally would. She wanted to feel her legs burning, to feel that dull stupor of fatigue that would surely, finally quieten her thoughts.

She completed her circuit and went home. She stood in the hallway, breathing hard as she bent to unlace her trainers.

Sirvan appeared in the living room doorway. "Where have you been?" he asked. Valeria indicated her running gear for an answer. "You didn't tell me you were going out."

"You were on the phone."

"Do not go out again without telling me." He didn't raise his voice, but Valeria could feel the weight behind his words.

She felt a surge of annoyance, but the schooling of many years took over. She dropped her eyes and said meekly, "Okay. I'll tell you."

He paused for a moment, hovering with uncharacteristic uncertainty, and then he said, "Zoran has been arrested."

She blinked, her mind so preoccupied with Athena that she could barely take this in. "Zoran?" she repeated.

"Yes. Mesut just called to tell me."

"Wait, isn't Zoran in Istanbul?"

"He should be," he said grimly. "He was arrested at the airport. They got him just before he boarded his flight."

Valeria composed her face into an expression of concern. Inwardly, she rejoiced that Zoran was in a cell. "What will you do?"

"I don't know." His face was even grimmer now. "I need to know what is going on. Police haven't been near us for ages, and now they suddenly pick up Zoran?" He paced up the hall, going to the bottom of the stairs and then back again. "That girl he lost," he said thoughtfully. "Maybe she went to the police."

"I guess she could've done," Valeria said, hoping that it had been Inna who had gotten Zoran behind bars.

"But then they pick him up just as he is about to leave the country?" Sirvan bit his thumbnail, talking more to himself than to her. "It's like they knew he was about to leave and had to get him before then. The girl would not have known anything about that. It can't be coincidence."

Valeria felt the unspoken words thickening in the small space of the hall. He was implying that someone might have talked to the police, and she had been in his world long enough to realise the implications of that. "Omer and Galip didn't seem that keen on him coming."

He looked at her sharply. "Even if that is true, this deal is important to them. They would be fools to risk it."

She wished she hadn't said anything. If Sirvan did have someone ratting him out to the police, then she was delighted. "Yes, I'm sure you're right," she said as soothingly as she could.

He went back into the living room, and a few minutes later, Valeria heard him talking on the phone as he paced restlessly up and down.

She went upstairs to shower. As the hot water sluiced over her, she wondered if the arrest would lead to the deal with Omer and Galip being called off. If so, getting arrested would be the one useful thing Zoran had managed to accomplish.

Maybe there was someone else in Sirvan's circle who didn't like the work that Zoran did. Well, more power to them if it helped stop the trafficking of women like Inna. But she wouldn't want to be in their shoes when Sirvan found out.

❖

As soon as Katya arrived in the salon the next morning, Valeria could tell that she had heard about Zoran. She shuffled off her coat and came straight to where Athena and Valeria were making coffee.

"I hear we won't be seeing that goat round here anytime soon?" she said in Russian.

"How do you know about that?" Valeria asked.

"Mesut told Azad, and he told Amina, and I saw her this morning when I was buying my paper."

Valeria rolled her eyes.

"Sirvan better hope Zoran keeps his mouth shut," Katya said.

"What's this about Zoran?" Athena said.

Katya and Valeria exchanged glances. "You might as well tell her," said Valeria. "Seeing as how everyone knows already."

"Zoran has been arrested at Heathrow," Katya said, switching back to English.

Athena's eyebrows rose. "Wow. Can't imagine he enjoyed that very much."

Valeria took a grim satisfaction in imagining Zoran's outrage at being clapped in handcuffs.

"You can forget chatting about holiday plans today," Katya said, sauntering to the front desk. "This gonna be all anyone talks about."

Athena looked at Valeria. "I guess it's a pretty big deal, huh?"

"Yes," she said, sipping her coffee. "Sirvan is not pleased."

Athena drew closer and lowered her voice. "What is he going to do?"

"I don't know. I don't think even he knows."

"I guess Omer and Galip will be relieved. Always seemed like they didn't take to him."

"Yes, I thought that too. But Sirvan is convinced they would not have had anything to do with this."

"Zoran wasn't exactly the subtle type, was he? Maybe some of the stuff he was doing finally got noticed by the police." Athena glanced swiftly around the salon and lowered her voice even further. "Do you think Inna went to the police?"

"She said she was going to," Valeria murmured. She could see Katya glancing curiously at them, so she moved away, saying loudly, "I have some extensions due at half-past. You can watch how to do them."

Katya was right; all the talk in the salon was about Zoran's arrest. He had cut a familiar figure in the area and was universally disliked. There was a lot of barely contained glee that he had finally had his comeuppance.

Shanaz and Athena had gone for their lunch break, and Azad was dozing in one of his chairs when Katya came and stood next to Valeria as she was cutting layers into her client's hair.

"So," Katya said in Russian, "who does Sirvan reckon tipped them off?"

"Tipped who off?" Valeria said distractedly.

Katya made an exasperated noise. "The police. Who tipped them off?"

"How should I know?"

"Someone must have talked to them. Too much of a coincidence that Zoran gets arrested just as he is about to leave the country, right?"

"Yes, probably," Valeria said, moving around her client's head. "But if it stops his business with the girls, then I'm happy."

Katya shook her head as if marvelling at her slowness. "Zoran's business is Sirvan's business. You gonna be happy if his business falls apart? What happens to your house and salon, then?"

"His house. His salon."

"What, you don't care if this all comes crashing down?"

Valeria knew that Katya would not like her honest answer to that question. She gently adjusted her client's head. "We almost done here, darlin'," she said.

Katya waited a few more moments and when Valeria said nothing further, stomped back to the desk, huffing angrily as she went.

Valeria's scissors moved with practiced ease as she contemplated what would happen if Sirvan's business collapsed. She felt a thrill of excitement at the thought. She imagined the salon, her house, and all of it falling down like a stage set, leaving the actors alone on an empty stage. Alone but free.

She was just beginning her last cut of the day when Sirvan came in. Shanaz and Azad had already gone, but Katya greeted Sirvan, and Athena gave him a brief smile.

Sirvan returned neither and instead walked over to Valeria, jerking his head to indicate he wanted to talk to her. She pushed down her annoyance and told her client she would be back in a minute. She walked with him through the washing area and into her tiny office. It seemed even smaller with him present, like he took up more space than he ought to.

His eyes ranged around the room. They lingered briefly on the filing cabinet, and Valeria was terrified that somehow, he knew about the stash. "What time are you done today?" he asked.

"About half six, same as usual."

"You come home straightaway, okay?"

"Sure."

"And when you get home, you stay home. No going running."

"What, I'm not allowed to leave the house now?" His look was steely, and Valeria dropped her eyes. "Okay."

He walked back to the main salon, and Valeria followed. Athena looked up from sweeping, and Valeria thanked God that she hadn't overheard Sirvan giving her orders. He left without another word to anyone.

Valeria went back to her client. Out of the corner of her eye, she could see Katya approaching. "Don't even think about it," she snapped in Russian.

"What?"

"Do not badger me about what he said."

"I wasn't going to say nothing about badgers," Katya replied hotly. The client's eyes widened in the mirror at the angry tone.

"Don't mind her," she said soothingly in English. "She's had some bad news today."

Katya took it upon herself to leave early and slammed the door a few minutes later. Valeria sighed and finished up her cut.

A little while later, she had locked the front door and was cashing up. As she took a handful of notes to the filing cabinet, she saw that the back door to the alley was open. She could hear Athena banging the bins around. She placed the money in the cabinet and then went and stood in the back doorway.

Athena was stuffing a black bin bag into the refuse bin. She turned. The light was already leeching from the evening, washing everything a pale grey.

"Are you okay?" Valeria asked.

"Me? Yeah, I'm fine."

"But you do not want to go jogging with me anymore?" Valeria said it with a playful tone, trying to mask her terror that Athena would say no.

Athena stuck her hands into the back pockets of her jeans and looked at the ground. "Look, I'm sorry. I know I made things weird last time."

"I asked too many questions."

"It's not that." She was silent for a moment, studying her trainers intently. "I just really like you. You know?" She glanced up anxiously.

Valeria grinned with relief. "I like you as well. So there is no problem?"

Some of the sadness had returned to Athena's eyes. "But it's more complicated than that, isn't it?"

Valeria's smile faded. "Yes. I know."

Athena looked at the darkening sky, and once again, Valeria had the sense that she was talking to someone much older. "I just worry that it won't end well and that you'll think badly of me."

Valeria took her hand and drew her into the doorway. "I would never think badly of you."

"You say that. But what if I did something terrible?"

"Like what?"

"I dunno. Like drop-kicked a kitten."

"I know you wouldn't do such a thing. And even if you did, I would think you had your reasons. Maybe it was a zombie kitten that was about to chew your leg off?"

Athena smiled weakly. "I guess there are always reasons. Even if it doesn't seem obvious at the time."

Valeria guided her inside and closed the back door. She pulled Athena into a kiss, slowly running her hands through Athena's thick hair. She returned the kiss, pressing her body against Valeria and slipping her arms around Valeria's waist.

Valeria placed her hands on Athena's hips and gently pushed her back against the wall, kissing her harder. As her tongue probed deeper, she pulled Athena's top up and let her hands roam over the soft skin of Athena's stomach.

Valeria's arousal grew. She needed more, much more. She unbuttoned Athena's jeans and slid a hand inside. She felt Athena's intake of breath, moved her hand, and moaned involuntarily as she felt warm wetness on her fingertips.

Athena shifted her hips, moving against Valeria's hand, and then Valeria became aware of her phone vibrating in her back pocket. She broke the kiss and withdrew her hand. Athena's face was flushed. "What is it?" she asked.

Valeria took her phone from her pocket and saw Sirvan's name flashing on the screen. She turned aside and answered it. "Hello?"

"Where are you?" His voice was terse.

"Still in the salon. I made a mistake with the cashing up and had to do it all again. But I'm coming home now."

"Okay. Don't be long." He rang off abruptly.

Valeria turned back to Athena, who had buttoned up her jeans again. "I have to go," Valeria mumbled, feeling ashamed of being summoned home like a teenager who had stayed out too long.

"Was that Sirvan?"

"Yes. I have to get home."

"Okay." Athena's voice was neutral, but Valeria felt the need to offer further explanation.

"He's worried. With Zoran being arrested and all."

"Sure. We wouldn't want anything to stop the exploitation of vulnerable girls, would we?" Athena furiously shoved her top into her jeans. Then she sighed and looked at Valeria. "Sorry. It's just, I hate him."

The passion behind her words took Valeria by surprise. She did not think of Athena as someone who hated. She always appeared so calm, so placid. "I understand."

"Do you? Do you really understand what he does to people? What he's been doing to them for years? For fucking *years*?" She took a step toward Valeria, her eyes burning with anger, and Valeria involuntarily stepped back until it was she who was backed against the wall. She held up her hands in a placatory gesture.

"He does terrible things. I know this."

Athena turned away, and her shoulders heaved once. When she spoke again, her voice was more normal. "I'm sorry. It just makes me so angry. But I know that you get it. And you have to go." She walked through into the main salon without looking back.

Valeria followed and watched her retrieve her jacket from the stand and put it on.

"I'll see you tomorrow, yeah?" Athena said.

Valeria stared, unable to believe the transformation that had taken place. Athena had gone right back to being her usual, casual self, as if the sudden show of anger had never happened.

"Yes. See you tomorrow." Valeria watched her leave and then collected her own things. Her mind was awhirl with confusion at Athena's sudden change of demeanour, but humming beneath it all, Valeria recognised the insistent throb of desire.

She returned home to find Sirvan sitting on the sofa with Mesut, both of them drinking whisky. The television was on, showing *Love Island*. Valeria would have laughed at the incongruity if it hadn't been for the stern expressions on their faces.

They both looked up as she entered. Sirvan nodded his approval that she was home, and Mesut stood to greet her.

"Have you eaten?" she asked.

Sirvan shook his head. "I don't want nothing to eat," he said. Mesut looked faintly disappointed.

"You want something, Mesut?" Valeria asked.

"Well. Maybe a little something," he said.

"I'll bring some bread and olives through for you."

His face creased in gratitude.

When Valeria came back in with the food, they were deep in discussion.

"I can still go," Mesut was saying.

"No," Sirvan replied. "I want you here. If the police are sniffing around, we need to be extra careful. Who else could go?"

"Hemin?" Mesut suggested, spearing an olive as soon as Valeria laid the dish on the coffee table.

Sirvan stroked his chin thoughtfully. "Is he definitely okay?"

"Hemin?" Mesut said, swallowing his olive in surprise. "He's worked with us for years."

"I know, but I'm thinking someone has talked to the police. And we don't know who."

Mesut speared another olive as Valeria laid out dishes of sliced bread and hummus. "It's gonna be hard, Sirvan. How are we saying who is definitely okay and who is not?"

Sirvan took another swig from his glass. Valeria glanced at his face and could see he was on a knife-edge of finely balanced tension. "Maybe the only way is to make sure either you or me are involved in every part of it," he said grimly. "Maybe we have to manage without anyone out on their side."

Mesut blew out his cheeks and reached for another olive.

"Do you need anything else?" Valeria asked.

"No," Sirvan said, reaching for the whisky bottle to refill his glass.

"Okay," she said. "I'll make myself something to eat. And then maybe I'll have a bath and an early night."

Mesut smiled vaguely, but Sirvan gave no sign of having heard, and Valeria retreated into the kitchen.

She made herself an omelette but after a few bites, concluded that she also wasn't hungry. Her stomach felt knotted with tension, and a bath seemed ever more appealing.

Half an hour later, she sank into a bubble-filled bath. She sighed as the water warmed her through. Her thoughts returned to Athena, and she moved her hand beneath the water, stroking over her thighs as she remembered the feel of Athena's body pressed against hers. She moved her hand between her legs as she replayed the unfinished encounter. It took mere minutes for her body to respond, and she pressed her lips together as she came, the release pulsing through her limbs.

As she returned to herself, she was dimly aware of Sirvan talking downstairs. A few minutes later, she heard both him and Mesut leave, the door slamming behind them. She sank into the water again and tried not to think about what they might be doing. She had just finished her preparations for bed when Sirvan came in. He was loosening his tie as he entered their bedroom, bringing the aroma of whisky with him. He looked tired, and the lines on his face seemed to have deepened over the course of the evening.

He sat on the edge of the bed and rubbed his hands over his face. Valeria heard Athena's bitter words echoing in her mind: "wouldn't want anything to stop the exploitation of vulnerable girls, would we?" But she had been Sirvan's wife for many years, and playing the part had become almost second nature. She sat beside him and laid a hand on his shoulder.

"Are you okay?" she asked.

He sighed heavily and lifted his face, staring vacantly at the bland furnishings of their room. "You need to give me your phone," he said.

She went cold. "What? Why?" Her mind raced as she tried to think if there was anything on her phone that would betray her affair with Athena. She had deleted all the messages between them as a precaution.

"We need to ditch all our phones." He held out his hand expectantly.

Valeria reached over to her bedside table and placed her phone in his hand. "Why do we need to get rid of our phones?"

"When they arrested Zoran, they would have taken his phone. They'll go through it, see who he has been calling, messaging, all of that. If they get our numbers, they can track us. We have to keep off them for now."

"But Zoran never called or messaged me."

"I can't take any risks." He ran a hand through his thinning hair. "The police are sniffing about. Omer and Galip, they are bloody furious. Zoran gets arrested, and they look at me like I've fucked up, like I'm running some tin-pot outfit. They start to doubt whether we can pull off the deal at our end. We have to. We have gone too far, invested too much. And if this goes tits up, every gobshite in London will know about it and think I am a bloody joke." He stood abruptly and paced up and down the room.

"You will go through with the deal?" If there was hope in her voice, it was the hope that Sirvan would say no, that the whole thing was off.

"Yes, I will go through with it. But I have to reassure them now, tell them that the police ain't about to shut us down." He stood for a moment, biting his thumbnail. "Zoran has not said anything. He knows the rules. He knows not to talk. But someone has talked."

He chewed on the nail, and Valeria averted her eyes. She could think of nothing to say that would soothe him in this moment, so she opted to keep silent.

"Maybe it was the phones, maybe they got taps going. Or maybe Zoran posted it on bloody social media." He resumed his furious pacing.

Valeria watched him, her heart knocking anxiously against her chest. She knew better than to ask any questions or risk agitating him further. After a few minutes, he finally came to a halt and drew a deep breath.

"So," he said. "No more phones. We have to be extra careful from now on." He looked sternly at her. "You understand?"

"I understand."

He sat on the bed and lay down, placing his head in her lap. Valeria was astonished. He had never done such a thing before. After a moment, she recovered and stroked his hair. "It's gonna be okay," she soothed. "It's all gonna work out fine."

She hated herself as she spoke the words. Everything working out fine for him meant the ruin of dozens of lives.

He sighed and mumbled into her stomach. "I can't fuck this up, darlin'. I got everything riding on this. I can't fuck it up."

"Shh. You're not going to fuck it up. Everything always goes well for you. You are always lucky. This will be the same, you'll see."

The words left a sour taste in her mouth, but she gritted her teeth and waited. He said nothing more, and after a moment, Valeria realised that he had fallen asleep.

Chapter Fourteen

Valeria arrived at the salon the next morning feeling groggy and tired after a restless night. Sirvan's tension had transmitted itself to her, and she had tossed and turned until daylight. She went at once to switch on the coffee machine.

Athena arrived a few moments later. "You desperate for a caffeine fix?" she asked. She smiled, and Valeria found herself annoyed that she showed no signs of discomfort or awkwardness following their exchange the previous evening.

"Yes. I didn't sleep well."

"Sorry to hear that. I almost messaged you this morning to see if you wanted company on your jog, but I'm glad I didn't disturb you."

"You wouldn't have done. I don't have my phone anymore."

"Did you lose it?"

"No. Sirvan has it."

Athena looked up from where she was logging on to the salon computer. "What do you mean?"

"He is paranoid about the police. He has decided that we're not using our phones anymore."

"He can't just take your phone," Athena said indignantly.

Valeria said nothing as the machine whirred. When it was done, she took the mug and sipped the coffee, closing her eyes to savour the moment.

"Valeria." Athena looked exasperated, but Valeria had no energy for a fight.

Through the window, she could see Katya approaching the salon door. She took her coffee to the back of the salon. "I'll be in my office. Come get me when my client arrives." She didn't wait for Athena's answer and retreated as fast as she could. She sat on the rickety swivel chair and sipped her coffee slowly. It was too much, she thought. She felt caught between Sirvan's control and Athena's expectations. And she was so tired.

As if to prove her point, Sirvan showed up a few hours later. Valeria could feel the eyes of the staff and clients follow him, trying to judge whether things were going well or badly.

He sat in Azad's corner, and Azad gave him a shave. Valeria tried to focus on her current client but felt Sirvan's presence as if a cold dark hole had opened up in the salon. The chatter amongst the women dampened.

When she had finished the cut, Valeria turned and brushed the hair off the woman's shoulders. She looked up as she did so and saw that Sirvan had finished his shave and was sitting in the chair flicking through a magazine. He looked up and caught her eye, a clear summons.

"Here," she called to Athena. "Can you do the blow-dry for me?" She handed over to Athena without meeting her gaze and went to Sirvan.

"We will have some guests tonight," he said with no preamble. "Mesut and a few others. We have a lot to discuss, so we'll need some food. But small things, you know? Things we can eat whilst we talk."

"Okay. I can do that."

"And no booze. We need clear heads."

She was faintly amused that he imagined that it was she who would control the alcohol intake of him and his men. "Okay." She waited. He said nothing further. He was looking at where Shanaz and Athena were working, and then his eyes moved to take in Katya on the reception desk.

Valeria found this surveying of her staff unnerving. "Is that all?" she asked.

His eyes moved back to her face. He nodded slowly, and she was dismissed. She walked back to where Athena was sweeping up the hair from Valeria's last client.

"Okay?" Athena asked.

"Yes," she said. She felt the weight of Sirvan's presence behind her stiffening her back with tension.

"You have to go home on time tonight?" Athena murmured.

"Yes. He has guests coming." She felt Sirvan's presence as chill tendrils reaching toward her, questioning and probing. She moved away from Athena to busy herself with her next client.

That evening, she closed up as quickly as she could. She had sensed the tension in Sirvan and knew it would not do to keep him waiting. She held the door open, waiting for Athena to gather her things.

As Athena came past, she stopped. "I'll be getting a coffee outside the park tomorrow morning," she said.

Valeria looked into the pools of her eyes and bit her lip. She wanted things to be all right again between them. "Okay," she said. "But it might be that I can't make it."

"That's fine. I'll wait until it's time to come to work." She smiled her brilliant smile and walked off down the high street, leaving Valeria to lock up.

When Valeria got home, Sirvan was not in. She set to work preparing and setting out a variety of dishes: flatbread, hummus and olives, and small cubes of roasted chicken. She had been at work for an hour or so when she heard the front door open, then voices in the hall. A few minutes later, Sirvan came into the kitchen.

There was a tightness around his jaw and at the corner of his eyes.

"You ready to eat?" she asked.

"Yes. We're in the dining room." He ran an eye over the dishes she had prepared and nodded, letting out a breath as he did so. He took up a few of the dishes, and Valeria followed him into the dining room, bringing several more.

Mesut and Amir, another member of Sirvan's inner circle, were seated at the table with a laptop open and a map spread out before them. They greeted Valeria cordially but with a distracted air. She set the dishes on the table and went back and forth with cutlery and drinks.

The men spoke in low, urgent voices, and she caught snatches of the conversation as she came in and out.

"We'll need someone to drive."

"…they arriving in Dover?"

"…going to a new place."

Once she had set everything out, she retreated to the kitchen and sat at the breakfast bar, flipping through the paper without taking anything in. The low, insistent hum of men's voices was like a fly droning in the next room.

After twenty minutes or so, she went back in, refilled drinks and replenished some of the food. As she moved behind Sirvan's chair, she glanced at the laptop screen and saw Omer's face on a video call. His expression was stern as Sirvan spoke to him.

"…so we have everything in place. We're good to go."

"Good. Because we had a deal, Sirvan. And we don't let people back out of deals with us." Omer's voice was tinny, but there was no mistaking the threat behind it.

Valeria moved around the table, giving no indication that she had heard anything. Sirvan's voice remained calm as he reassured Omer that everything would go according to plan.

She went back into the kitchen and repeated her aimless flicking through the paper. She did not want to go back and be polite to these men who were planning misery with such precision. But she was also afraid of the tightness in Sirvan's face. After what she judged to be the correct interval, she returned to the dining room. The laptop was closed, and the men were sitting back in their chairs, running hands through hair or across their faces. Sirvan was folding up the map.

"Would you like tea or coffee?" Valeria asked.

"Tea," Sirvan said without looking up.

By the time she returned with three glasses of tea, the mood in the room had shifted from tense to exhausted. Mesut's face looked almost grey as he took the tea and immediately spooned in several helpings of sugar.

Sirvan glanced at Mesut as he stirred his tea, the spoon clinking rhythmically against the glass. "You gonna be ready?"

Mesut's back straightened. "Absolutely."

"We'll give you everything you need. Map, car, phone, cash."

Mesut nodded. He took a gulp of tea, but it was too hot. He spluttered, almost dropping the glass.

Valeria went into the kitchen and returned with a tea towel for him.

"Thanks," he said, patting at where he had spilt tea on his trousers.

Sirvan watched him in silence and then said, "Why don't you take the time between now and next Tuesday to relax? Have a break from work."

Mesut looked up. "I don't need a break. I'm ready for this."

"I know. But I think you will be even more ready if you have some time to rest beforehand. Amir can cover for you."

Amir nodded enthusiastically. "Sure thing," he said.

Mesut shot an annoyed look at him and turned back to Sirvan. "I don't need a rest. There is lot to prepare in time for Tuesday."

"And I've said you don't need to worry about it." Sirvan's voice was entirely neutral, but there was a quiet force behind his words.

Mesut looked at him for a moment and then conceded. "All right," he said. "I'll go fishing for a bit until next week."

"Good. Now, Amir. You got things to get ready at Zoran's new place, right?"

Amir nodded again, almost puppy-like in his enthusiasm. "It's all under control. I'm making sure we've got room for the girls and have got everything in place."

"Okay. I'm gonna come tomorrow and see for myself."

Amir licked his lips but nodded again. "Sure, sure. That's no problem."

"I want to talk to all the guys involved in Zoran's place," Sirvan said. "I'll come and stay with you for the night so I can see that everything is ready."

Amir's smile faltered. It was still plastered on his face, but a glassy look came into his eyes. "Sure. Okay," he said, sounding anything but sure.

"Good. Now, I will open a single malt I've been saving for a special occasion." Sirvan rose and ushered the men through the doorway into the living room as Valeria cleared the table.

She took the things into the kitchen and began clearing up. She had not eaten anything that evening, but her stomach felt knotted and tense. She could not remember the last time that Sirvan had spent a night away, and ordinarily, she would have been excited at the thought of having time by herself, away from his scrutiny. But she could not forget the "business" he was engaged on. Even now, there might be girls preparing to go to sleep, excited about the future they imagined awaiting them. Valeria shuddered and wished with all her might that she could see Athena. She looked at the clock and calculated the number of hours until she could see her again.

CHAPTER FIFTEEN

They polished off the single malt that evening, and Sirvan was still asleep when Valeria awoke the following morning. She slipped out of bed and got dressed in her running gear. She let herself out as quietly as she could. She knew that Sirvan would not approve of her going out on her own, but if he didn't see her, he had no chance to forbid her from going.

A light rain was falling, and Valeria practically sprinted to the park, she was so eager to see Athena. She was there, leaning against a plane tree inside the entrance and clutching a coffee cup. She was not dressed in jogging gear but in her usual jeans and jacket, her hood pulled up against the rain.

"Hi," she said, raising her cup in greeting.

Valeria had to resist the urge to fling her arms around her and hold her close. "Hi," she said. "You're not jogging this morning?"

"No. I thought we could just go for a walk round the park instead. You want a coffee?"

"No, thank you." Valeria couldn't abide the thought of queuing and thus losing time with Athena. They set off at a slow stroll around the path. Everything was dripping in the drizzle, and the smell of wet earth hung in the air.

"I thought you might not make it," Athena said. "You seemed worried yesterday."

"Yes, I'm worried. But I woke up before Sirvan." She turned to look at Athena, but the hood of her jacket partially obscured her face.

Athena took a sip, then said, "Would he have stopped you coming?"

Valeria didn't reply immediately. Every time they mentioned his control of her life, she felt herself shrink in Athena's eyes. Surely one day, she would become so tiny that she would disappear entirely. "I don't know," she said finally. "He is very tense at the moment and worried about his deal. I don't know what he might do."

"His deal is still going ahead?"

"Yes." She winced at having to make the admission.

Athena's eyes followed a squirrel as it scampered across the path in front of them and straight up the trunk of an oak tree. "It must be soon if he's so jumpy."

"Next Tuesday, I think. That seemed to be the day they were all talking about."

Athena's jaw tightened, and Valeria sensed she was holding her words back. She tried to think of something to say, something that would make it better but there was nothing.

"Where are they bringing these poor girls to?" Athena asked.

"Some place that Zoran had."

"They must be coming through one of the ports, right?"

"I suppose so."

Athena pursed her lips as she looked away. "Poor things."

They had come to the belt of trees, and Valeria found her steps slowing of their own accord. She thought of the previous occasions when they had disappeared into the undergrowth and made love on the earth and leaves.

Athena slowed and turned back. The rain began to fall harder, spattering against her jacket. She seemed to follow the direction of Valeria's gaze and sighed. "A bit wet for that." Valeria blushed. "Would be nice to do it in an actual bed sometime, eh?" There was an edge of bitterness to her voice that twisted Valeria's heart. She opened her mouth, but Athena held up a hand. "I know, I know. You don't have to tell me."

"I'm sorry," said Valeria helplessly.

"Yeah. Me too." They looked at each other as a wind ruffled

the branches of the trees and set the leaves to whispering. The dank heaviness of the morning seemed to thicken, and Valeria found that she could not see Athena's face clearly. She squinted, trying to read her expression but that just seemed to make her fade even farther into the thick grey air.

Athena puffed out her cheeks and said, "I might go and grab some breakfast on the high street before work. I'll see you in the salon."

"What? But we've only just got here."

"I know, but..." Athena shrugged.

"You were the one who suggested meeting," Valeria said. She had hoped that Athena suggesting they meet meant that things were going to be all right between them once more.

Athena grimaced and turned back to the belt of trees. "I know I did. But you shouldn't be gone too long. Sirvan might notice." She walked off, leaving Valeria fighting back tears of frustration that Athena could be so close to her but a million miles away.

Sirvan was still asleep when she got back and had not woken by the time she left for work. The day in the salon dragged unbearably. Valeria found herself constantly glancing at the clock, wishing that the hours would pass. She could only summon the most desultory chat with her clients, who soon gave up and took their phones out.

She saw Shanaz looking from her to Katya and Athena and frowning. "Geez, ladies. What's up with you all?" she said.

Katya grunted and Athena said, "Nothing." She tried her winning smile, but it had nowhere near its usual power, as if the batteries were running out.

"Might as well be working in a funeral parlour, know what I mean?" Shanaz said to her client. The woman smiled nervously, glancing at Valeria as if checking that it was okay to smile. In normal times, Valeria would have said something to reassure the client. She had always said that she didn't want her customers feeling nervous around her just because she was Sirvan's wife. But she had no energy to do so. She just wanted the day to be over.

When closing time finally came, Valeria rushed to get through everything she needed to do. She still found time to add to her stash in the filing cabinet, even if it did not give her the same illicit thrill it once had. The quiet house that she held in her mind seemed impossibly remote when compared with the tiny stack of money in the drawer.

Athena did not attempt her smile as she said good-bye. But her eyes lingered on Valeria's for a moment longer than was necessary, and Valeria once again wished that she could find the right words. There had been a time when words had tripped easily off her tongue. She had always known the right thing to say at any given moment. With the men who frequented the bars she'd worked in, she had known when to joke or when to be serious. She could read the mood of her clients equally well and knew when to chatter to put them at ease or when to leave them be.

But it seemed that knack had deserted her. She watched Athena melt into the early evening press of people on the high street. Everything that she had once been or had thought herself to be seemed to be slipping away from her. And she had no idea what would be left once it was all gone.

Sirvan was in when she got home. He was standing in the hallway, and Valeria started when she saw him. The discomfiting thought crossed her mind that perhaps he had been waiting in the hallway all afternoon for her to come home.

"Are you okay?" she said warily. She closed the door and stayed where she was, clutching her bag as if it was a shield. She instinctively looked at her watch. She wasn't late so he couldn't be holding that against her.

"Yeah, I'm fine." He chewed his thumbnail and looked at her intently. His eyes seemed to be burning, and her shoulders tensed. "Come here," he said.

She moved cautiously toward him, her chest tightening.

He looked into her face with that same intent gaze. "I'm gonna show you something."

"Okay."

He turned and opened the door of the cupboard under the stairs.

Valeria blinked. Whatever she had been expecting, it was not this. He ducked into the cupboard and motioned for her to join him.

Feeling faintly ridiculous, she squeezed in beside him. It was a small space and with both her and Sirvan, impossibly cramped. The cupboard itself was virtually empty, with none of the usual clutter normally found in other people's houses. Sirvan did not like clutter anywhere. The only thing in the cupboard was the safe, which had been built into the brick wall.

He gestured to it. "This is the safe."

"Yes."

"You know what's in it?"

"The cash from the salon." Her hands went clammy as she thought that he must have noticed that small amounts were being skimmed from the takings, and this was his way of letting her know that he knew. She was so panicked that she almost missed what he said next.

"Not just that. In here is everything that is important to the business. And right now, what's the most important thing to the business?"

"The deal with Omer and Galip." She prayed it wasn't a trick question, but he nodded.

"Yes. Everything rests on this deal. If it goes wrong, I'll lose all the honour and reputation I have. And if that happens, the business goes as well. And if the business goes, this house goes, everything we have goes. You understand?"

She felt a flash of irritation at his use of "we" but said simply, "I understand."

"Good. I am showing you this because the deal must go through. Whatever happens." He punched in a code on the safe and turned the small lever. He opened the door and took out a large brown envelope. "In here is everything Mesut needs for Tuesday. It has the map, the car keys, a phone, and some cash for him. I'm not giving any of it to him yet in case he gets picked up by police. But I am telling you that this is here so you can give it to Mesut if you need to."

"If I need to? Why would I need to?"

"In case something happens to me. The police might arrest me."

"But if you get arrested, the deal would be off. Wouldn't it?"

"No." His face was set in hard, chiselled lines. "If I get arrested, I'm telling the police nothing. And they have nothing on me. So Mesut can still go ahead with the deal."

"What if he is arrested too?"

"Then it will be Amir."

"And what if—" She saw his face and stopped herself.

"If we are all arrested, then it's not just the deal that is off but everything. Everything would be lost."

She composed her face into a serious expression so that he would not see how exciting that prospect was to her. "I understand," she said gravely. "I will know what to do."

"Good. Now look carefully." He closed the door of the safe and punched in the four-digit code. He opened it and looked at her. "Did you get it?"

"Yes. Five, five, three, eight."

"Good. You have to remember that. You cannot write it down anywhere."

Valeria blinked, unable to quite believe that Sirvan was finally telling her the code to the safe. "Okay."

He was still looking at her intently. "Will you remember it?"

"Yes." She felt another flash of irritation at being spoken to as if she was a child.

"Okay. I will ask you later today to see." He placed the envelope back and closed the safe.

Her annoyance was so great that it prompted her to throw caution to the wind and ask the question that had been dogging her for many weeks. "Where does the money go?"

"What money?" he asked, not looking up from checking that the safe was locked.

"The money I give you from the salon. Where does it go?"

He looked at her curiously. "I take it to the bank."

"Which bank?"

"My bank."

"And if you get arrested, how will I have money?"

"One of the guys will take care of it for you."

"And if you are all arrested? And everything is over? What will I do then?"

His eyes glittered at her in the dim light. She could see the hairs of his eyebrows and could at once pick out the ones that had first turned grey. His face was so familiar to her, and yet there was no comfort in that familiarity.

"If that happens, you'll be looked after. I promise." He said it with almost ostentatious gravity, as if he was making a solemn vow.

"But I would rather look after myself."

He took both her hands. "I promised you I'd always look after you, and I will. You don't need to worry about this." He smiled and touched her cheek. "All you have to do right now is remember the combination."

He retreated back into the hallway, and she followed, choking down her frustration. She could be trusted enough to know the combination of the safe but not to have access to any of the money she earnt from the salon.

He closed the cupboard and went upstairs. She went into the kitchen and opened the fridge to assess the options for dinner. She could hear him pacing back and forth. She was taking out some peppers and wondering whether to stuff them when she heard his tread on the stairs, and he reappeared in the kitchen, a holdall in his hand.

"I need some clean shirts for tomorrow," he said. Valeria looked at him blankly. "I will be staying tomorrow night at Zoran's place with Amir."

"Oh yes, I remember. I can wash some for you after dinner."

He proceeded to give her a list of all the things he would need. He rarely spent a night away and seemed especially anxious, checking the smallest details with her. He finally seemed satisfied that she was capable of packing an overnight bag for him. He dug in his pocket and drew out a couple of fifty-pound notes that he laid on the counter. "I will leave this here before I forget. This is for anything you need whilst I am gone."

Valeria was reminded of her wrinkled babushka, pressing warm coins into her palm whenever she and her mother visited. "When will you be back?" she asked.

"I will be back the day after tomorrow in the evening sometime. I have to check that Amir has got everything ready. Nothing can go wrong." He looked at her intently. "You will be okay?"

Valeria knew that this was not a question about her well-being but about her conduct. "Yes. I'll be at work tomorrow, and then I'll come straight home."

"Good. If you need anything, talk to Azad."

"Okay."

He turned and went back upstairs. She let out a sigh of relief. She went back to chopping the pepper and thought about what it would be like to have an evening in the house to herself. She could not remember the last time she had been alone for a night. She tried to imagine what she might do, what other women would do in the same situation. Should she flop on the sofa, eating ice cream and watching TV? She had never much cared for their leather sofa. She found its dark smoothness vaguely sinister. Should she crack open a bottle of wine and read a book in the bath? She did not drink much these days, fearful of losing the iron control that was necessary to maintain her demeanour around Sirvan.

She wished idly that Athena could be with her, and then, just as the thought was flying from her mind, she called it back. She almost dared not think it, as it felt so transgressive. Katya had only been to the house once, as far as she could remember. And they had both sensed that Sirvan was not best pleased, though he said nothing. And that had been it. For the years afterward, it had only been a steady stream of Sirvan's men who had come over.

Valeria thought of Athena being in the house, of her scent wafting through the rooms like a cleansing balm. She imagined her in all the different rooms, but her mind balked when it got to the bedroom. She pulled herself up.

No, she thought. She could not allow herself to get carried away. It would be beyond reckless to have Athena in the house whilst Sirvan was gone. How could she possibly explain that if discovered? She focused instead on deseeding the pepper and tried to push all the images of Athena floating through the house out of her mind.

Chapter Sixteen

Sirvan woke early the next morning, which meant Valeria did too. She had packed his bag for him the night before, but that didn't stop him from barking questions at her all morning, making her check and recheck the bag several times.

He was seriously stressed, that much was obvious. Valeria hid her exasperation and patiently reassured him that he had everything he needed for a single night away. Then she made him a hearty breakfast, which seemed to calm his nerves.

She got herself ready for work, and by the time she came downstairs again, he was standing in the hallway, ready to leave. He kissed her briefly on the cheek and held her by the shoulders, looking into her face. "You will be okay?" he asked again.

"Yes, I'll be fine. It is only one night."

"I know, but things are tense right now. Everything is resting on this deal, and the police are sniffing around."

"It's okay, it's okay," Valeria said, smoothing her palm over the lapels of his jacket. "I understand how difficult things are at the moment. You go and concentrate on your deal. You don't need to worry about me."

His face relaxed. She hadn't entirely lost the ability to say the right thing. He went to open the front door, then turned as a thought seemed to strike him. "What's the number to the safe?"

"Five, five, three, eight."

He allowed himself the tiniest of smiles. "Good." And then the front door closed behind him. Valeria heard a car start and move away. She stood in the empty house, which already felt warmer now that Sirvan had gone.

She arrived at the salon feeling more upbeat than she had in a while, and Katya noticed at once. "Why you in such a good mood?" she demanded, as if affronted that anyone could be so cheerful.

"No reason."

Katya glared at her suspiciously but did not push any further. Valeria made her a coffee and spent some time talking with her at the front desk. Katya was at first grumpy and brusque, but Valeria persisted, and eventually, they had something approaching a normal conversation.

When Shanaz arrived a little while later, she smiled at the sight of them talking. "That's better," she exclaimed. "Honestly, you could've cut the atmosphere between you two with a knife." Athena was the last to arrive, just after Azad. "Hey," Shanaz said as Athena hung up her jacket, "these two are mates again."

"Thank God for that," Athena said.

"I know, right? Now we can get our good vibes back."

"There was always good vibes with you around," Valeria said, patting Shanaz affectionately on the shoulder.

"Yeah, you got vibes to spare," Athena said. Shanaz laughed, and to Valeria, it felt as if the good humour had been restored to the salon.

It persisted throughout the day. Everything just seemed less fraught. Valeria could once more chat easily with her clients and found herself taking a genuine interest in their various life dramas. She had just finished sympathising at great length with a lady complaining about her son-in-law's inability to hold down a job. She went to make herself a tea whilst Katya took the payment.

As she sipped her drink, she wondered if this was what life would be like without Sirvan's presence casting a shadow. Would everything feel lighter and freer?

Athena came up to the machine and busied herself making coffee for the clients. "Katya keeps going on about what a good mood you're in," she said.

"I know. I must have been a miserable cow for a long time."

"Nah, you ain't been that bad," said Athena graciously. "But you do seem super chirpy today. Have you had some good news?"

"Sort of." She leaned closer and said in a low voice, "Sirvan has gone away for the night."

Athena raised her eyebrows. "I see. Where's he gone?"

"To Zoran's place, I think. To check everything is ready." She handed Athena some milk sachets. "He never goes away on business, so I'm not used to being home alone."

Athena placed the coffee on a saucer alongside the milk and one of the little chocolates they always gave to clients. She met Valeria's eyes for a moment. "You should make the most of it," she said. And then she moved away.

Valeria stood for a moment, watching the sway of her hips. Had that been some kind of an invitation? The previous evening, she had indulged in thoughts of Athena being in her home but had quickly dampened them. But was Athena right? Was this an opportunity to take advantage of? Her heart began to beat faster just at the thought. Sirvan would not be happy if he found out that Valeria had invited someone into their house of her own accord. But she could think of a reason to explain it. And Sirvan was so distracted at the moment that it would be a small matter compared to the importance of his deal.

Valeria shook herself and went to tackle her next client. She knew that the habit of conforming to Sirvan's wishes was ingrained deeply within her. But she had already defied him in a multitude of ways. What difference would it make to add another defiance to the list?

She ruminated on this as she worked her way through her appointments that afternoon. Everything she had done with Athena had taken place outside of the house, and that had given it a feeling of distance, of separation from the life she ostensibly shared with Sirvan. Bringing Athena into the heart of his carefully controlled life felt like a whole additional level of defiance. And she wasn't sure if she was brave enough to take that step.

When closing time came, she took her cash to the filing cabinet and wasn't surprised when she heard Athena enter the office behind her. She turned from locking the cabinet and looked at Athena leaning against the door frame with her arms folded.

Athena raised her eyebrows questioningly. "Well?" she said.

"Well, what?"

"Come on, Valeria," Athena said with a smile. "Are you really not going to ask me?"

Valeria felt heat rising to her face. "Ask you what?"

"You've got the house to yourself. Which you've already said never happens. So?"

Valeria looked at the floor, feeling as bashful as a teenager. "I know. I've thought about it. But I'm worried that Sirvan will find out."

"So he finds out you had a friend over whilst you were on your own. Is it really that bad?"

"I never have friends over."

"And he never goes away. You just say you were nervous or something and that you fancied some company." She said it with such easy assurance, Valeria felt a pang of envy.

"I don't know," she began, but Athena drew close and looked into her eyes.

"Wouldn't it be nice to be together somewhere that isn't the salon or the bushes?"

Valeria's breath caught in her throat at the thought of doing *that* in Sirvan's house. It had been lurking in the back of her mind, but she hadn't allowed herself to properly entertain the idea.

Athena pressed her mouth against Valeria's. Her lips were warm and soft, and Valeria returned the kiss. She delighted in the feel of Athena's lips opening to her tongue, and for a few minutes, she lost herself in the embrace. When they finally pulled apart, Valeria knew something had shifted.

"Okay," she said, still catching her breath after the kiss. "Okay. You can come over this evening." Athena grinned in delight, but Valeria held up her hand. "But you need to wait until it's dark."

"All right. Whatever you want."

"And if anyone asks, you say that I asked you over because I was afraid to be in the house by myself. Okay?"

"Sure. That's a great cover story."

"I don't want any trouble to come to you. It has to be all my idea."

Athena's face twisted as if with a sudden pain, and she turned away for a moment.

Puzzled, Valeria reached out to touch her arm. "Hey, it's okay."

"It's not," Athena said. "I hate that it has to be like this."

"I know," Valeria said. "But look, I'll cook you something nice to eat, and we can at least enjoy tonight."

Athena's shoulders rose as she took a deep breath. "All right," she said with a lightness that sounded forced to Valeria's ears. "That's an offer I can't refuse."

When Valeria got home, she at once set to cleaning the house with an almost manic energy. She cleaned regularly, but the thought of Athena being in the house spurred her to make everything spotless.

Then she turned her attention to dinner. She realised she had no idea what food Athena liked and was struck by the thought that Athena could be vegetarian. Or even vegan. She pulled herself back from a panicky spiral by recalling that Athena took cow's milk in her coffee, so she couldn't be that vegan. She decided to make a meat-free meal, just in case.

She threw together some spring onions and lemon to make a simple risotto, and as it was bubbling on the stove, she slipped upstairs to get changed. And here there were further quandaries to resolve. She had thought to change into a dress, but looking at all her dresses now, it seemed faintly ridiculous that she should wear one around the house. And she realised that these dresses had been bought with Sirvan's gaze in mind, and that immediately put her off wearing them.

In the end, she opted for changing into a fresh version of what she normally wore to work: jeans and a well-fitting shirt. She styled her hair and sprayed a spritz of perfume around her.

She set the kitchen table ready to eat. She had always disliked the dining room with its heavy, dark wood furniture and preferred to eat in the kitchen.

When the doorbell rang a little while later, she smoothed her hands over her thighs, taking a deep breath. She was a bundle of nerves. The thought of Athena being here, in what had always been Sirvan's house, made her stomach tighten. But there was an edge of excitement to the nerves, a thrill that she was doing something so out of character. It gave her hope that she was not as "all set" as she might appear to be.

Athena was standing on the doorstep with her hand in her pocket, looking like a prom date who was trying to play it cool. She stepped inside quickly, and Valeria closed the door behind her. They stood in the hallway looking at each other shyly.

Athena held out a bottle. "I brought some wine. I went for white. I hope that goes with whatever you've made."

"Yes, it'll go very well." Valeria stood for a moment, holding the wine and looking at Athena, unable to quite believe she was really standing there. Then she roused herself. "Come into the kitchen," she said and led the way down the hall. She placed the wine in the fridge and stirred the risotto. "Are you ready to eat?" she asked.

"Yeah, I'm starving." Athena stood beside Valeria and looked into the pan. "Looks good."

"I hope it'll be okay. I didn't know if you were vegetarian or not."

"I'm a, what'd you call it, a reducetarian. I'm trying to cut down how much meat I eat."

"Ah, good. And I have some baklava for dessert."

"Do you want me to do anything?"

"You can pour the wine. The glasses are in there." Valeria gestured to a cupboard. Whilst Athena took care of the wine, Valeria spooned the risotto onto plates and garnished with some fresh parsley. She placed them on the table along with a bowl of grated parmesan.

They sat opposite each other, and Athena raised her glass. "Cheers."

"Cheers." They clinked glasses and began to eat. Valeria looked at Athena and realised that despite all the intimacies they had shared, she had never done something as simple as have a meal with her. "You know," she said, "I realised tonight that I don't even know what your favourite food is."

"Just so happens, it's risotto," Athena said with a grin.

"What a coincidence." Valeria smiled and took a sip of wine. She was aware that the last time she had asked Athena questions about herself, it had seemed to annoy her, and she did not want to spoil this precious time they had managed to steal together. Yet there was still so much she didn't know. "Are you parents pleased about your job?"

Athena looked up. "My job?" she repeated.

"Yes. You've told them about your work in the salon?"

"Oh, right. Yeah, they're pleased. They're happy I'm working."

"What are their jobs?"

"They're both retired now."

"Really? You seem too young to have retired parents."

"They took early retirement. But what about your mum? What did she do for a living?"

"She was a cleaner. I would go with her to cleaning jobs because there wasn't anyone else to look after me. She used to clean in a salon, and that was where I first decided I wanted to be a hairdresser. I thought the salon seemed like such a magic place." She smiled at the memory. "If I was to see it again now, I would probably think it was a dive, but back then, I thought it was the most wonderful place on earth."

"You got your dream, eh?" Athena chased a ball of her risotto around her plate.

Valeria watched her, finding the gusto with which she attacked her food rather endearing. "For a while, yes. I thought I had my dream. But not anymore."

Athena looked up, her dark eyes resting on Valeria's. "What's changed?" she asked.

"I realised that nothing I had was really mine. It was all Sirvan's. And I always knew that his business was not legitimate. But I didn't think about it because I was safe, and that mattered more to me. But

I realise the damage he does. And I'm a part of that." She looked at her food, her appetite gone. "And then," she said, looking up at Athena, "there was you. You've changed everything."

Athena's face was very still. Her eyes looked into Valeria's for a long moment. "You could escape from all this, Valeria. There are thousands of other lives you could be living out there."

Valeria gave a tight smile. "I know. I've imagined many of them. Sometimes, you are there as well."

Again, Athena's face was almost unnaturally still. Her mouth twisted as if there were words fighting with each other to come out. "I wish, I mean, I hope that will be possible one day." She dropped her eyes and took up her fork again. "But Sirvan would need to be out of the picture."

Valeria was silent, her eyes roving around the kitchen. Out of all the rooms in the house, this felt most like her space but only because she spent so much of her time here. But just the like salon, everything in the kitchen belonged to him.

"Valeria?" Her attention was pulled back to Athena. She was staring intently. "Do you love him?"

"No," said Valeria, and she was surprised at the question, as it seemed so self-evident to her. "I never loved him."

Athena's shoulders dropped, and her face seemed to come to life again. "Okay. So when the time is right, you can walk away from all this."

"You make it sound easy."

"I know it won't be easy. I know that he controls everything, that he owns everything. But I also know you can do it." It was another of those moments where she appeared wise beyond her years.

"He does control everything," Valeria admitted. "But I think that things are changing, that maybe he trusts me more now. He even told me the combination to the safe yesterday."

Athena's fork halted in mid-air. "Did he really?" she said.

"Yes. He's worried about something happening to him, I think. This is the first time he has ever trusted me with anything like this."

Athena resumed eating and said through a mouthful of rice,

"Yeah, but did he give you the actual combination? Maybe he just told you a load of random numbers so you would feel better."

"No, it's the real code. I saw him punch it in."

"Have you tried it yourself?"

"Well, no," Valeria admitted. "I haven't needed to yet."

Athena put her fork down. "You should try it now. Make sure it works, and he's not just having you on."

Her words sowed a sudden doubt in Valeria's mind. Was she right? Was Sirvan simply playing a cruel joke on her? Making her think that he trusted her to keep her on his side? She pushed back her chair and rose. She went out into the hall and opened the understairs cupboard. She was aware of Athena following, but she barely noticed. She was consumed with fury at the thought that Sirvan might have played a trick on her. She had to know right now.

She punched the code into the safe and turned the latch. The door opened smoothly on its hinges.

"Huh," said Athena, who was standing just behind her and looking over her shoulder. "Look at that. He does trust you."

Valeria looked at the open safe, not knowing how she felt.

"Is that where the cash from the salon goes?" Athena asked.

"Yes. But then Sirvan takes it to the bank."

"Shame. Would be nice for you to have access to the money you've earnt, wouldn't it?"

Valeria closed the safe and heard a click as it locked again. She could feel the closeness of Athena in the confined space. As she turned, their hips brushed against one another. Valeria's lips sought out Athena's almost instinctively, and they kissed in the awkward confines of the cupboard until Athena broke off, laughing.

"If it's not bushes, it's cupboards."

Valeria took her by the hand and pulled her back into the hallway. She closed the door behind her and led Athena upstairs. She felt that, with each stair they climbed, she was crossing further and further toward a point of no return. There could be no plausible explanation or easy excuse to get out of this. And she found that she relished it, relished the feeling of finally owning the space she had lived in for so many years.

She drew Athena into the bedroom. Athena hesitated by the door, her eyes resting on the double bed. Valeria diverted her attention by kissing her hard. She pushed Athena onto the bed and sat astride her, cupping her face as she kissed her.

Her need was almost overpowering, and it wasn't long before she had pulled Athena's top off and unbuttoned her jeans. Athena gasped as Valeria moved a hand inside her knickers, and then her head tipped back as Valeria explored with her fingers. Valeria buried her face between Athena's breasts as she worked her hand back and forth, and it wasn't long before Athena's hands were twisting in the bedsheets as she came.

And then Valeria took her time. She trailed kisses across Athena's neck and worked her way slowly down to her breasts. She spent a while there, licking, nibbling, and sucking as Athena moaned and writhed beneath her. And then Valeria moved on, kissing her way down Athena's stomach until her head was between Athena's legs.

She tasted the rich, earthy flavour, coating her lips and tongue with it. And then she spent a while exploring Athena's sex with her tongue, investigating all the hidden recesses. She licked the hard nub of Athena's clitoris and felt the shock of the contact travelling up Athena's body. She wrapped her arms around Athena's thighs and worked her tongue back and forth in a steady rhythm. She could feel Athena's orgasm building as she went, could feel the tremors in the muscles of her thighs.

When it finally broke, Athena's entire body went rigid except for her sex, which fluttered and pulsed against Valeria's mouth. Valeria lay there for a few moments and then raised her head. Athena was lying with her arm flung across her eyes, and as Valeria lay down beside her, she was shocked to see tears running down Athena's cheeks.

"What is it?" she asked, reaching out to touch Athena's face. "Did I do something bad?"

Athena rolled onto her front and buried her face in the sheets. "No," she said, her voice muffled. "It's nothing. Ignore me."

"You can tell me," Valeria said, stroking her bare back. "Whatever it is, you can tell me. Especially if it's something I have done that's made you feel bad."

Athena took a few deep breaths and then raised herself on her arms. "No. It's nothing you've done." She scrubbed at the tear tracks on her cheeks and sighed. "I really wish you weren't so nice to me."

"What? You want me to be horrible to you?" Valeria was smiling despite her confusion.

"Yeah. Sometimes." Athena leaned across and kissed her, slowly at first, then with more urgency. Her hands moved across Valeria's skin, never staying in one place for long. Then she rolled on top, and her weight was a delicious pressure along Valeria's entire body. Athena pressed her hips down as her tongue probed Valeria's mouth.

Propping herself on one arm, Athena used her other hand to trail across Valeria's breasts, her fingertips barely grazing the skin. Valeria closed her eyes and sank into the sensations as if she were slipping beneath warm, lapping waves. Athena's touch on her breasts became firmer until Athena was kneading and squeezing as her hips pressed down.

All of the sensations in Valeria's body seemed to focus down to a fine, hot point between her legs, and when Athena finally rolled to the side and entered her, Valeria almost moaned with relief. She raised her hips and allowed Athena to go deeper, to touch the deepest part of her. She lost all sense of time as she felt Athena move inside her. She could not have said if the steady rhythm of Athena's hand had lasted one minute or ten. For a while, she could not have said who or where she was. Everything faded except for the bright white heat that built from her core and erupted outward, engulfing everything.

The next thing she was aware of was Athena lying beside her, her head resting on Valeria's shoulder and an arm thrown across her stomach. Valeria put her own arm around Athena and felt the sheen of sweat on her back. She planted a kiss on Athena's forehead, and Athena raised her head.

"Thank you," Valeria said, stroking Athena's cheek.

Athena grimaced. "Oh my God, Valeria. Please. You don't have to thank me."

"Why not? No one else has made me feel this way."

Athena turned her head away. "It's just sex."

Valeria felt a stab of hurt. "No, it isn't," she insisted. "Not for me. And not for you either."

Athena turned her face back to Valeria. Her eyes darkened. "How do you know?"

"Because I know you. I mean, I don't know everything *about* you, but I know who you are. And I know what you feel."

Athena's face was still, her eyes unblinking. "You can't know everything I feel."

"No? Why don't you tell me?" There was a long moment of silence as they looked at each other.

Then Athena took a deep breath. "I think I love you," she said.

Now it was Valeria's turn to be still, every muscle frozen in case a sudden movement should disturb this fragile moment. "I don't have to think," she said. "I *know* that I love you."

There was once again a twist in Athena's face, as if she had felt a sudden sharp pain somewhere. She closed her eyes briefly. "I'm sorry," she said.

Valeria cupped her face. "You don't have to be sorry. I'm not sorry. I know things are complicated, but everything will be okay in the end."

"Will it?" Athena's voice was small and sounded as if it was coming from a long way away.

Valeria wrapped her arms around her and pulled her close. "Of course, it will," she said, feeling her own heart twist with the knowledge that she had no idea how things would be okay.

Athena buried her face in Valeria's neck, and nothing more was said. After a little while, Valeria pulled the duvet up to cover them. Athena's breath deepened against Valeria's throat, and as Valeria felt sleep claim her, she remembered that they had not gotten around to eating the baklava.

When Valeria awoke, she had to spend a few minutes figuring

out where she was. Her own bed had become strange to her. She rolled over, tangling herself in the sheets as the previous evening replayed itself in her mind.

Morning light was weakly attempting to break through the curtains. Valeria sat up and looked about. Athena was nowhere to be seen. Valeria was just beginning to wonder if she had slipped away during the night when she heard a noise downstairs. She couldn't pinpoint what it was exactly, just that someone was moving around.

She lay very still for a moment. The thought occurred to her that maybe it was Sirvan, back early. In which case, it was good that Athena might have left already. But had she left? What if she had simply gone to the bathroom, and now Sirvan was downstairs, and he would see the remains of their dinner and—

Valeria reined her thoughts in sharply. She got up at once and quickly dressed in a pair of shorts and an oversized T-shirt. She went out onto the landing and paused, listening intently.

She could definitely hear someone moving about in the hallway. Her heart began to beat faster. She was convinced that it had to be Sirvan because if Athena was still here, what would she be doing in the hallway?

Valeria padded softly down the stairs, mentally rehearsing the different explanations she could give to Sirvan. Athena had come for dinner, had gotten a bit drunk, and so Valeria had suggested she sleep it off before heading home. That sounded plausible enough and would appeal to Sirvan's sense of honour.

Valeria rounded the bottom of the stairs, her face ready to show surprise. But it wasn't Sirvan standing in the hallway, it was Athena. She was standing by the kitchen door, just opposite the cupboard under the stairs. She was dressed in the clothes she had been wearing the night before and looked a little crumpled and blurry around the edges.

She jumped when saw Valeria. "Jesus! You nearly gave me a heart attack."

"What are you doing?"

"I was going to make some coffee."

"In the hallway?"

"I couldn't find anything in the kitchen. I thought I'd come back upstairs, but I didn't want to wake you." She smiled sheepishly. "I was hovering here having a moment of indecision."

Valeria took a deep breath. "I thought you were Sirvan."

"Oh shit, sorry. Is he due back?"

"Not till this evening."

"But I suppose I shouldn't hang around too long?"

"You can hang around long enough for a coffee." Valeria moved past her and took Athena's hand as she went, drawing her into the kitchen.

Athena had clearly not tried very hard to find coffee, as the cafetiere was sitting right on the side. Valeria pointed this out teasingly, and Athena blushed. "I'm not at my best in the mornings."

"You should go for a run every morning. It sharpens the mind," Valeria said as she spooned coffee into the cafetiere.

Athena leaned back against the counter, her arms folded. "I'm impressed by your dedication."

"It is the only time I get to myself." She poured hot water on the coffee and let it brew. She glanced at Athena and saw a look of pain on her face.

"It won't always be this way," Athena said. "I promise you. Things will change."

"Sure," Valeria said, wanting to lighten the tone. "Everything changes." She poured out coffee for them, and they stood by the open back door and watched the morning light slowly brighten over the roofs of the houses. Birds sang and flitted from one fence to the other.

"You should think about what you would do if Sirvan wasn't here," Athena said, her eyes following a blackbird as it hopped across the lawn.

"I do think about it. I have my dream house sorted out."

"No, I mean properly think about it. Make a plan."

Valeria looked at her. "Are you planning to slip some arsenic into his tea or something?"

"No. But you said it yourself. Everything changes."

Valeria was silent as she looked out at the familiar row of terraced houses. The sound of the traffic was faint at this hour, but she knew its tempo would increase as the day wore on. She thought of her small stash of money, hidden away at the salon. She had been planning for something, although she had never articulated to herself what that something was. But perhaps, deep down, it had always been for a life without Sirvan.

She took a deep breath, feeling anxiety tightening across her chest. "But you don't know whether the change will be for the better," she said.

Athena reached across the doorway and took her hand. "I know it's scary. But I just want you to be ready when it comes. And..." She took a deep breath. "I want you to remember what I said to you last night. That was true, you know?"

Valeria squeezed her hand. "I know. It was true for me too."

"No matter what happens, remember that it's true." Athena's eyes searched hers, and she again experienced the strange sensation that Athena had aged before her eyes.

Her chest tightened again. "What do you mean? What's going to happen?"

"I don't know. That's the whole point. Things will change, and I just want you to remember that last night was real, properly real, yeah?" Athena was gripping her hand so tightly that it was painful.

"Okay," Valeria said. "I promise. I will remember."

"No matter what happens?" Athena pressed.

"No matter what happens."

Athena released her hand and looked back out over the garden. She took a deep breath and released it slowly. Valeria studied her face, trying to discern what she was thinking. There was a tightness around her jaw that robbed her face of its usual open, sunny appearance. Valeria sensed that there was something at work in her, a dark shape moving beneath the surface that she could only catch glimpses of.

Athena drained her cup and turned to place it back on the kitchen side. "I should probably get going."

Valeria glanced at the clock. "It's still very early."

"Yeah, but if I go now, there's less chance of being seen, right? And I need to go home before work."

"All right. But won't you stay for some breakfast?"

"Nah, I'll grab a pastry or something on the way home." She kissed Valeria lightly on the lips and made her way to the front door. Valeria followed, thinking that once again, they were set for an awkward parting.

Athena turned at the door, took Valeria's face in her hands, and kissed her again. It was a deep, passionate kiss, and Valeria felt a creeping dread that this was the kind of kiss you gave someone when leaving them forever. The thought made her hold Athena tightly, and she returned the kiss with just as much ardour.

When they finally pulled apart, Valeria saw a stricken, helpless look flit briefly across Athena's face. And then she saw Athena trying to set her features to their usual open expression.

"I'll see you at the salon," Athena said, trying to smile. Everything about her manner was so clearly forced that Valeria felt like she had just received a paper cut. It smarted and sang with pain.

"Okay," she said, unable to force any more words out.

When the front door closed behind Athena, Valeria leaned against it and felt tears springing to her eyes. Something was happening that she did not understand. All she knew was that it was taking Athena further away from her.

Chapter Seventeen

Valeria mechanically prepared herself for the day. She cleared all traces of last night's dinner and tidied up the bedroom. She stripped the sheets off the bed, and as she did so, Athena's scent filled the room. She remembered all they had done and said last night, and tears threatened to overwhelm her again. It all seemed so fragile, so easily destroyed.

Once she had showered and dressed, she began to feel more like herself. She ate some toast while looking out at the back garden and thought of what she had said to Athena about everything changing. Something would have to change. She loved Athena, and she could not continue to snatch moments with her in the salon or in the park. She wanted more. She wanted a proper life with her.

Her own desires terrified her because she knew they would set her on a direct collision course with Sirvan. People who crossed Sirvan had a habit of disappearing, never to be seen or spoken of again. And they had been on the outskirts of Sirvan's circle. She could not imagine what he would do if someone closer betrayed him. A shiver passed through her, and she pushed the thoughts away. They felt too huge and serious to deal with right now.

She arrived at the salon and went through all the usual tasks of setting up for the day's business, but her thoughts dwelt on Athena, on the way she had looked as she told Valeria that she loved her. Valeria alternately smiled and grimaced at the recollection as it brought both joy and fear all at once.

Katya arrived, and Valeria exchanged pleasantries with her. "You have a chance to play whilst the cat was away?" Katya asked.

Valeria felt herself tense. "No," she said. "I just had a quiet night in."

"Look at your face." Katya hooted. "It's all right, I know you wasn't out clubbing all night."

"How would you know that?" Valeria asked too abruptly.

Katya frowned. "I was joking, Valeria."

"Yes, I know." Valeria realised she couldn't convince Katya with that line and tried a different tack. "Sorry, I'm just a bit stressed at the moment. Sirvan never goes away, so that means he must be stressed about something."

Katya nodded sympathetically. "I know, darlin'. If Sirvan's nervous, he makes all of us nervous too, eh?"

"Yes, that's it."

Katya heaved a sigh and looked out at the bustling morning traffic. Valeria looked at her lined face and remembered the Katya she had first met all those years ago. Even then, Katya had seemed world-weary and worn.

Valeria said, "Do you ever think about how your life could have turned out differently?"

Katya looked at her. "Different how?"

"I don't know. Different anyhow. If you'd made different choices."

"No. I don't never think about that. Because there is no point."

"But your life would have been very different if you had stayed in Russia, no?"

"Yes. It would have been worse. I'm glad I came here."

Valeria looked at the traffic crawling along the high street. A cluster of pigeons were gathered on the pavement, pecking at someone's discarded takeaway from the night before. "Is it everything you dreamed it would be?"

A sad smile flitted across Katya's face. "Darlin'," she said gently, "nothing is ever what you dream it will be. My cornflakes this morning were not what I dreamed my breakfast would be. But they stop me being hungry, and so they will do. I'm not starving or homeless or getting beaten every day. That is enough."

"Is it?"

"For me, yes." Katya reached out and gripped her arm. "And it should be for you too. When you start thinking that the grass is greener somewhere else, that's when the trouble starts."

Valeria was saved from answering by Azad arriving. He nodded a solemn greeting to them and walked to his part of the salon. Valeria watched him and found herself wondering about whether Azad had the life he had dreamed of. She had never thought much about what his dreams might have been; she had always vaguely imagined that he was born at the age he was now.

Shanaz arrived a few minutes later, relentlessly cheerful as always. "Hey, do you guys know what a fronted adverbial is?"

"It sounds like a lizard," Katya said.

"It's something to do with English. The kids are doing it at school and keep asking me about it, and I ain't got a clue. Like, I know what a verb is."

Valeria left Shanaz and Katya discussing grammar whilst she looked up her appointments for the day. Her schedule was full, which she was glad about, as that would give her less time to think.

She made herself a coffee and began checking that she had everything she needed for her first appointment. She looked toward the salon door and frowned. As if reading her thoughts, Katya asked, "She sick today?"

"I don't know. She hasn't called."

"It's not like her to be late, eh?"

"No." Valeria clenched her jaw.

"She's probably got a hangover or something," Shanaz said.

Valeria said nothing. Athena was never late, and she knew for a fact that she wasn't hungover. Was something wrong? Her brain at once went into overdrive, thinking of all the different scenarios: sudden illnesses, bus crashes, family emergencies. And then there was the worst scenario of all: that Athena had simply left. And wasn't that a more likely explanation than any of the other disasters?

Their declarations of love the previous night didn't change the fundamental fact that Valeria had precious little to offer. And so maybe it made sense to Athena that she should cut her losses and leave. And hadn't Valeria sensed a farewell in that kiss?

Valeria's hands began to shake with agitation, and she forced herself to take a deep breath. Her first client of the day arrived, and she focused as best she could. She listened as the woman described what she wanted, but her eyes kept drifting to the salon door, waiting for Athena to come.

Finally, when Valeria was halfway through her client's cut, the door opened, and Athena appeared. That relief that flooded Valeria was so intense that her knees almost gave way.

"What time do you call this?" Katya asked.

"Sorry," Athena mumbled. She looked tired, and Valeria wanted to go to her at once, but she made herself carry on with her task, smiling and chatting to her client.

From the corner of her eye, she watched Athena getting ready to start work and tried to figure out what was going through Athena's head. As ever, her expression gave nothing away. Apart from the dark circles under her eyes, there was no indication that anything was amiss.

When she had finished the cut, Valeria passed her client over to Katya and went through to the sink room where Athena was washing the hair of Mrs. Karim, Valeria's next client.

"Come and see me in my office when you are done," Valeria said loudly, so Katya and Shanaz would hear. They would be expecting Athena to get a ticking off for being late.

Valeria went into her office to wait. On impulse, she opened the filing cabinet and counted her stash. It still seemed absurdly small, but it was better than nothing. She replaced it in the cabinet, and Athena appeared a few moments later. Close up, Valeria could see the lines of tension stretched across her face.

"I'm sorry I was late," Athena said. "Won't happen again."

"Where were you?"

"I went home to get changed, and I fell asleep."

"You don't look very well slept."

"Thanks a lot."

"Sorry, I did not mean—"

"No, I'm sorry." Athena ran her hand over her eyes. "I've just got a lot on my mind at the moment, you know?"

Valeria badly wanted to hug her, but she did not dare take the risk with the salon full. "I thought you might have left. For good."

"Of course not. I meant what I said last night." Athena said it wearily, as if it was tiresome to have to reassure her.

Valeria felt her throat tighten, and she took a deep, shuddering breath. She had felt so relieved at seeing Athena walk through the door, but now, it felt as if Athena was still nowhere near her. "Then why do I feel like you are about to leave me?"

Athena's face twisted. "I'm not. I promise. It just hurts that I can't be with you, that's all."

"I know." They looked at each other in silence for a moment, Valeria thinking how beautiful Athena was.

She tried to think of what she could say that would make things better, but Athena shook herself and said, "I suppose I better get back to Mrs. Karim."

Valeria made a concerted effort to pull the fracturing parts of herself together. "Okay. But make sure you look like I gave you a bollocking. I don't want the others thinking I've gone soft."

Athena smiled weakly. "I'll do my best."

Shanaz and Katya exchanged glances as they both re-emerged into the main salon, Athena looking suitably contrite. Valeria began work on cutting Mrs. Karim's hair, going through the motions whilst her mind was again walking through the fantasy house of her imagination. This time, she didn't hesitate to put Athena in it, to imagine their life together of making meals, sleeping in the same bed. All simple, everyday things that took on a magical aura in her imaginings.

Whenever her glance alighted on Athena, she noticed how tense and worried she looked, and her heart twisted painfully. She wanted so badly to make things better.

"So I told her, you ought to just do it. Don't wait till you're old and full of regrets."

Valeria met Mrs. Karim's eyes in the mirror. "You told your daughter this?" Valeria desperately tried to recall the conversation she had only been half listening to.

"Yeah. 'Cos it seems like you have years and years, but really, you don't. It can be gone like that." She clicked her fingers to emphasise the point.

"Your husband died young, didn't he?"

Mrs. Karim looked at her in the mirror. "You got a good memory."

"I remember you telling me. I was shocked because he was so young, and it was very sudden. I always think how brave you've been."

"Nah, sweetheart. I ain't been brave. If I'd been brave, I would've taken my kids and gone back home to my mother. And then maybe Yusuf would never have got into trouble. But I stayed here because I was too afraid to leave everything familiar behind me. And I was too proud. I thought going back home would be admitting I had failed. I don't want my girl to make the same mistake I did."

"How do you know it was a mistake to stay?" Valeria asked.

Mrs. Karim tapped her chest. "I feel it in here," she said. "I should've gone."

Valeria's hands were still in Mrs. Karim's hair. She glanced around the salon, every inch of it as familiar to her as her own body. But it was not hers and never would be. And then her eyes fell on Katya, her dearest friend, who would go on doing the same thing year after year and would always advise Valeria to do the same.

She swallowed hard and resumed cutting. Almost involuntarily, her hand fluttered above her own chest, in imitation of Mrs. Karim's gesture. She knew what she felt in there. The feelings had been lurking for a while but had been drawn out by her relationship with Athena. And now they were no longer just feelings but had coalesced into a decision. She could not go on like this. Her life could not continue in its current groove.

She replied absently to Mrs. Karim's remarks as the resolve settled and hardened within her. It all seemed so simple, so blindingly obvious. Valeria could not carry on with this life, with its pretence and the sheen of normality that overlaid its rotten foundations. She knew with crystal clarity that she wanted out.

Chapter Eighteen

The hours of the day wore away, and eventually, Valeria was finishing off her final client as Katya tidied up, and Athena swept. When the last customer had been seen out the door, Valeria began the cashing up as Katya put her coat on. She could hear the sound of Athena rinsing down the sinks out the back.

Katya looked at Valeria, and Valeria could feel that she was working up to say something.

"Yes?" Valeria said.

Katya's eyes were softer than usual. "You know, I remember when I first met you. At that kebab shop. You remember?"

"I remember it very well."

"I knew at once that you needed someone to look out for you. You were like a little bird that had fallen from its nest." Valeria smiled at the memory. "You could easily have been crushed, you know? Like all the other girls we knew." Katya leaned forward and placed a hand over Valeria's. "I know sometimes you might look around and think, what if? But I'm telling you, the grass is not always greener. Those other girls? They would look at you now and think you were the luckiest woman alive."

Valeria dropped her eyes. There was a time when Katya's words would have made a deep impression on her, when she would have treated them as precious jewels of wisdom to be cherished. But that Valeria seemed a long way away. "I understand why you say that," Valeria said. "And you've been a good friend to me. But things change, Katya."

Katya frowned. "What do you mean? What is changing?"

"Me, for starters. I am not the same as the girl in the kebab shop. What I wanted then is not the same as what I want now."

Katya looked positively alarmed. "What are you talking about? You ain't going to do nothing stupid, are you?"

"When have I ever done anything stupid?"

Katya did not look reassured and seemed about to argue further when Athena emerged from the back. "All done there," she announced.

"Good. Can you do the bins before you go?" Valeria said. Athena did as she was asked, and Valeria turned back to Katya. "You can go now. I'll see you tomorrow."

Katya scowled. "Don't do nothing stupid," she barked in Russian as she left.

Athena looked up from where she was emptying the bin.

"She told me not to do anything stupid," Valeria explained as she locked the front door.

"Oh, right. Good advice." Athena carried the bin bag through to the back, and Valeria followed her and held the back door open as Athena deposited the bag into the bin in the alley and came back inside.

Valeria took her gently by the arm and drew her into the office. "I want to show you something," she said. She unlocked the filing cabinet and drew out her stash of notes. "There's a good amount here."

"Yeah. A good little rainy-day fund."

Valeria bunched the notes into her back pocket and took Athena's hands. "Every day is a rainy day. I want to change that."

"What do you mean?"

"There's not much here, but there's enough to last us a little while."

"Last us? What are you on about?"

"I want to leave here. Leave Sirvan, leave everything." Athena's eyes widened. "I want to have a life with you. And we can only do that far away from here."

Athena looked stunned. "Wow. That's...I mean, that's great, I guess."

"We can leave tonight."

Athena blinked and then laughed uncertainly. "You're not serious."

"Yes, I am. I want to leave now. How can I go back to Sirvan after last night? I love you, and you love me. So let's go and start again somewhere else."

"But you can't just leave. What about the salon?"

"What about it? It's not mine."

"Okay, but what about Katya?"

"I'll always love Katya, but I can't live my life by her advice anymore. She'll be okay."

"But I can't just up and leave my life," Athena protested.

"We can start a new life somewhere else."

"But my parents are here."

"I'm not saying we go to the moon. We go somewhere else, settle for a bit, and then you can come back and see your parents when it's safe."

"Safe?" Athena repeated.

"We'll need to keep our heads down for a bit. Sirvan will be furious."

"Exactly. It's not safe, Valeria."

"But it will never be safe. Sirvan is not going to let me leave him. He would...he would kill me." She swallowed hard. She had barely allowed herself to think this, let alone say it, but she was in no doubt that it was true. She would become another one of those people who simply vanished. "The only chance we have is to run away together."

"Okay, okay." Athena took a step back and made a calming gesture with her hands, as if she was trying to pat down water rising around her. "But we don't have to go right now. Let's give it a while to make some proper plans and then—"

"Athena, I can't go back to him tonight. I'll have to sleep in that bed with him and..." She shuddered. "I can't do it."

"I know it'll be hard. But it doesn't have to be for long. Just until we've got a plan."

"What plan?"

"I don't know. An idea about where we'll go and the money we'll need and everything else that we need to think about."

Valeria bit her lip. The decision had seemed so obvious in her head, but Athena's objections were bringing her back down to earth with a bump. "Okay," she said, taking a deep breath. "I understand this has been a bit sudden for you. So I will go tonight. And then I can get a message to you when I am somewhere safe."

Athena's eyes widened. "No, you can't do that!" Her vehemence took Valeria by surprise.

"What? Why not?"

"Because…it's too sudden."

Valeria almost laughed. "I can't leave Sirvan gradually. I have to go when he isn't expecting it. And I told you, I can't go back there tonight."

"You have to," said Athena, taking hold of Valeria's arm. "Just hang on for a bit longer, okay?"

Valeria shook her arm free. "No. I won't spend any more of my life like this. Why are you trying to make me stay with him?"

"I'm not. I'm just asking you to wait a little longer."

"Wait for what?" Valeria said, exasperated.

"Wait until Thursday, at least."

"Why? What is happening on Thursday?"

"Things might have changed by then."

Valeria threw her hands up in frustration. "What are you talking about? You tell me you love me, then you tell me to stay with Sirvan. Who I thought you hated?"

"I do hate him. Which is why I want to be sure he goes down for what he's done."

"Oh, and he's going to go down on Thursday, is he?"

"I bloody hope so!"

They stared at each other, the walls of the tiny room ringing with their raised voices. Athena swallowed, and Valeria could see her trying to regain control of herself. It was unsettling. Valeria again had the sense that there was something moving under the surface of Athena, something that was about to break into the open. There was something terribly wrong, but Valeria could not say what it was.

"You said you loved me," Athena said quietly. "If that's true, just please give it a few days. Okay? And then..." She stepped forward and put her arms around Valeria's waist, looking up in her face. "And then you and me can go wherever we want. I promise."

Valeria looked down at her. Athena's face was so lovely, so familiar. And yet. "Thursday," Valeria said. "It will all be okay by Thursday?"

Athena's expression faltered. It was a flickering of the eyes, a slight blurring of the picture, and Valeria felt her heart contract painfully within her. She disengaged herself from Athena and took a step back.

"How do you know that?" she asked.

Athena attempted a smile. "'Cos you told me his big deal is tomorrow, right? So if he's going down, it's going to be because of that."

"But you're very sure. Why are you so sure?"

"Because it's a risky venture. If he's ever going to be caught, it's going to be now."

"No. You're telling me to wait because it's a certain thing. How can you be so certain?" Athena didn't answer. She just looked at Valeria with her beautiful eyes, as if that would be all the answer needed. Valeria slammed her hand onto the desk, making Athena jump. "Tell me!"

Athena held out her hands. "Okay, okay. I know that the police are planning to arrest Sirvan when this deal takes place tomorrow."

Valeria felt the blood drain from her face. "How do you know that? How can you possibly know that?"

There was silence and, in the stillness, Valeria saw the now familiar expression cross Athena's face. A painful twisting, as if something was being forcefully wrenched from her.

"Because..." Athena began and closed her eyes briefly. When they reopened, there was a sad resignation in them. "Because I'm a police officer."

Valeria felt the ground shift beneath her feet. She put a hand out and touched the cold metal of the filing cabinet. She placed her palm flat against it, steadying herself. "A police officer? Since when?" She had a moment's wild thought that perhaps Athena meant that she had literally just joined the police. But one look at Athena's face told her it was much worse than that.

"For about five years now. I'm working on a team dedicated to bringing Sirvan and his business down."

Nausea rose in a wave from Valeria's stomach, as if she was gazing down at a sheer drop, the wind howling about her ears. She looked at Athena, a woman she'd thought she had known, that she had been ready to leave her well-ordered life for.

Athena took a step toward her. "And we're so close, Valeria. So close. This deal of his tomorrow? That's when my team will make its move and arrest Sirvan and all the rest of them red-handed. We'll have the evidence to put him away for the rest of his life. But we just need to keep things quiet for a little longer. Do you see? If you do a runner now, Sirvan will know something is wrong, and it could jeopardise the whole operation."

Valeria struggled to pay attention to her words because she was so distracted by her voice. It sounded completely different, deeper and older somehow. And Valeria realised she had heard her speaking in this voice before, all those times where she had been caught off guard or had appeared older than her years. That had been her real voice.

"Who are you?" Valeria asked. And there it was again, the sudden twisting of Athena's face. "Is Athena your real name?"

"No. My real name is Andrea."

"Andrea." Valeria repeated, the syllables feeling horribly false and gritty in her mouth. She thought back to all the basic facts that Athena had told her about her life. "Do you really live in Enfield?"

"No. But that's not important, Valeria. What's important is what happens now."

But Valeria didn't hear her. Her mind was feverishly replaying every interaction she'd had with this woman who was not Athena.

She was trying to find something solid, something true in any of it. "Are you even Greek?" she asked.

Andrea made an impatient sound. "Valeria, you have to listen to me. You have to keep this under wraps for now, just until Sirvan is arrested."

That dragged Valeria's attention back to the matter in hand. In her world, *arrested* was a word fraught with danger, with a sense that someone somewhere had messed up. "Sirvan is going to be arrested?" she repeated dazedly.

"Yes. We know when and where this shipment of trafficked girls is arriving. We can get Mesut and Galip and Omer's men. When they're safe, we can take Sirvan. All you need to do is keep schtum a little longer, and you'll be free." Her face was alight with confidence, her eyes fired with satisfaction.

Valeria felt her body respond to how beautiful Athena looked in that moment, and she had to shake her head to remind herself that this woman was not Athena. She was a stranger. "How can you know where the deal is taking place? Sirvan has been paranoid about phones and emails and all of that. I don't know where it is meant to be. Even Mesut will only know exactly where it is when Sirvan gives him the envelope from the safe—"

She stopped. She saw it so clearly in her mind's eye. Her, punching in the number to the safe as Athena watched. And then the next morning, coming downstairs to find Athena hovering in the hallway, right by the cupboard where the safe was.

"You opened the safe," Valeria said. "And you looked."

Andrea's shoulders sagged. She gave the barest of nods. And now Valeria's mind was in overdrive again, thinking back to all the times she might have said something.

"I told you about Zoran going to Istanbul. And about Omer and Galip coming round. And you..." She stopped and had to take a deep breath as her head spun. "And you turned up at the house." And then she saw it. Athena apparently calling an Uber and holding her phone up as Omer and Galip were in the hall. "Did you take a photo of them in the house?"

Again, the merest hint of a nod. And then Valeria was thinking of all the times in the salon when Athena had flirted with the men, had even taken selfies with them. Selfies with them. How simple it had been. Even Sirvan, with all his caution and paranoia had not twigged. And Valeria had never suspected anything because she had been so infatuated with Athena.

"You got a lot of photos," Valeria said.

"Yes. I needed to gather as much evidence as possible. We had to make sure our case was watertight."

"I must have been very useful to you, no? I told you all sorts of things about Sirvan and his business."

"I didn't have a definite plan for any of this. My brief was just to work in the salon and see what I could pick up. I never expected that you and I—"

"You really think I'm gonna believe that?" Valeria burned with humiliation as she remembered how she had made the first move. "God, you must have seen me coming a mile off."

"It wasn't like that," Andrea said firmly. "I liked you from the start, but I was surprised when you kissed me. And I never expected that I would fall in love with you."

"Don't you dare say that." Valeria's voice rose. "You used me. You used me to get information about Sirvan."

"Yes, I did. Because he has to be stopped. But it doesn't change the fact that I love you."

Valeria shook her head, disbelieving. "You're mad. How can you think I would believe that? Everything you've ever said to me has been a lie!"

"Not everything," Andrea insisted. "I know I told you lies, and I'm sorry I had to do that. But if it puts that man away, then it's all been worth it." She took another step forward. "But I never lied about the way I feel about you. I love you, Valeria."

Valeria pushed her away. "Liar," she choked.

A look of anguish crossed Andrea's face, but it was only fleeting. The hardness that Valeria had glimpsed before returned. "It's the truth. But all right. I can understand why you wouldn't believe me. But you're not going to stand there and defend Sirvan to me, are you? You're not going to say that he shouldn't be stopped."

Valeria hated her at that moment. She hated Andrea's inexorable, relentless pushing about Sirvan. She hated it because she knew that Andrea was right. And she didn't want her to be right about anything. She wanted to hate this woman cleanly and without complication, but she couldn't.

"He destroys people, Valeria." The fire was back in Andrea's eyes. "You think I used you? It's nothing to the way Sirvan uses people. They are destroyed once they've come into contact with him. There are girls in a truck right now, thinking they're coming here to start a new life, a better life. And Sirvan will have them selling sex for him. And when they stop being useful for that, he'll chuck them away. He'll destroy them, like he destroys everything. Like he's almost destroyed you."

Valeria closed her eyes. She didn't want to hear this. She wanted to keep being angry, to keep feeling the smart of shame and humiliation that would fuel that anger. But Andrea was relentless.

"I've seen what he does, Valeria. I've scooped the bodies off the streets, seen the wreckage he's left behind. I've interviewed women so scared, their hands never stop shaking. I've seen little kids wetting themselves with fear when his name is mentioned. You can hate me for what I've done, but you can't let that endanger the best chance we'll ever have to put a stop to him."

She had drawn closer again, and Valeria couldn't help but notice how beautiful she looked with the fire and animation in her face. It was the flashes of what she had occasionally glimpsed before, what had been lurking under the Athena mask, and now she could see it in all its glory.

But the wound was too deep and too painful. Being so close to her made Valeria think of all the times they had been intimate...but it had been a false intimacy because Andrea had been acting a part the whole time. The burning humiliation returned.

"Get out of here," Valeria said. "I don't want to see you ever again."

Andrea's jaw tightened. "Okay. I can leave today and not come back if that's what you want. But promise me you won't say anything to Sirvan."

"Promise you?" Valeria said, incredulous.

"You don't need to do anything." There was an edge of desperation in Andrea's voice. "Just carry on as normal for a day until Sirvan is arrested. Please, Valeria. You know it's the right thing to do."

Andrea was practically pleading with her. And all because of Sirvan. As usual, everything in her life was owned by him somehow. Even Athena, the one thing that Valeria had thought was hers and hers alone turned out to be nothing but a lie to trap Sirvan. Valeria felt tears gathering in her throat but was determined that she would not cry in front of Andrea.

"All right," she said, her voice choked. "All right. But please just go."

Andrea's face registered her relief. "Thank you. And Valeria?" She swallowed hard. "I do love you. I want you to remember that."

Valeria turned away as the tears spilled from her eyes. She heard Andrea's footsteps fading, and a few moments later, she heard the sound of the front door being unlocked and closed behind her.

Valeria sank to the floor, resting her cheek against the cold, unyielding metal of the cabinet as her tears flowed unchecked down her face.

Chapter Nineteen

W hen Valeria made it home a little while later, Sirvan was already back. He emerged from the front room as soon as Valeria closed the door behind her. She felt a jolt of revulsion at the sight of him, swiftly followed by crushing sadness that she had thought she was on the verge of a new life with Athena, far away from him. He stood and looked at her as she took off her jacket and bag.

"You're back," she said, his scrutiny like ants crawling across her skin.

"What's wrong?" he asked.

"Nothing." She attempted a smile. All she wanted was some time to herself, some time to think. "Did everything go okay with Amir?"

"Yes. All is good. Mesut will come first thing tomorrow. We must give him a good breakfast."

"Okay. I bought some *sucuk* yesterday. He'll like that. Are you hungry? Have you eaten yet?"

She moved past him into the kitchen and couldn't help recalling Andrea's words: "He destroys lives." She had always known this, but she had pushed it away. And was Andrea right that Sirvan had destroyed her own life? She had always told herself that he had saved her, that he had given her safety and security at a time when she had needed it most. And she had been so grateful for so long that she had been able to ignore what it was he did for his so-called work.

He followed her. "I'm not hungry," he said.

"Okay. I might make myself something." She had no appetite at all, but she wanted something to do to keep her busy. Sirvan's quiet, watchful presence was unnerving her.

She moved about the kitchen, half-heartedly preparing an omelette and salad for herself. As she placed a pan on the stove, Sirvan came and stood next to her. She kept her gaze on what she was doing, but she could feel his eyes on her face, moving and probing.

"What's the matter?" he said.

"Nothing."

"Something has happened. What is it?"

She clenched her jaw. She was furious with herself that he could read her so easily, even after all the years she had spent concealing her feelings. She did not think she could brush him off again without making him angry, so she said, "It's nothing. Athena has quit, that's all." She swallowed hard.

"Quit?" he repeated sharply. "Why?"

"I dunno. She said the job wasn't for her. Maybe it's not a bad thing. She was late today."

"You said she was a good worker."

"She was. But she has been getting sloppy recently. Turning up late, taking too long on lunch break, you know the kind of thing." With a huge mental effort, she kept her hands steady as his eyes didn't move from her face.

"Did she say something to you? Something that upset you?"

"No. She was okay." She folded the omelette over. Sirvan was still staring at her with his unblinking gaze, and she felt she needed to explain herself further. "I'm just disappointed, that's all. She was good with the customers. So friendly, so charming. Everyone liked her." She stopped speaking, feeling a lump come to her throat. She turned away from Sirvan and pretended to look for something in the cupboard so that she could hide her face.

"That's a shame," he said. "She was a good girl. She was good for the salon."

Valeria retrieved a plate from the cupboard and nodded, not

trusting herself to speak. "Are you going out again tonight on business?" she asked, keen to change the subject.

"No. I want to rest tonight, to make sure that I am ready for tomorrow."

She flipped the omelette onto the plate and tried to hide her disappointment. She would have given anything to have had the house to herself for a while, to be able to be alone with her thoughts. "Okay. I'm tired, so I might have a bath and an early night after I eat this. I'll get up early tomorrow to make sure Mesut has a good breakfast."

Sirvan nodded slowly, his eyes still searching her face. Then finally, to Valeria's intense relief, he went back to the living room.

She put the omelette on a plate and scattered some salad leaves next to it. She sat at the table and poked the meal with her fork, her mind running over her conversation with Andrea again and again. She thought back to all the interactions they'd had and tried to determine if there were signs, things she had missed. And then she felt her anger and shame rising afresh within her. God, she felt like such an idiot. Had Andrea simply been laughing at her the whole time? Had she immediately known that Valeria would be a patsy, that she could so easily pull the wool over her eyes?

Valeria forced down a few mouthfuls of food and then pushed the plate to one side. She got up and walked up and down the kitchen agitatedly. A few hours earlier, she had actually thought that she and Athena could leave and start a new life together. But now, there was no such person as Athena. There never had been. It was as if the Athena that Valeria had loved had crumbled into dust before her eyes. She leaned on the kitchen counter and put her head in her hands.

She didn't know how long she remained like that, but she was stirred from her position by the sound of the living room door opening and Sirvan's footsteps approaching. She straightened at once and took up her plate, emptying the uneaten food quickly into the bin.

She was at the sink, washing up when he entered.

"I thought you were having a bath," he said.

"I lost track of time," she said, glancing at the clock. "Is Mesut okay?" She had no interest at all in how Mesut was feeling, but she did not want any more questions. She felt as if she was hanging by a thread, as if her whole being was glass with cracks running across it.

"Yes," he said. "Things are all in place for tomorrow. But he's worried about the police. We all are."

"The police?" she echoed faintly.

"We still don't know how they knew about Zoran. That girl who got away might have told them some things, but they couldn't know he was about to leave the country. The guys are worried someone is leaking information to them."

Valeria placed the washed plate carefully onto the dish rack. "Why would anyone do that?"

"Someone who doesn't like me. They are angry, resentful. So they get their own back by telling the police stuff." He tapped his thumb thoughtfully against his teeth. "But how would they know about Zoran going to Istanbul? We only talked about that with Galip and Omer." Valeria took a sponge and wiped down the already spotless kitchen surfaces in order to give herself something to do. "We didn't even text about it or nothing. So how could someone know?"

"Maybe Zoran told someone," Valeria said.

Sirvan pursed his lips. "Maybe. He was not always the best at keeping quiet."

"Exactly. He was always chatting away."

Sirvan folded his arms and frowned at the kitchen floor. "You're right. In the salon, he was always chatting with your girls."

Valeria's shoulders tensed as she mindlessly wiped the sponge back and forth. She could sense it coming, could feel the air grow heavy with foreboding.

"You think anyone in the salon said anything?" He said it with studied casualness, as if he was asking about something as trivial as whether it would rain tomorrow. But the question was loaded with consequences, with a darkness that pushed and strained beneath the apparently innocuous words.

She moistened her lips. And as she did so, she remembered the feel of Athena's lips pressed against her own. Not Athena, Andrea, she corrected herself. And the sting of the betrayal came again, enough to bring tears to her eyes.

"Definitely not Shanaz or Katya," she said. "They barely spoke to Zoran. And besides, I've known them for years." There was a silence after she spoke, and Valeria dared not turn round and meet Sirvan's eyes. She could hear his breathing, could feel his solid mass in the room.

"Yes," he said in the same neutral tone. "I would say the same for Azad. It was Athena that was always chatting to him."

"And taking pictures," Valeria added. She turned to look at Sirvan as she said this. She could see the words strike home. And then she could see him repeating the process she herself had been through, reviewing all the interactions with Athena. She saw a shift in his face, a tightening around the eyes that was always a sign of anger with him.

Her stomach clenched painfully as she realised that now it had been half said, it could not be recalled. She wished that she had not said anything, that she had just remained silent. She tried to think of something to say to divert him, but he was already turning away, going out into the hallway.

She followed him into the hall and stopped. He was pulling his coat on and grabbing his car keys. There was a look of chilled determination on his face, and Valeria felt a wave of cold sickness pass over her. She placed a hand on the wall for support.

It was okay, she told herself. It was okay. Athena was not a real person. It had been Andrea all along, and she was a police officer. That meant she was protected, safe. She had said she would not come back to the salon anyway, so there was nothing to worry about. And why should she worry anyway? Andrea had lied to her and used her.

Valeria tried to summon some of the anger and hurt she had felt a moment before, but she could only recall Andrea's eyes fixed on hers as she'd said, "I never lied about the way I feel about you."

Sirvan looked up at her with cold fury in his eyes.

"What will you do?" she asked, her voice shaking.

"I'm going to take care of it."

"It could have been anyone," she said desperately. "You can't know for sure."

"I will know soon enough." Something of her terror must have shown itself, for his face softened slightly. He came forward and placed his hands on her shoulders. "Don't worry about it, darlin'. I'm going to sort it out. You go and have your bath."

She knew an order when she heard one. She turned and walked slowly upstairs. By the time she reached the bathroom, she heard the front door slam and the sound of Sirvan starting his car. She sat on the edge of the bathtub, turned the taps on, and watched the water falling into the tub. She felt hollow, as if everything that had ever been of worth within her was pouring out like the water.

It would be okay, she kept saying to herself. Andrea was a police officer; she would be fine. She imagined Andrea sitting in a police station somewhere, surrounded by high fences and barbed wire, but the image did nothing to quell the anxiety clawing at her insides.

❖

Valeria was acutely aware of the absurdity of effectively being forced to have a bath, but nevertheless, she undressed and got into the tub. She sat there miserably, watching the water eddying around her body.

Eventually, the water went cold, and she got out and towelled herself dry. She dressed and then stood irresolute on the landing. What should she do? The question rooted her to the spot. She looked at the neutral walls and carpets of the upstairs landing and felt as if they were closing in on her, smothering her with their bland lifelessness.

She went downstairs and began cleaning the oven. She scrubbed at it mindlessly, reducing her world and her thoughts to the removal of the crusty black residue. She scoured until her arms and shoulders ached, and then she kept going, finding relief in the pain.

Eventually, her knees and arms could take no more, and she sat back on her heels. She looked up at the clock. Sirvan had been gone for several hours. What could he have been doing all this time? She couldn't bear to consider the possible answers to this question, and so she got up stiffly from the kitchen floor and went into the front room. She switched the TV on and scrolled listlessly through the channels.

She generally spent very little time in the living room when she was not cleaning it or waiting on Sirvan's guests. She and Sirvan never sat together and watched television. When he did watch TV, he watched violent crime shows which she found actively distressing.

She shifted on the sofa, thinking how much she disliked the cold, slippery feeling of the leather. She found a rerun of a detective drama set in the nineteen thirties. Characters wandered around a chocolate box village bathed in sunshine whilst debating who had committed the murder in their midst. Valeria watched it with a kind of revolted fascination. Was murder and violence more palatable if it took place in a charming village rather than in a stinking alleyway? She watched as the convoluted motive was explained by a dapper detective. She had known people killed for much less, for practically nothing, in fact, a misdirected glance or straying into the wrong postcode.

A soothing theme song and roll of credits heralded the end of the drama, and another episode began, almost indistinguishable from the last. Unbelievably, Valeria felt her eyelids grow heavy. The burbling of upper-class voices lulled her to sleep.

The front door slammed, and her eyes jumped open. The TV was now showing an eighties action film. An absurdly muscled man was spraying bullets into a roomful of henchman. The incongruity with the detective drama was so stark that, for a moment, Valeria could only gape at the TV whilst her brain struggled to make sense of what she was seeing.

She heard voices in the hallway and the sound of something being dragged along the floor. She went to the doorway and was just in time to see Sirvan look back over his shoulder as Mesut and someone else went ahead of him into the kitchen.

"Ah, you're still up," Sirvan said when he saw her. "Good, you can come and talk to her."

"Talk to who?" she said automatically, but her chest tightened because she knew the answer. Sirvan motioned her into the kitchen.

Andrea was sitting on a kitchen chair with her arms pulled behind her. Mesut was bending and tying her wrists with a cable tie. Andrea looked groggy, her head lolling from side to side. Valeria saw the red marks on her face and throat and felt her blood turn to ice in her veins.

Sirvan strode around the kitchen, running his fingers through his hair. "You heard Zoran say something in the salon, right?" he said as if resuming a conversation partway through. "You heard him say something about going to Istanbul. And then you tell the police this."

"I don't know what you're talking about." Andrea's voice was thick. Her eyes met Valeria's. Valeria looked away immediately, not trusting herself to keep her expression neutral.

Sirvan shook his head and spoke quietly, almost to himself. "I'm an idiot. I see you in the salon, chatting with them, taking pictures with them. Then you show up at my house just as they happen to be here. I didn't see it. I didn't see any of it." He stopped and looked at Valeria. "I didn't see it until you pointed it out to me."

Valeria kept her eyes on him, fixed them on his face so that she did not have to look at Andrea. She could see the pale oval of Andrea's face in the edge of her vision and dreaded what she would see if she were to look into her eyes.

"Everyone at the salon talked to them," Andrea said. "So why isn't Katya here instead of me?"

"Katya was not taking pictures with them."

"Jesus, I was trying to be nice. I thought you wanted me to be nice to them?" She sounded hurt by Sirvan's apparent misinterpretation.

"Why did you quit the salon?" he said.

"'Cos I can get paid more in town."

"And you decide you're going to leave just now?"

She blinked at him in confusion. "What do you mean?" She looked from him to Valeria pleadingly. "Look, I'm sorry if me quitting makes a problem in the salon. I can stay on a bit longer if that would help?"

Valeria looked at the floor. Andrea was playing the role of Athena beautifully, right down to the story Valeria had given about her quitting. Valeria couldn't help admiring her performance.

"I want to know what you have told the police."

"I haven't told them anything."

Sirvan backhanded her across the face. Her head snapped back at the impact, and Valeria started forward. Blood leaked from Andrea's split lip as she blinked rapidly.

Sirvan crouched before her, his finger in her face. "You're lying. I'm thinking about all the times you were hanging around at the salon. The pictures you took. That time you turned up here. And then you quit with no reason. I know someone has been talking to the police about my business. I know it was you. So now, I want to know how much you told them."

"Please, Sirvan, I don't even know what your business is." Her eyes were wide.

He straightened and turned to Valeria. "You ever say anything to her about my business?"

Valeria's entire body prickled with heat as she remembered all the times she had done exactly that. She wondered what his reaction would be if she confessed the truth. "No, of course not. I never talk about your business to anyone. You know that." She risked a quick glance at Andrea and saw relief in her face.

His mouth twisted in displeasure. He put his hands on his hips and looked at Andrea. And then he looked at Mesut, who had been standing silently behind her. Sirvan motioned with his head, and he and Mesut stood in the kitchen doorway, conversing together under their breath.

Andrea looked at Valeria. The blood from her lip had trickled down her chin. Valeria expected to see anger and hurt in her eyes, but there was nothing but concern. "Are you okay?" Andrea mouthed. Valeria turned away, unable to look at her bloodied face.

Sirvan nodded curtly as he finished his conversation with

Mesut. Then, very slowly and very deliberately, he ran his fingers over the knife block on the side. He let them trail over the wooden handles, lingering first on the bread knife and then the carving knife.

Valeria's entire body stilled, as if a breath out of place might tip him into doing something unthinkable. Her eyes flicked to Andrea. Her face was pale, making her eyes appear even darker.

Sirvan drew the carving knife very slowly out of the block. He held it and hefted it as if he was checking the weight and feel. He looked at Andrea, who met his gaze unblinkingly. "You're telling me you never said nothing to the police?" he asked conversationally.

"That's what I've been telling you all along," Andrea said. She spoke calmly. She wasn't being Athena now; she was clearly someone different. It seemed so obvious to Valeria that she was sure that Sirvan would notice.

"I don't believe you," he said, holding the knife so that its tip pointed upward.

"I can't help that."

He walked slowly around the chair. Andrea kept her gaze firmly focused on the ground in front of her. "I think," he said as he orbited her, "that you aren't taking me seriously. You think this is a game."

"You just hit me in the face. I know this isn't a game."

"I can do much worse than hit you." He came to a halt directly behind her. Her eyes briefly met Valeria's, and the fear in them made Valeria's heart lurch. She knew that violence underlay everything Sirvan did, but she had never before seen it with her own eyes.

He grabbed a handful of Andrea's hair and yanked her head back hard. He pressed the blade of the knife against her exposed throat. Valeria started forward with a cry but stopped as she saw him digging the point of the knife into Andrea's skin, drawing a small globule of blood.

Andrea's body was rigid as he spoke softly into her ear. "You tell me the truth, or I will kill you right here."

"Sirvan. Please. You cannot do this." Valeria could hear how high and tight her voice sounded even as she fought to stay calm.

He raised his eyes slowly to hers. "If I have to kill her, I will," he said.

"Don't!" Andrea's voice was strangled, but the terror in it was unmistakable.

Something gave way inside Valeria. "You can't kill her! She is police!"

She could not remember the last time she had seen Sirvan taken by surprise. His eyes widened, and the hand with the knife fell away from Andrea's throat. "What did you say?" he asked.

Valeria clenched her fists. "You heard me. She is a police officer. If you murder her, they will never let you be."

He released his hold on Andrea, pushing her head roughly away. He took a step toward Valeria and pointed at her with the knife, his eyes blazing. "How do you know she is police?"

Valeria moistened her lips. "'Cos she told me." She was entirely winging it, hoping that the words would come to her and that somehow, she would be able to divert Sirvan from his path.

"When? When did she tell you this?"

"Earlier today."

"Ah." He nodded slowly. "And you didn't tell me. Why was that?" His voice was gentle, which Valeria knew was a sign that she was in serious danger. She had seen burly men begin to shake when Sirvan spoke in that voice.

Her mind raced as she tried to think of some plausible explanation. "I…I didn't—"

"I threatened her," Andrea said. Sirvan's head swung back to her. "I wanted her to tell me what she knew about your business, but she wouldn't. I told her I was a police officer and that she would go to jail if she didn't tell me." Andrea shook her head slowly as if marvelling at Valeria's loyalty. "But she wouldn't say anything. So I told her that if she said anything to you, I'd make sure that armed police would raid her salon, and they would be forced to shoot her in self-defence."

Valeria stared at Andrea in disbelief. She could not comprehend why Andrea was coming up with a story to protect her. Valeria had betrayed her to Sirvan. Andrea had no reason to try to defend her.

Sirvan looked at Valeria, waiting for her to say something. Behind him, she was aware of Andrea's eyes fixed on her. They were pleading with her, and she could feel the force of it as if Andrea was shouting at her.

"Yes," she said hoarsely. "I was too scared to tell you. I thought the police would kill me."

He looked from her to Andrea and then looked at Mesut. He seemed to get no help from any of them, and for the first time, Valeria could sense he was at a loss. He placed the knife on the kitchen side, and the whole house seemed to exhale with relief. "You were the one who pointed out that she was pally with Zoran, taking pictures and all that. But you didn't tell me she was a police officer?"

"I'm sorry," she said desperately. "I couldn't think straight. I wanted to warn you somehow, but I was afraid to tell you everything." He looked at her, his eyes glittering. His face was entirely still, and Valeria felt sick with fear. "I'm sorry," she said again. "I should have told you."

His arm shot up with incredible speed, and his hand was around Valeria's throat before she had time to react. His hand seemed impossibly large, encircling her neck as if it was a mere twig. Valeria could feel pressure, and panic surged through her. Her hands scrabbled at his.

"Yes. You should have fucking told me." His eyes bored into hers, his anger cold and focused. Dimly, Valeria was aware of a commotion behind him. Andrea was trying to get to her feet and struggling with Mesut, who was holding her down. Valeria could hear shouting somewhere beneath the pounding of blood in her ears. The pressure on her throat increased, and black spots began to appear before her eyes, mercifully blotting out the cold mask of Sirvan's face.

Was he going to kill her? Was this how she would die? She felt bitterly disappointed to be meeting such a tawdry end in a kitchen she had never really liked.

The pressure on her neck ceased, and light flooded her vision. She took a great gasp of air, falling back against the kitchen worktop.

"You're lucky," he told her. "Anyone else would die for this." He turned his attention back to Andrea. She had lost the battle with Mesut, who was restraining her with an arm about her neck. Sirvan took a deep breath and ran his fingers through his hair. "All right," he said, as if he was trying to calm some overexcited children. "Let's start again. How much do the police know?"

"Valeria! Are you all right?" Andrea's voice was muffled by Mesut's arm.

"You don't get to say nothing to her," Sirvan said coldly. "You talk to me, you understand?"

"Get this bastard off me," she said.

Sirvan nodded to Mesut, who released his hold. Valeria met Andrea's gaze but was wheezing too hard to say anything.

Sirvan snapped his fingers in Andrea's face. "Hey! I asked you a question. How much do the police know?"

Her gaze returned to him, and Valeria could see her weighing the options. "We know that you have contact with Omer and Galip and that Zoran was going out there to do some kind of business with them."

"That's why you arrest him? To find out what he knows?"

"No, we arrested him because he runs a brothel and is a serial abuser. We didn't want him leaving the country and escaping."

"How did you know he was going to leave the country?"

Andrea gave him a pitying look. "'Cos he told me. He was very excited about it."

"He wouldn't tell you. He knew it was all hush-hush."

Andrea rolled her eyes. "Yeah, and he wouldn't be so careless as to let one of his girls escape, would he?"

His jaw tightened in fury, and Valeria swallowed hard. "What was the plan after Zoran was arrested?"

"To gather as much intel as possible on your so-called business."

"And you try to get this intel from my wife?" He sounded disbelieving, as if this was the stupidest thing he had ever heard.

Andrea grimaced. "Any source was worth pursuing."

Valeria's breathing was finally returning to normal. She flinched at being described as "a source" and caught Andrea's darting glance toward her.

"What intel have the police got about my business?"

"We know about the brothel that Zoran ran for you. But obviously, he said you had nothing to do with it."

He smiled. "Keep going."

"We know you've got this whole borough stitched up. Protection rackets, extortion, money laundering."

"What else?"

"What do you mean? What else is there?" Andrea looked at him keenly.

He leaned back against the breakfast bar and folded his arms. "Wow. You must have a tonne of evidence on all of this. Which is why I have been a free man all this time, yes?"

Andrea looked at him with pure hatred.

He stuck his hands in his pockets and walked back and forth. "Let me get this straight. The police are so desperate to know what I'm doing that they send you, *you*, to work in my wife's salon. So what? You are gonna catch me handing over a briefcase of used fifties whilst I have a shave?" He stopped in front of Andrea and looked at her with pity. "The police must be really desperate," he said, "if they are relying on you for information."

Andrea looked at him for a moment, then very deliberately spat in his face.

He gave a cry of fury and wiped his eye. Mesut wrapped an arm around Andrea's neck again, pulling her tight against him. Sirvan drove his fist into Andrea's stomach.

"Sirvan!" Valeria cried, but it came out as croak, and he didn't notice. He punched Andrea in the stomach again and then stood back, having apparently relieved his fury. Mesut released her, and Andrea flopped forward, only her bound hands stopping her from folding over completely. Her mouth hung open as she gasped for air.

Valeria stepped forward, almost falling to the ground as she did so. She felt lightheaded, and her throat burned, but she didn't care. She had to get Sirvan to stop. She knew that appealing to any sense of mercy in him was pointless, so she tried a different approach.

"Sirvan," she said, trying to force her voice through her bruised throat. "It's getting late." He looked at her appraisingly, as if reevaluating who she was. Yet Valeria knew exactly who he wanted her to be in this moment. "There is not time for this now."

He looked at the clock and scowled. He and Mesut spoke rapidly, their heads bent together behind Andrea's chair.

Valeria stood against the counter, watching Andrea as surreptitiously as possible. She was still bent over, her eyes closed, and her breathing coming in small, shallow gulps. Valeria ached with longing to go to her, but she balled her fists and pushed down hard on her emotions. She had to keep this all under control for now.

Sirvan turned to her. "Go and give Mesut the stuff like I showed you."

Valeria nodded and stumbled out of the kitchen, Mesut following her. She felt sick at the thought of leaving Sirvan alone with Andrea, but she had already had one narrow escape from his wrath.

She opened the cupboard under the stairs. Her vision swam, and it took her several attempts before she punched the correct code into the safe. She withdrew the brown envelope. Her thoughts returned to the morning she had come downstairs and found Andrea hovering by the cupboard. Andrea had looked inside the envelope, which meant that surely the police were ready and waiting for the handover?

She handed the envelope to Mesut, praying she was right. He took it from her in silence, and they both returned to the kitchen.

Andrea was sitting back in the chair, her eyes closed, and pain etched in her face. Sirvan leaned against the counter, his arms folded, and his eyes fixed unblinking on Andrea. "Ready?" he asked Mesut.

"Ready," Mesut said.

"I'm relying on you. You got to make sure this thing works."

"I will, Sirvan." Mesut clasped Sirvan's hand, and Sirvan nodded gravely at him. And then, Mesut was gone.

Valeria stood in the kitchen doorway, watching Sirvan, who was watching Andrea. Every muscle in Valeria's body was pulled as tight as a drum, waiting to see what Sirvan would do next.

He walked to the back of Andrea's chair and checked the cable tie on her hands. Then he opened the back door and motioned to Valeria to step outside. She followed him, and he closed the door. Through the glass, they could see Andrea clearly. Her eyes were still closed, and she was motionless, only the movement of her chest indicating that she was still breathing.

Sirvan took out a cigarette and lit it, blowing smoke into the blackness of the night. "I meant what I said. If it had been anyone else, I would kill them for keeping a thing like that from me."

She lowered her eyes, trying to ooze remorse from every pore. "I know," she said, softly. "I let you down. I'm sorry. I was just so afraid at the thought of being gunned down in my salon." She shivered, helped by the coldness of the night air. Sirvan drew on his cigarette and said nothing. "How did you find her?" she asked after a pause.

"I sent her a text from your phone, asking to meet." He sounded almost bored by how easy it had been to entice Andrea into a trap. Valeria looked at the peeling wood of the decking bathed in the yellow glow from the kitchen. She tried not to think of Andrea receiving the text, perhaps with a surge of hope that Valeria had wanted to talk, then the horrible moment when Andrea realised that Valeria was not the one meeting her. She must have thought Valeria had done it deliberately, had connived with Sirvan to trap her.

She closed her eyes briefly, shame and remorse almost threatening to overwhelm her. And yet Andrea had still tried to protect her from Sirvan. Her overtaxed brain struggled to process this, to sift through the emotions to work out what it all meant.

"We have been married a long time, yes?" She opened her eyes and saw him looking at her, his face softer than before.

"Yes," she agreed. She had no desire to count up the exact number of years she had been with him, to enumerate precisely how much of her life she had spent under his control.

"You've been a good wife," he continued. "You've never caused me trouble." This was high praise indeed, and Valeria knew a response was expected.

"You have been...good to me." She struggled to force the words out, and her hand went unconsciously to her throat.

He seemed to note the gesture. "I don't want to hurt you," he said. "But the business is everything. You understand?"

"I understand."

"I have enemies everywhere. From other guys in London, from the guys I do business with who think they can do better than me. And the police. The police are always trying to take me down." He drew on his cigarette, and his eyes moved restlessly around their small garden as if he was searching for any police officers that might be concealed in the bushes. "This is the closest they have ever got. And they did it by putting a pretty girl into my salon." He shook his head. "There is no fool like an old fool."

Valeria almost wanted to laugh that he was finally acknowledging that it was his salon. But she mastered the urge and said, "You couldn't have known. None of us knew."

"But now I have a problem. And I need you to help me." Her stomach tensed. "That girl needs to disappear."

The air was chased from her lungs. "What...what do you mean?"

He looked at her, the light from the kitchen behind him throwing his face into shadow. But she could still see his eyes glittering in the darkness. "I can't simply let her go. She will go back to the police and tell them everything."

"But she doesn't know anything. She clearly knew nothing about this deal of yours." She fought to keep her voice under control.

"She knows enough to cause damage. And I can't allow it to be known that I had a police informant in my business and did nothing." He took a final drag on his cigarette and ground the stub beneath his heel. "She needs to disappear tonight. And I'll need you to help me. I don't want anyone else knowing about this."

She swallowed. There was no doubt in her mind about what "disappearing" Andrea meant. It seemed for a moment to be absurd that he should be so calmly discussing this in their back garden, but she had known, had always known, that this was what his business boiled down to.

An icy clarity came into her mind. She knew what he intended, and she knew just as certainly that she had to prevent it. She glanced at the slumped figure of Andrea in the chair, and the vulnerability of her made Valeria's heart ache. Andrea had assured her repeatedly that she loved her, and Valeria had not believed her. But Andrea had tried to protect her, even though she had delivered her to Sirvan. That showed more than words ever could, and Valeria could not pretend otherwise.

"I understand," she said. "But you cannot do it here. You'll have to take her somewhere else."

His face registered surprise, and Valeria felt a grim satisfaction. It was as if all her life thus far had been training for this precise moment. She knew exactly what he wanted of her, what part she was required to play.

He nodded slowly, and an approving smile tugged at the corners of his mouth. She swallowed the bile that was rising up her bruised throat. "Yes, I can't do it here," he agreed. "But I have a place I can use."

She turned aside, afraid she was in danger of being physically sick. She shouldn't be surprised, she chided herself. She had known, somewhere deep down, she had always known.

He heaved a sigh, as if he was about to begin a tedious and unwelcome task. He looked at his watch. "Okay. We need to move quickly. Mesut will be taking delivery of the shipment soon, and I don't want any distractions. I will call Amir to come and watch her whilst I get things ready."

"Amir?" Valeria got her face under control and turned back to Sirvan. "You don't need him to come and watch her. I'm here, aren't I?" He looked at her sternly. Valeria risked laying a hand on his arm. "I know I let you down before. Let me help you now. We don't want to involve more people in this than we need to, right?"

It was too dark to read his expression, so she waited in the silence. She focused all her energy on keeping her hand flat against his arm, resisting the urge to grip it. She had no idea what she was going to do, but she would have no chance if he brought more of his men to the house.

Finally, she felt him shift his weight. "All right," he said. "But you have to be careful, yes? She is not sweet little Athena who made the good coffee. She is a lying bitch who wants to destroy me." The hatred in his voice chilled her to the bone.

"I know," she said. "I know exactly who she is." And for the first time, she felt that she really did.

When they went back inside, Andrea was sitting up straight in the chair again. She looked pale but still defiant. Sirvan twisted the gold signet ring on his finger as he looked at her.

"We got a problem now, eh?" He spread his hands apologetically. "I can't let you go, can I?"

She pressed her lips together but said nothing.

He turned to Valeria. "I need to get some stuff from the loft. You shout for me if you need me. Okay?"

"Okay."

He looked into her face, his eyes moving restlessly over her features as if probing for a sign of weakness. She met his gaze resolutely. He finally seemed satisfied and left the kitchen.

"Valeria," Andrea croaked, "Are you——"

"Shh!" She shook her head, trying to signal with her eyes that Andrea should keep silent. She heard Sirvan's footsteps going up the stairs and heard the sound of the loft ladder being pulled down. At the creak of his step on the ladder, she opened a kitchen drawer and drew out the heavy kitchen scissors.

She went straight behind Andrea and slid the blade of the scissors underneath the cable tie. It was so tight, she had to press the blunt side of the blade hard into Andrea's skin. The scissors made no impression against the hardened plastic, and she almost screamed with frustration. She pressed with all her might, sawing the scissors back and forth.

"What are you doing?" Andrea whispered.

"Getting you out of here. Pull if you can."

Andrea pulled her wrists apart as Valeria sawed with the scissors. She could hear Sirvan moving about in the loft, shifting things across the rafters. Finally, she cut through the plastic ties, and Andrea's hands were free. She sighed with relief as she moved her arms and rubbed at her wrists.

Valeria helped her to her feet, wrapping an arm around her

waist. She nodded to the back door. "Go now. Get over the back fence and go left, and you will be on the street."

"You're coming with me." Andrea leaned a hand on the kitchen table to support herself as she looked into Valeria's face.

Valeria shook her head. "No. I will stay here to keep him busy whilst you get away."

"No way. I'm not leaving you here with him." Andrea's jaw was set in a determined line.

Valeria wanted to howl with impatience. She took Andrea's face in her hands. "You have to go call your police colleagues. Sirvan still has my phone and yours. Find someone with a phone and call them. I'll keep him busy as long as I can for you."

"No," Andrea said, her eyes wide. "I can't leave you."

Valeria leaned her forehead against Andrea's. Despite the fear that coursed through her, she revelled in the feeling of being close to Andrea again. "Listen to me. I know you love me. I didn't believe it at first, but now, I know it's true. If you love me, please go. If you leave it much longer, he will come back, and then we have no chance at all."

"I can't." Andrea's voice was choked.

"Please, Andrea. Please go. Now."

There was a creak from overhead. They both jumped at the noise, and Andrea finally seemed galvanised into movement. She went to the back door, opened it, and cast a look back at Valeria, her eyes moist. "I'm coming back for you," she said.

Valeria nodded, too overwhelmed to speak.

Andrea staggered down the garden, clutching her side. Valeria could just see her scrambling awkwardly over the back fence. Then she heard more movement overhead and the sound of a creak on the ladder. She went out into the hallway and looked up the stairs. Sirvan descended the ladder from the loft, the steps creaking as he came. She held herself steady, prepared to face him. She had never before defied him openly, and she felt almost drunk with a mixture of fear and reckless euphoria. She was no longer all set. She had finally done something that no one would have expected.

He had a bundle of things under his arm, and as he laid them on the floor of the landing, her stomach turned. A tarpaulin, thick rolls of masking tape, and a gun.

She blinked to make sure her eyes had not deceived her. But, no, there was a gun lying on the carpet of the landing. He'd brought it down from the loft in the same way that other people took down their Christmas decorations. She had occasionally caught glimpses of guns tucked beneath jackets, either Sirvan's or one of his associates. She had never asked about them and preferred not to think of them at all. This was the first time she had seen one in plain sight, and the thought of what he intended to do with it made her sick. She forced her mind back to the present moment and ran feverishly through all the possible ways she could detain or distract him until Andrea got help.

He tucked the gun into the back of his trousers, picked up the tarp and masking tape, and walked down the stairs. When he saw Valeria standing at the bottom, he said sharply, "What is it?"

"I came to see if you needed any help taking stuff down."

He placed the things in a pile on the hall floor. "No, I have everything I need." He rolled up his sleeves. "I'll need you to help me get her to the car."

As he made to go past her and back to the kitchen, Valeria placed her hands on his chest. He looked taken aback and stopped in his tracks. She leaned forward and placed her lips on his. She tried to make herself soft and inviting against him, using all the willpower she possessed to resist her body screaming at her to get away from him.

He pulled his head back and looked at her as if she was mad. "What are you doing?" he asked.

"I'm kissing you."

"Now is not the time for that," he growled.

"I want to make up for not telling you about Athena straight away," she said, lowering her eyes demurely.

His face softened. "I know, darlin'. But I have a lot going on tonight, okay? You can make it up to me later."

She kept her hands against his chest, desperate to delay him just a little longer. Every second made it more likely that Andrea would make it. "It will be quick for her, won't it?"

His jaw clenched. "If it wasn't for the shipment coming, I would make it very slow. But lucky for her, it will have to be quick."

"That's good. I know she is police, but I don't want to think of her suffering."

He frowned. "I told you, she is not sweet little Athena. She is police scum who deserves everything she gets." And with that, he swept determinedly past her and toward the kitchen.

She took a deep breath and prepared herself to face his fury as best she could.

He walked into the kitchen and stopped. His head snapped to the left and right as he scanned the kitchen. "Where is she?" he demanded.

Valeria came to the door and assumed a look of surprise. "I don't know where she is," she said.

He ran to the back door and wrenched it open. He sprinted down the garden, withdrawing the gun from his trousers as he did. He pulled himself up to the back fence and looked down on the other side. And then he was back again, his face twisted with rage.

"How the fuck…" he began, and then his gaze snagged on the cut cable ties on the floor behind the chair. He walked over to them and held them up, observing the clear break where the scissors had finally cut through. He raised his eyes slowly to Valeria. She met his gaze calmly, feeling no fear, only a kind of grim resignation.

It felt inevitable that this moment would arrive, that there would come a point where the version of herself that she had cultivated for so long would crumble, and it seemed fitting that it should happen before Sirvan's eyes.

He gripped the broken cable ties in his fist. "What is this?" He spoke quietly, in the way that always signalled danger.

She briefly considered blustering, trying to buy more time by pretending ignorance, but she was so sick of pretending. "I cut through the ties," she said.

"Why did you do that?"

"Because I couldn't let you kill her."

"She will bring the police down on us."

"I know."

"We could lose everything!" he shouted.

She could not remember the last she had heard him raise his voice. Perhaps, she thought with a detached satisfaction, it was not only she who was finally revealing her true self. Perhaps Sirvan's careful, calm front was also beginning to crumble. "*You* could lose everything. I have nothing to lose."

"Nothing? You calling this house, the salon, nothing?"

"It is your house and your salon. They are nothing to me."

He stared at her. "What the hell is wrong with you? You want me to end up in jail? You want to end up on the streets?"

"I don't care what happens to me. Your business is rotten. I hope the police tear it all down."

His mouth dropped open. Valeria had never spoken to him like that in her life, and he looked at her as if she was a stranger. And essentially, she was. She had never let her guard down with him, but the cracks that had been showing in her carefully constructed facade had widened into deep ruptures, and there was no stopping her true self from bursting through.

"I always knew what your business was," she continued, emboldened. "I knew it was based on exploiting and terrorising people. But I was scared, so I stopped myself from thinking about it. I was a coward. But I'm not afraid anymore. Andrea helped me to see you and this life for what it really is."

"Andrea?" he repeated. "Is that…is that *her* name?" His thoughts seemed to race behind his eyes. "What the fuck has been going on?"

"We've been seeing each other." She had no energy, no will for hiding it anymore. And she couldn't deny the grim satisfaction at seeing the shock on Sirvan's face.

"Seeing each other? You saying that you and her…" He couldn't seem to finish the sentence. He could only stare at her uncomprehendingly.

"Yes. I didn't know she was a police officer at first, and I thought I was in love with her. When she told me who she really was, I was so angry. But now I know that I still love her. I love her more, in fact, now that I've seen who she really is."

He looked at her in stunned silence. And then he threw his head back and laughed. Mocking, contemptuous laughter that dashed against her like a wave. "That is the best joke I have ever heard! You're telling me you have been a dyke all this time?"

"I don't know who I've been all this time. But I know now."

His mirth halted as abruptly as it started. "I tell you who you are now," he said. "You're a dead woman." He drew the gun and pointed it at her.

She looked down its stubby barrel to the cold eyes behind it. For the second time that night, she considered that she would die in this wretched kitchen. But at least this time, she would die as herself.

She looked into his eyes and waited patiently. She thought of her grandmother and the icons she had prayed before every day. She thought of her mother and hoped that there was an afterlife and that she would see her again. She thought of Katya and almost smiled at what she would make of all this. And she thought of Andrea, and then she did smile, smiled with relief that she had known and loved her and had been able to save her at the last. That alone had made her life mean something.

She straightened her shoulders and waited for him to pull the trigger. He frowned as he looked at her down the barrel. "Why the fuck are you smiling?" he asked.

"You wouldn't understand."

His finger tightened, and she closed her eyes. She heard a loud bang and waited for the pain to come. Then she heard shouts and opened her eyes. Another bang came, and this time, she knew it wasn't the gun but someone banging on the front door, breaking it down. And then there was the sound of splintering wood and shouts of, "Police!"

Sirvan's head turned toward the doorway and the hall beyond it. Hope surged within Valeria, warm and sweet. Andrea had done it. She'd given them a chance, and Valeria had to seize it She dived behind the breakfast bar, just as Sirvan swung back toward her.

Hot, searing agony detonated in her lower back before she even registered the bang. She hit the floor, the breath exploding from her lungs. She gasped for air and turned her head toward Sirvan, scrabbling desperately to haul herself away.

He was facing the kitchen doorway, his hands in the air. Very slowly, he bent and placed the gun on the ground. And then he lay on the floor, stretching his arms out by his sides. A swarm of black-clad figures surrounded him, and he disappeared from view.

There was shouting, so much shouting. But fortunately, the sound seemed to be fading with every passing second. Valeria felt a hum in her ears as the pain in her back bloomed and spread its tendrils along her bones. A black hole of sorrow opened within her. She had almost made it. She had been so close to finally getting away.

She closed her eyes, unable to focus on anything else. She opened them again when someone touched her. Faces swam above her. Calming voices asked her how she felt, where the pain was. She opened her mouth but could not form words. The pain seemed to be squeezing her lungs, forcing any last remaining breath from her.

Andrea's face came into focus above her. Valeria tried to smile, to reassure her because her face was contorted with panic. It's okay, Valeria wanted to say, I'm okay. She was so glad that Andrea was safe, that Sirvan…but now she couldn't remember what he had been going to do, and she couldn't remember how she had ended up on the kitchen floor. It was all too tiring, and her back hurt so much.

Valeria closed her eyes. God, she was tired. She just wanted to rest, to go to sleep for a while. She felt someone gripping her hand and whispering in her ear. She couldn't take in the words, but they were comforting. The noise and the pain slowly receded as she sank into blissful darkness.

CHAPTER TWENTY

It was the beeping. Valeria didn't notice it at first, but it persisted and intruded into her consciousness. She went to open her eyes and found that she had to put an inordinate amount of effort into raising her eyelids. When she did so, the light was painful. It took a few more attempts to open her eyes properly.

She was in a hospital. That explained the bleeping. And the smell. She moved her arms experimentally, and they felt okay. She shifted her legs, and pain flared in her lower back. She gasped.

There was movement somewhere in the room beyond her field of vision. Someone came forward and stood by her beside. "Valeria? Are you awake?" It was Katya. The familiarity of her voice made Valeria want to weep.

"Katya." Her voice was weak and cracked.

Katya laid a hand on her shoulder. "You had us worried. There was a time it looked like you weren't coming back to us." Her eyes were moist and red around the edges. Valeria couldn't remember ever having seen Katya cry. Her mind dragged itself back to that kitchen, to her lying on the floor and looking at Sirvan.

"Sirvan," she croaked. "Where is he?" She remembered that he had a gun; he had been going to shoot her. She gripped the high sides of the bed, and Katya rubbed her shoulder, making hushing sounds.

"It's all right," she said. "The police have him. He's not going anywhere. You are safe."

"He shot me."

"I know, darlin'."

"He wanted to kill me."

"He would have too, if the police hadn't arrived." Katya reached for a water jug and poured some into a plastic cup. She put her arm around Valeria's shoulders to support her as she drank. "This is why I was always afraid for you, why I always wanted you to keep him happy."

Valeria lay back against her pillows. "I couldn't do it anymore, Katya. All those people he hurt for all those years, and I did nothing."

"What could you have done?" Katya demanded. "You have seen what he is capable of."

"I never should've stayed with him. I knew what he was, but I wanted to feel safe."

Katya took hold of her hand. "That's what we all wanted." Valeria squeezed her hand with as much feeble strength as she could muster.

The door opened, and Andrea came into the room holding two Styrofoam cups.

"She is awake," Katya said to her.

Andrea seemed like she might drop the cups in her haste to come to Valeria's bedside. She stood on the other side to Katya, handed her a cup, and then laid her hand on Valeria's forehead. Her eyes were filled with tenderness. "How do you feel?" she asked.

"Awful. But alive. Unless I'm not, and this is heaven."

Andrea smiled. "Nah. Heaven would have better coffee."

"What about the girls? The girls that were in the lorry. What happened?" Valeria began sitting up in agitation, but Andrea laid a hand on her shoulder.

"They're safe. We got to them just as Mesut did. He and the others were arrested, and the girls are okay."

"What will happen to them?"

Andrea pulled a face. "Some of them might be able to claim asylum and stay here. Some might get sent back. But they're safe from the life that Sirvan had planned for them."

"Are you all right? Sirvan—"

"I'm fine. Just some bruising that's healing nicely."

Valeria reached up and touched her face, relieved beyond words that she was there and standing before her. Andrea's eyes flicked over the bed, and Valeria turned her head and saw Katya looking at them with mingled suspicion and bewilderment.

"Ah," said Valeria.

"I'm thinking I haven't been told the full story," Katya said accusingly.

Andrea held up her hands. "It's not just my story to tell."

"I think maybe Valeria could do with something to eat. Why don't you go get her a snack?"

Valeria was about to protest that she wasn't hungry, but she caught Katya's eye and thought better of it.

"All right," Andrea said. "I'll be back soon, okay? I'm not going anywhere." She squeezed Valeria's hand and left the room.

There was a brief silence. Valeria wondered if she could get away with going back to sleep.

Katya pulled up a chair and sat. "Okay," she said, "you're gonna tell me the whole story. From the very beginning."

"I'm tired, Katya."

"The sooner you start, the sooner you can go back to sleep."

"I don't know where to begin."

"Start from when Dalia left."

Valeria took a deep breath and cast her mind back to the day when Andrea had first walked into the salon. It seemed like a lifetime ago, when Valeria had been an entirely different person.

She told Katya everything, and for once, Katya did not interrupt. Her voice was hoarse by the end, as she reached the moment when she had lost consciousness on the kitchen floor, convinced that she was dying.

She lay back on her pillows, exhausted with the effort of speaking. She waited for the inevitable onslaught from Katya, the recriminations and the expressions of disbelief. Katya was silent for a long while, looking first at Valeria and then at her hands resting in her lap.

Valeria was unsettled by this uncharacteristic silence. "Well?" she said. "You're not going to say anything?"

"Why didn't you tell me any of this?" Katya asked quietly.

Valeria would have laughed if she'd had the energy. "Because you would've told me that I was crazy, that I had a good life with Sirvan, that I shouldn't rock the boat."

Katya looked at her hands again.

"Wouldn't you?"

"Yes," Katya whispered. "That is what I would have said."

Valeria closed her eyes. Dark waves of fatigue were lapping at her, and the ache in her back was a constant nag. "I have to sleep now," she mumbled. "Tell Andrea I'm sorry we couldn't talk for longer."

As she drifted beneath the waves, she heard Katya saying, "I'll tell her."

The next time Valeria awoke, there were doctors who asked how she felt and explained the surgery she had undergone to remove bullet fragments from her back. They told her how lucky she was that the bullet had not lodged in her spine, but she would need to spend some time in hospital, recovering. Valeria managed to stay awake long enough to eat some rubbery hospital lasagne before slipping back beneath the dark waves.

Whenever she awoke, either Katya or Andrea was there, sometimes both. Andrea would sit by her bedside and talk about her work, her family, and every aspect of her life. It was as if she was making up for all those times when as Athena, she had brushed off questions about herself.

"Your sister really is called Briony," Valeria remarked as Andrea finished a roll call of close family members.

"Yeah. And she really does live in Newcastle, which is why I don't see her often."

"And what about Sarah?"

"Sarah?"

"You said you had an ex-girlfriend called Sarah."

"Ah. No, there was no Sarah. That was just the first name that came into my head."

That was not the first time they'd had an awkward moment as Valeria unpicked the truth from the necessary deceit. Andrea looked as if she was about to apologise, but Valeria stopped her. "It's okay," she said. "We are starting from the beginning. It's like we are on a first date. But with much worse food."

And then Valeria would need to sleep again, and the next time she awoke, it would be Katya by her bedside. Katya would read from the papers and celebrity magazines she bought in the hospital shop, and neither of them would speak of anything that had happened.

On one of the occasions she awoke, Valeria found Katya sitting beside her bed. Next to her sat a man and a woman, both unsmiling and dressed in grey suits. Katya explained that they were detectives who needed to take a statement. Katya held her hand as she tried to tell them everything she had ever known about Sirvan's business. She told them about helping Inna, about Omer and Galip coming to the salon, the dinner she had cooked and the snippets she had overheard. The detectives peppered her with questions. What exactly had she seen? Who had been there? Could she recall the date? Finally, they had asked Valeria to recount in detail what had happened on the day Sirvan had shot her. She went through it as dispassionately as she could but was unable to stop her voice shaking as she relived the pain and the horrible certainty that she would die on the kitchen floor. Katya's grip tightened as Valeria finally reached the end of the story.

The detectives' expressions remained impassive throughout. They presented the statement for Valeria to sign. Valeria was so exhausted that she struggled to grip the pen.

As she scrawled her name, Katya asked the detectives, "What's gonna happen to all the money Sirvan made?"

"If he's convicted, all his assets will be forfeited," the female detective said.

"And he will be convicted, right?"

"We are seeking to gather all the relevant evidence," she said with studied neutrality. Valeria laid down the pen and fell back on to the pillows, remaining conscious just long enough to hear Katya quizzing the detectives about whether all police officers had terrible haircuts.

Her periods of wakefulness gradually increased, and she was able to leave her bed for the first time and shuffle experimentally up and down the hospital corridors. Her legs felt wasted from lack of use, and her back pained her, but she gradually regained her strength.

After two weeks, the doctors declared that she could be discharged, and Katya announced that Valeria would stay with her until she was fully recovered. On the day of her discharge, Andrea appeared with a large bunch of flowers and drove them all back to Katya's small, one-bedroom basement flat. When they arrived, Valeria was installed in Katya's bedroom, with Katya insisting that she would be fine sleeping on the sofa. Valeria lay on Katya's bed, exhausted by the short trip from the hospital and listened to Katya and Andrea talking in low voices in the living room next door. Katya was giving Andrea a detailed shopping list, right down to specifying the exact brand of tinned tomatoes.

"And if they don't have it there, then go to that big place in Palmer's Green."

"What? That's miles away."

"You better get going, then, so you got time to get it before they close. That car of yours crawls along, eh?"

"There's nothing wrong with my car."

"Oh, you just choosing to drive like a snail?"

Valeria was already drifting off to sleep, but the sound of their good-natured bickering brought a smile to her face.

Valeria had no other clothes apart from those she had arrived in at hospital. The next day, Katya did a sweep of the charity shop and returned with faded jogging bottoms and T-shirts, of the kind that Valeria would never have worn in her old life.

Over the next few weeks, Valeria spent a lot of time watching TV and reading the books Andrea brought from the library. She had never had such a period of enforced idleness before. She found that her thoughts kept returning to the past, to memories of her mother and her childhood. She recalled again her youthful hopes and dreams and began to wonder if they were still within reach.

Katya went to work each day. She had found a job at a new salon, and she said nothing about the old place. Valeria didn't ask anything about it, apart from enquiring after Shanaz.

"She is a stylist at another salon in town," Katya said. "She gets paid a lot more."

In the evenings and at weekends, Valeria would go out for walks with Katya. At first, she was nervous of meeting people she knew, but Katya told her not to worry.

"Everyone is relieved that Sirvan ain't around anymore. They don't have to pay money to him, don't have to worry about offending him in some way. People are glad he's gone."

Valeria thought that Katya was just trying to make her feel better, but on one occasion, they met Mrs. Karim coming out of one of the many small groceries that lined the high street. She stopped in front of Valeria and looked her up and down. Valeria didn't know what to say and gripped Katya's arm, hard.

"I'm glad to see you're okay," Mrs. Karim said.

"Thank you," Valeria said. Her eyes strayed to Mrs. Karim's hair.

Mrs. Karim patted it self-consciously. "You let me know as soon as you are back in business," she said. "No one did my hair as good as you." And then she wished them a good evening and carried on.

Valeria had been staying with Katya for about three weeks when they ventured out one Saturday and walked around the park. Her strength had been gradually returning, and their trips out had been getting longer. They rested on a bench at the halfway point of their walk. It was the first few weeks of spring, and great banks of daffodils were nodding gently in the breeze as families with children ran across the grass.

Valeria stretched her legs out in front of her and winced.

"Does it still hurt?" Katya asked.

"Yes, but not as much as it used to. It gets better every day."

"That's good." Katya stared ahead of her, watching a toddler running around, delightedly brandishing a stick.

Katya was unusually quiet these days. She did not speak about

Sirvan, Andrea, or anything that had recently happened. Most of their conversation revolved around the early days when they had first known each other, and Katya had even told Valeria stories from her own childhood in Russia that Valeria had never heard before.

As Katya watched the little girl swiping her stick in the air, she said, "You remember I told you about my younger sister, Masha?"

"Yes. I remember you saying she died when she was a teenager."

"When I first met you, you reminded me so much of Masha." The little girl toddled to her father and proudly showed him the stick. Her dad reacted with overblown delight, and Valeria smiled. "She had a boyfriend with a motorbike. He was not a good boy. He drank too much. He was drunk when he came to pick her up one night. My mother was out, but I told Masha she shouldn't go with him. She ignored me, naturally. And he crashed the bike and killed them both."

"I didn't know that," Valeria said. "I'm so sorry."

Katya grunted. "I always thought I should have tried harder to stop her going with him. You know, tackled her, locked her in her room, something like that. I was her big sister, but I didn't keep her safe." She turned with tears gathering in her eyes. "In my mind, you were Masha, do you see? I had to keep you safe."

"I understand. And you were a good friend to me in those early days. I don't know what I would've done without you."

Katya turned away, her jaw tightening. "You might have done better. I pushed you toward Sirvan because I thought he would keep you safe."

"I made my own decisions."

"I always thought of you as Masha. But you're not her. You are your own person."

"I am now." Katya looked at her, questioningly. "I've spent so long being someone else, someone who wasn't even real. And now, for the first time, I can be me."

Katya placed a hand over hers. "I'm sorry," she said. "I was always telling you to be safe, whatever the cost. But the cost can be too much."

Valeria held her hand. "I feel safer now than I've ever felt before. Even if I have no money, no job, and nowhere to live."

"You can live with me for as long as you like. And the job and the money…" Katya waved a hand as if those things were not worth worrying about. "And you got Andrea now. That girl is devoted to you."

"Is she?" They had not spoken about Andrea since she had first told the story from her hospital bed.

"Is she?" Katya repeated, shaking her head. "You can't see the thing that's in front of your own face? She was there every day at the hospital. She would be here every day too, but she wanted to give you some time."

"What? You've talked to her about me?"

"Yes, we talk about you all the time. 'Cos we both love you and want you to be happy."

Valeria's heart was too full for her to speak. She twisted her hands in her lap.

"You know," Katya continued, "I have to go out tonight. I've asked Andrea to come round to keep you company." She said it with studied neutrality, but Valeria wasn't fooled.

"Oh, really? And where are you going?"

"To the bingo."

"You? Playing bingo?"

"What? That's what old women like me do, right? We play bingo."

"But you hate things like that. Things with other people."

"Yes, I do. But it's important that you and Andrea talk properly to each other about everything that has happened. And decide what you're going to do."

"Are you giving me advice?" Katya smiled grimly.

"Yes, yes, I know. You don't want no more advice from me. And I swear, this is the last time I will give you any. I don't understand what was going on with Athena not being Athena after all and being this Andrea girl. But I do know that Andrea loves you. I ain't gonna give you any advice about what you should do about that. But I think that being loved like that is a precious thing that you shouldn't let go of lightly."

Valeria stared. She had never heard Katya talk like this before and felt again as if the ground was shifting beneath her as people became both familiar and unfamiliar all at once. She looked back at the nodding daffodils and reached to take Katya's hand. They sat together on the bench in silence for a long while.

CHAPTER TWENTY-ONE

Valeria sat on the sofa and watched as Katya put a pack of bingo dabbers into her handbag.

"You're really going to do it?" she asked.

Katya's face was set in an expression of grim determination, as if she was about to go for a serious operation rather than a night of bingo. "When I say I'm gonna do something, I bloody well do it." Katya plumped the cushions on the sofa and generally fussed around until Valeria told her she would be late. She stood in the doorway and wagged a finger. "I'm doing this for you, remember. You make sure you talk honestly with your girl."

In the silence that followed Katya's departure, Valeria wondered if she could really think of Andrea as hers. If she was in Andrea's shoes, she would be tempted to extricate herself from this mess as soon as possible. Valeria might be free of Sirvan, but she still had nothing to offer. No job, no home, and no assurance of what the future would hold. Why would someone like Andrea stick around for that?

By the time the doorbell rang a little while later, Valeria had convinced herself that Andrea was coming to say good-bye. Despite this, she still felt a jolt of excitement when she opened the door and saw Andrea on the doorstep. Andrea, for her part, looked uncharacteristically shy, and they stood looking at each other until Valeria remembered to ask her in.

Andrea held up a small bag. "I talked to the officer in charge of the case and got some of your things back for you." Valeria opened the bag and looked through the assortment of clothes and toiletries.

"Not much to show for it all, is there?" she remarked.

"No," Andrea agreed. "But at least these clothes fit you."

Valeria placed the bag on the floor. She wasn't even sure that she wanted to wear those clothes again, clothes that had been purchased with Sirvan in mind. "Would you like a coffee?" she asked, changing the subject.

"I'll make one," Andrea offered, but Valeria waved her away.

"I can manage," she said. "You go make yourself at home." She shooed her into the front room and went into Katya's tiny galley kitchen and made two mugs of instant coffee.

She brought them in and set them on the small table by the sofa. She sat next to Andrea and found herself blushing like a teenager on a first date.

"How are you feeling?" Andrea asked, sipping her coffee.

"Better every day."

"Good. I haven't been deliberately keeping away, you know. I just wanted to give you some time."

"Yes, Katya said." Valeria sipped her coffee. "Time for what, exactly?"

Now it was Andrea's turn to blush. "A lot has happened. I figured you'd need some time to process it all."

"I have processed it," Valeria assured her. "Sirvan is not coming back, right?"

"He's pled guilty to all the charges so there won't be a trial. The evidence was overwhelming, especially with Mesut's statement."

"Mesut gave a statement against Sirvan?"

"Yep, spilled the beans big time. He cooperated so he could get a reduced sentence."

"Sirvan was always so sure of him."

"Not just Mesut. Even Zoran ended up dishing the dirt. Turns out, once the fear factor was removed, there wasn't much loyalty left."

"How long will Sirvan be in jail for?"

"Sentencing is next month, but he should get a hefty term."

Valeria sipped her coffee, almost giddy with relief. For the first time, she began to feel the dark tendrils of Sirvan's control receding from her.

"He might easily spend the rest of his life inside," Andrea continued. "You don't have to be afraid of him anymore."

Valeria shifted in her seat slightly and felt the dull ache in her back, a reminder of the way Sirvan had hurt her.

Andrea leaned forward and laid a hand on Valeria's knee. Her touch was warm and firm. "You could do anything you want, Valeria. Anything at all."

"I don't know what I want to do."

"You always wanted to have your own salon, right?"

"Yes. But I have no money. I have nothing."

"That's not true. You have the same skills you had before. And you have people around you who will support you no matter what."

Valeria looked up and saw a flush come across Andrea's face. She thought of Katya wagging her finger and took a deep breath. "Are you saying that you…you want to stick around?"

Andrea put her mug on the table. "Yes. I want…I want us to start again." Her gaze was fixed on Valeria's face, but Valeria couldn't yet bring herself to look into her eyes. She had been so convinced that Andrea was coming to say good-bye that she couldn't quite comprehend what she was hearing. Andrea shifted closer. "Look, I know that I lied to you and deceived you about who I was. And that's not an easy thing to overcome, I know that. But if you can forgive me, well, then, I'd like to give it a try."

Valeria finally looked at her. Andrea's eyes were wide and full of hope. "Give it a try?"

"Yeah. You know, like go out for dinner together and that kind of thing."

Valeria felt a surge of joy at her words, coupled with disbelief that Andrea was actually saying them to her. Yet the ingrained habit of caution and reserve was hard to overcome. She cleared her throat. "Why?" When Andrea blinked, she added, "Why would you want to do that with me?"

"Because I love you."

Valeria looked away. Half of her wanted to fling herself into Andrea's arms, to say that she loved her too. The other half held back, terrified that it wasn't true, that it couldn't possibly be true.

"Don't you believe me?" There was a note of anguish in Andrea's voice.

"I want to," Valeria said. She forced her eyes back to Andrea's face. There was still hope there, but she could see Andrea keeping it in check, preparing for the worst.

"Tell me what I have to do to prove it, and I'll do it," Andrea said.

Valeria looked at her for a long moment. "When I kissed you that first time, you were surprised. But then later, you kissed me back. Did you do that because you liked me or because you thought it would help you get information on Sirvan?"

Andrea's gaze dropped to her lap where she'd twisted her hands together. "A bit of both. I was so desperate for the operation to succeed that I think I would've done anything." She raised her eyes. "But I always liked you. I saw that you didn't like what Sirvan did, and I saw you take a big risk in helping Inna. The more I liked you, the more I hated that I had to lie to you and use you to get the information we needed." She dropped her eyes again and sighed. "I told myself that if we could just get through to the end of the operation, I would be able to tell you the truth and that..." She broke off and grimaced. "Well, I had a little fantasy that we could start a new life together somewhere."

"I had a similar idea. I pictured a house out of the city where you and I could live."

"And now?" Andrea was very still as she waited.

Valeria looked through Katya's window at the feet of people walking past on the street above. "I was in love with Athena, and I was so angry because I felt like you took that from me. The one thing I had that was truly mine." Andrea closed her eyes briefly. "Athena was never real. But then...neither was I. I had been playing the part of Sirvan's wife for so long that I'd no idea who I was anymore. And maybe I still don't."

The silence stretched out between them, broken only by the

sounds of the footfalls from the people outside. Andrea waited, and Valeria could see the tension in her face.

She took a deep breath. "I saw how you tried to protect me, even when you must have known I had betrayed you to Sirvan." She moistened her lips, her chest tight with the enormity of what she was about to do. "That told me a lot about who you were. But…I would like to know you better."

Andrea's face was still unmoving. "Do you really mean that?"

"Yes. If you're willing to get to know me…whoever I might be."

The dazzling smile that Valeria had first admired burst across Andrea's face. "Thank you," she said.

"But we have to be totally honest with each other. No lies, no deceit."

Andrea leaned forward and took Valeria's hands. "I promise, I will never lie to you, ever again."

"Good. You can begin by telling me if risotto really is your favourite food."

They sat together talking in Katya's tiny front room for a long time. They unpicked the events of the last few months as if it had been a tapestry, pulling out the threads that they could use to create something new.

Katya returned a few hours later and stood in the doorway, looking at them. A smile creased her face. "Aha. You two have had a good talk, eh?"

"Yes," Valeria said, smiling. She took Andrea's hand. "We've decided to start again, to get to know each other as if we had just met."

Katya shuffled to the armchair and flopped into it with a sigh. "Good. 'Cos I ain't going to bingo again." She jutted her chin at Andrea. "You still remember how I take my coffee?"

"I won't ever forget," Andrea said, getting to her feet. "I got it wrong one time and never heard the end of it." She went into the kitchen, and Valeria smiled at Katya.

"You look good," Katya said. "I ain't seen you smile like that since…forever."

"I know. I can't remember the last time I felt like this. Like I can just be me." Katya's face creased into smiles of her own.

Andrea returned from the kitchen and handed Katya a mug. "Hey, what's happened to your face?"

"Don't give me your cheek." Katya waved a regal hand toward the sofa. "Take a seat, darlin'. I got lots to tell you about the bingo."

Andrea sat next to Valeria and put an arm around her. Katya rubbed her hands with glee and launched into a long and detailed account of why bingo was the worst activity in the world.

Valeria leaned into Andrea's shoulder, enjoying the solid feel of her. She thought of the unknown future that lay ahead, and for the first time since she had arrived in London all those years ago, she felt excited by the all the possibilities that were open to her.

Andrea laughed at something Katya said, and then Katya laughed too, the sound echoing around the tiny flat. Valeria closed her eyes briefly, revelling in the joyful moment and feeling certain this was the first of many to come.

About the Author

Cathy lives in the UK with her wife and daughter. She writes stories at every opportunity, usually whilst fending off her cat's attempts to contribute. When not writing, she enjoys being outside in all kinds of weather—cycling, walking, and playing sports.

Books Available From Bold Strokes Books

A Cutting Deceit by Cathy Dunnell. Undercover cop Athena takes a job at Valeria's hair salon to gather evidence to prove her husband's connections to organized crime. What starts as a tentative friendship quickly turns into a dangerous affair. (978-1-63679-208-8)

As Seen on TV! by CF Frizzell. Despite their objections, TV hosts Ronnie Sharp, a laid-back chef, and paranormal investigator Peyton Stanford have to work together. The public is watching. But joining forces is risky, contemptuous, unnerving, provocative—and ridiculously perfect. (978-1-63679-272-9)

Blood Memory by Sandra Barret. Can vampire Jade Murphy protect her friend from a human stalker and keep her dates with the gorgeous Beth Jenssen without revealing her secrets? (978-1-63679-307-8)

Foolproof by Leigh Hays. For Martine Roberts and Elliot Tillman, friends with benefits isn't a foolproof way to hide from the truth at the heart of an affair. (978-1-63679-184-5)

Glass and Stone by Renee Roman. Jordan must accept that she can't control everything that happens in life, and that includes her wayward heart. (978-1-63679-162-3)

Hard Pressed by Aurora Rey. When rivals Mira Lavigne and Dylan Miller are tapped to co-chair Finger Lakes Cider Week, competition gives way to compromise. But will their sexual chemistry lead to love? (978-1-63679-210-1)

The Laws of Magic by M. Ullrich. Nothing is ever what it seems, especially not in the small town of Bender, Massachusetts, where a witch lives to save lives and avoid love. (978-1-63679-222-4)

The Lonely Hearts Rescue by Morgan Lee Miller, Nell Stark & Missouri Vaun. In this novella collection, a hurricane hits the Gulf Coast, and the animals at the Lonely Hearts Rescue Shelter need love—and so do the humans who adopt them. (978-1-63679-231-6)

The Mage and the Monster by Barbara Ann Wright. Two powerful mages, one committed to magic and one controlled by it, strive to free each other and be together while the countries they serve descend into war. (978-1-63679-190-6)

Truly Wanted by J.J. Hale. Sam must decide if she's willing to risk losing her found family to find her happily ever after. (978-1-63679-333-7)

A Good Chance by Ali Vali. Harry, Desi, and Desi's sister Rachel are so close to getting everything they've ever wanted, but Desi's ex-husband is coming back to get his revenge and rip apart their chance at happiness. (978-1-63679-023-7)

A Perfect Fifth by Jaycie Morrison. Streetwise pianist Zara Keller and Lady Jillian Stansfield couldn't be more different, yet their connection brings a new awareness of who they are and what they truly want in their lives—including each other. (978-1-63679-132-6)

Catching Feelings by Ana Hartnett Reichardt. Andrea Foster expected to catch a lot of pitches from the Alder Lions' star pitcher, Maya, but she didn't expect to catch feelings. (978-1-63679-227-9)

Defiant Hearts by Lee Lynch. In these stories, you'll find your lovers, friends, and lesbians you wish you knew—maybe even yourself. (978-1-63679-237-8)

Love and Duty by Catherine Young. All Princess Roseli wants is to marry her three lovers, but with war looming, she must instead marry Princess Lucia to establish a military alliance between their planets. (978-1-63679-256-9)

Serendipity by Kris Bryant. Serendipity brings jingle writer Annie Foster and celebrity pop star Bristol Baines together, and their undeniable attraction keeps them close, but will their different paths drive them apart? (978-1-63679-224-8)

The Haunted Heart by Jane Kolven. A ghost, a ring, and a quest to find a missing psychic—it's a spell for love. (978-1-63679-245-3)

The Rules of Forever by Nan Campbell. After reconnecting at their high school reunion, Cara and Lauren agree to embark on a textbook definition friends-with-benefits relationship, but trying to keep it uncomplicated is harder than it seems. (978-1-63679-248-4)

Vision of Virtue by Brey Willows. When virtue and desire come together, be prepared for sparks in this next installment of the Memory's Muses series. (978-1-63679-118-0)

The Artist by Sheri Lewis Wohl. Detective Casey Wilson and reclusive artist Tula Crane are drawn together in a web of passion, intrigue, and art that might just hold the key to stopping a killer. (978-1-63679-150-0)

Cherry on Top by Georgia Beers. A chance meeting leaves Cherry and Ellis longing for a different life, but when Ellis's search for truth crashes into Cherry's insta-filter world, do they have any hope at all of a happily ever after? (978-1-63679-158-6)

Love and Other Rare Birds by Angie Williams. Ornithologist Dr. Jamie Martin and park ranger Rowan Fleming are searching the Alaskan wilderness for a bird thought to be extinct, and they're about to discover opposites really do attract. (978-1-63679-108-1)

Parallel Paradise by Mayapee Chowdhury. When their love affair is put to the test by the homophobia of their family, community, and culture, Bindi and Rimli will need to fight for a chance at love. (978-1-63679-203-3)

Perfectly Matched by Toni Logan. A beautiful Cupid named Hannah, a runaway arrow, and just seventy-two hours to fix a mishap that could be the best mistake she has ever made. (978-1-63679-120-3)

Slow Burn by Missouri Vaun. A wounded wildland firefighter from California and a struggling artist find solace and love in a small southern town. (978-1-63679-098-5)

The Inconvenient Heiress by Jane Walsh. An unlikely heiress and a spinster evade the Marriage Mart only to discover true love together. (978-1-63679-173-9)

The Value of Sylver and Gold by Michelle Larkin. When word gets out that former Boston Homicide Detective Reid Sylver can talk to the dead, the FBI solicits her help on a serial murder case, prompting Reid to assemble forces once again with Detective London Gold. (978-1-63679-093-0)

Wildflower by Cathleen Collins. When a plane crash leaves seven-year-old Lily Andrews stranded in the vast wilderness of Arkansas, will she be able to overcome the odds and make it back to civilization and the one person who holds the key to her future? (978-1-63679-244-6)